Strange Bedfellows

The Hell Hole Saga:

Book III

S.L. Kotar and J.E. Gessler

Ahead of the Press Publishing
St. Louis, Missouri

Library of Congress Cataloguing-in-Publication Data

Strange Bedfellows
The Hell Hole Saga: Book III
/ S.L. Kotar and J.E. Gessler / authors
/E.J. Rossi / illustrator

| ISBN | Paperback | 978-1-950392-10-0 |
| ISBN | KINDLE | 978-1-950392-11-7 |

Ahead of The Press Publishing
St. Louis, Missouri

Table of Contents

SUMMARY OF HELL HOLE SAGA BOOKS
First Draw

Book I

Hellhole, Kansas, was no ordinary town. Like other places, it was comprised of desultory businesses, saloons, livery stable, bank, and clapboard homes, clinging to life by their figurative fingernails. What set this hider town apart from other post-Civil War outcroppings of civilization was that it also housed a United States Marshal's office. Hellhole was known to the authorities in Topeka as the place where lawmen went to die.

Claw Kiley had served in the Union Army during the Civil War, being discharged, as he had entered, a private. That fact hardly qualified him for a Federal position, yet he knew something about deputing, having served under the legendary Marshal Jack Duvall before the War. Duvall was widely regarded as the best man ever to wear the badge, yet he had been gunned down on the street of some unnamed town by a man seeking a reputation. Kiley had been the youth who outdrew the man who killed Jack Duvall. That alone made his resume worth considering, and as his life expectancy was deemed to be short, the government agents offered him the job on the expectation he could do little harm in the time he served in the position.

Bright-eyed and with faith in the almost mystical power of the badge he wore, Marshal Kiley drew three rapid conclusions about his new town: the residents of Hellhole still seethed over the outcome of the War Between the States; a girl working at the Lowdown Saloon would become very important to him; and outlaws held no respect for the Law. His first order of business was to teach the citizens to put the late conflict behind them and develop a respect, if not a friendship for the Federal man. His second, get to know Miss Cougar Bradburn; the third, to survive against those who took what they wanted by the power of guns and sheer audacity. How he succeeded would determine not only his own fate, but how the law of the land was to be carved out of hell.

Audition for a Legend

Book II

The post-Civil War era in the American West was a troubled, turbulent time. With hatreds still seething, men often took it upon themselves to enforce their own brand of justice. When they did, it brought them in conflict with those few who attempted to apply a standardized set of rules and regulations to a rawboned civilization.

Convincing men who did not fall into the category of outlaws but who were, rather, self-appointed vigilantes to follow the law was not a simple task, yet that was what Marshal Claw Kiley faced when he confronted a gang of mountain men from West Virginia, out to punish renegades for dishonoring a woman. Not unsympathetic to their cause, yet well aware how easily vengeance turned to slaughter, Kiley was forced to risk his life in order to let the law judge and sentence the guilty.

To survive past the one-year life expectancy the Federal men in Topeka had given him, the marshal will need all the help of trusted friends. Not only did he face the task of keeping peace in the brutal environs of Hellhole, a town existing solely as a half-way point where buffalo hunters gathered to sell their hides to Back East buyers, but he also faced the threat of drifters, gunfighters, and outlaws, all eager to try their hand at bringing the new "Badge" down. If Kiley lived, he would become a legend; if they gunned him in the street, he would fill a grave on Boot Hill – next to those who had come before and failed.

DEDICATION
"Strange Bedfellows"

A great many people have touched our lives along the years but perhaps no one has had such a profound influence on our medical careers that Preben Bjerregaard, M.D. We first met Dr. Bjerregaard in 1990 when he hired us to work at St. Louis University Medical Center in what became known as the Electrocardiographic Monitoring Laboratory. Throughout our nearly 25-year association that eventually expanded to the John Cochran Veterans Hospital, we worked with him on many projects, including his ground-breaking studies on Short QT-intervals. More that a professor and a teacher, he remains in contact, and it is with great pleasure and honor e dedicate this novel to him.

SLK and JEG

Hellhole Saga

"Strange Bedfellows"

Book III

CHAPTER 1

The stationary was a pale blue, like a clear summer sky. The aura of familiarity clung to it, like must, although it had been a long while since the writer had composed a letter.

The page lay before her, naked, empty, cloudless. It awaited only the touch of a steel-tipped pen, the scratching of devil's black ink, the transmission of thought to paper, as easy, one might suppose, as rain issuing forth from ink-black storm clouds.

But as so often happens, the rain did not fall and the land, parched for want of water, dried and withered. So, too, did the writer's heart.

The woman had every excuse not to write, she told herself, adjusting the hand-knit shawl around her stooped shoulders. She was unsure of the recipient's name; uncertain, even, how the missive would be received, if ever it found its way into the intended's hands.

She shivered, though the late summer day was warm, not chill. That was a symptom of old age, she imagined: being cold while others complained of heat. While not elderly by chronologic years, the would-be writer was worn, not by the wearing away of decades, but rather from the constant erosion of seconds.

Working through the perfunctory task of selecting a pen, the woman's ever-active mind calculated her age. If the year were 1868, which it was, and the month September, then she was forty-two years old. Not ancient by most standards, yet she felt the weight of time pressing down upon her rock solid, New England frame.

Born of parents recently immigrated from Scotland, in the year of Our Lord 1826, Ada Carter had been a hale, hearty child, with a jaw jutting out two feet in front of her, if her father's oft expressed words were to be believed. She was known for her temper and her ability to stare anyone - man, boy or woman - in the eye, and never blink before they did. The game was called "owl," and at age five, Ada Carter was the owl champion of three surrounding counties.

The oldest of seven children, she had become, in effect, a second mother to her siblings. Although of hot blood and fierce temper, Ada was never heard to complain of her lot in life. Everyone, her parents included, were surprised, therefore, when she announced late one evening in June, 1842, that she had taken an advert out in several Western newspapers, offering to hire herself out as a governess, domestic or other position suitable for a "woman of dignity."

No one had ever heard of such a thing. Yet, once the extraordinary announcement had settled in, her mother dried her tears, her father went back to sharpening the blade of his plow and the smallest Carter began crying. No more was said on the subject, and for all practical purposes, it was a dead issue.

Until the letter arrived.

Very little information was imparted to the recipient. A stage ticket was enclosed, along with seven dollars, cash money. "Miss Ada Carter" was requested to present herself in one month's time at the residence of one Mister Adam Burnham, where she would immediately assume "such tasks and duties as befit a woman of dignity."

"You'll be walkin' into a wolf's lair," her father commented with less interest than befit the situation.

Ada Carter thought, but did not say, if it were no better than going from the frying pan into the fire, she would have little in which to complain.

A fortnight later, Ada was on the stage, headed for "parts unknown." Her mother was ill and did not make the trip to the depot. Her father deposited her at the station, offered her twenty cents "travelin' money," which she pocketed without thanks, then remarked that before she embarked upon this "wondrous journey," she ought to "have the goodness to change the baby," which had been toted along for lack of someone responsible to watch her. He then slipped away to have words with the blacksmith about straightening the rim of a wheel.

Ada did as requested. When her father did not return before the stage departed, Ada pursed her lips and made a difficult decision. It did not tax her judgment to decide the baby had been left with her, without any thought of it returning home with its father. But the Ada Carter, who stood, poised on the running board of a new world, was not the same child who had wordlessly raised a multitude of smaller Carters.

She had no intention of taking an infant with her; her "parenthood" ended when she set foot on the stage. Begging the driver to wait a moment, Ada wrapped the baby in her shawl than ran with it to the church, the doors of which were locked, it being a weekday.

Without bothering to write a note, the girl child deposited the baby child on the doorstep, whispered a short prayer, then hurried away, with a stolid New England conviction that whatever happened was for the best.

She departed on the stage and never looked back.

Ada Carter passed through so great a number of towns they became a whirl to her, and she stopped trying to remember their names and distinctions. At first it had been her thought to keep a journal of her travels, but as the weary days and nights blurred into one single mass of time, the newness wore away. It was not until she reached St. Louis and saw the mighty, puffing steamboats that her heart caught in her throat.

Here, certainly, was a wondrous, a great thing to behold. Pouring forth steam more like a train engine than a boat, its whistle shrieking in a pitch not unlike that of a hunting owl, the boat quivered and shook, stimulating her impressionable mind with thoughts of what could be, rather than what were.

On impulse, Ada marched to the ticket office and inquired the cost of one ticket for an unaccompanied female working her way west. When asked her destination, she replied, "Anywhere down river."

First class passage to New Orleans, she was informed, which included a berth in the "Ladies Wing," and all meals, was $25.00. Staggered by the enormity of the sum, she then inquired whether there might be some other, less expensive mode of transportation down river.

"There's steerage," the clerk suggested, picking his teeth with the tip of his pocket knife. Because he had just used the tool to sharpen a lead pencil, he blackened his lips in the process.   Ada saw no good reason why she should suggest he wipe his mouth.

"What type of boat is 'steerage'?" she asked.

"It ain't a type o' boat. It's passage in the hold."

"And what is a 'hold'?"

The clerk started at her with lizard-eyes, then grinned wickedly.

"That means the bowels o' the boat."

To a woman having raised a multitude of babies, the word was hardly shocking.

"How much is steerage?" she demanded.

"Four dollars; don't include no meals."

"How does one eat?"

"You kin either git off at a wood stop an' buy food, which is mighty durn expensive, or you kin purchase some crackers an' cheese befer you board, an' be frugal wid it," he advised.

Ada winced at the man's uncouth language, but accepted his advice.

"I shall buy one ticket, steerage," she decided, pushing nearly the sum-total of her worldly fortune under the man's drumming fingers.

It never occurred to Ada that she write Mr. Burnham, informing him of her decision to respectfully decline his offer and refund his advance. Nor did she give any more than a passing fancy toward informing her parents that she was bound for New Orleans, rather than Kansas City. They would, she determined, be too busy, to read her letter.

Ada Carter never made it to New Orleans. Along the route the ship struck a sandbar and grounded. Steerage passengers were required to "retire themselves to the shore," while the crew attempted to maneuver the now lighter craft back into the water. The process was a long and arduous one, which explained, as one first cabin passenger remarked, why the captain forgot to invite the steerage passengers back aboard.

Abandoned by their boat, the eighty-seven men, women and children left stranded on the bank had no other choice than to set off on foot. Without food, water or the wherewithal to procure sustenance, they had one factor in their favor: by following the Mighty Mississippi as it twisted and turned its way toward the Gulf of Mexico, they could not get lost.

That optimistic statement was made before any of the foot travelers discovered that walking by the side of a river bank was not as easy as imagined. There was, they ascertained, no actual shore upon which to travel. Banks were steep, the water rapid and of grossly varying widths, while the limited foot space was littered with dead tree branches, debris discarded from steamboats, broken timbers from sunken and decayed rafts and a collection of rocks jutting from the shallow water.

One by one, or in small family units, the steerage passengers broke away from the larger group. Some, too weary to continue the trek, camped by flats along the river side, hoping to attract the attention of another passing vessel. Others, jaded by past experience, opted to follow wispy trails of smoke they saw floating into the calm, azure sky, which deceivingly obscured vast distances into hopes of short journeys.

Still others, allured by the prospect of "homesteading," dug their toes into the clay of the banks and declared themselves landowners, without the slightest idea to whom or by whom the land was actually owned.

They were immigrants, most of them, foreigners, seeking new chances in a new land. If Fate had declared they be set ashore and forgotten, who were they to complain of God's Divine Plan? The soil appeared reasonably fertile, there was water with which to sustain the crops and trees to cut and fashion into cabins.

Then, there were those who, unable to either keep pace or read optimism into Revelations, fell by the wayside, broken in body and spirit. For them, the New World was no better than the Old and they died as they had lived, destitute and forgotten.

Sixteen-year-old Ada Carter was one of those who made it to Trapper's Landing, a small, unkempt, depressingly squalid "town," constructed on a shifting sand dune which wore away a foot or more after every storm. The residents did not seem to mind, however. They simply knocked down the walls of any cabin which found itself suspended over a newly carved-out bank and reconstructed it back a yard or two.

The settlers had no food to barter away, nor any hope to offer the motley company working its way toward New Orleans. When a castaway asked how far they had to go to reach their destination, one man scratched his head, shrugged his shoulders and declared, "a fur piece."

When further inquiry was made, seeking his guess as to how far they had walked, he declared, "Not so fur a piece."

That news, by itself, could hardly be considered encouraging.

There were no women in Trapper's Landing. Several squaws had once resided there, accounting for the group of half-naked children seen hiding behind the trees, frightened by the unexpected appearance of strangers, but they had all run off when a band of "Injuns," escaping from the nearly continuous squabbles of "upstream," had passed close by.

Of the five women remaining in the party of former steerage passengers, only one left Trapper's Landing. The others opted for brief ceremonies and a chance to get off their feet.

Ada Carter was the lone woman. Striking out on her own, a banded kerchief knotted at the base of her neck to protect her hair, her dress bound around her legs with strips of latigo and the twenty cents traveling money she had been given by her father, she made good time. Without the worry of old men getting lost in the bushes, boys scampering away until they were out of earshot, and the continual stream of moans and groans of those less hearty, she covered eight miles before stopping to set a fishing line in the river.

The fish were not biting, or perhaps she failed to properly cover her bent pin with the reddish brown night crawler dug from the clay. Abandoning the attempt after an hour, she gave the half drown worm its freedom and lay down to sleep, only too well aware that the cramps of hunger she experienced were only a preview of what was to come.

The teenaged woman was not one to look back. She did not brood over the life she left, or the opportunities missed. Survival was her only goal, and that, because the alternative was death. Having little faith in the promise of Eternal Reward for those who perished in the faith of the Savior, whose power on earth seemed limited, at best, she awoke the next morning, made her small toilet and continued onward, face to the wind.

It was on the third day of her lonely journey that she saw the man on the raft. It was the type of conveyance a poor man made, binding rough-cut logs together with rope and steering with a pole. He was a man of medium height, with long, flowing locks, a straw hat pushed back on his head and a pair of britches rolled up to the knees, so as not to let the over-long trouser legs get soaked with every wave which washed aboard.

He was a man in the same way she was a woman; deserving the title not from a great achievement of age, but rather from the fact he faced the world alone. His eyes were bright blue, his nose sunburned into a state of permanent red, and his left hand was wrapped in a protective rag to spare it from the inevitable splinters of the pole and the equally debilitating blisters inherent in his task.

What set this man-boy apart from others she had viewed and let pass on their way down stream was the book he clutched in his right hand. Since leaving home, Ada had seen no reading material of any kind. With curiosity peeked, she stepped from the bank and returned his cheerful call.

It took him all of an hour to pole the raft to shore. Fighting the current, and his seeming inability to part with the book for more than a moment at a time, Ada had ample opportunity to study the stranger. She liked what she saw, but even if she had not, the moment she revealed herself to him, her die was cast.

When the raft was rutted to shore, then dragged up into the bank and attached by rope to a tree trunk, the river poler introduced himself.

"My name's Jack," he said, grinning and squinting into the sun she had purposely placed at her back. "What's yours?"

"Ada."

"Ada. That's a nice name. Where you headed?"

"New Orleans."

"I'm going to Natchez. Ever heard of it?" She shook her head. "It's a riverboat town. I read an ad in the paper. They're lookin' for a law man. I'm by way of being the man they're lookin' for."

"How do you know?"

"The paper said they can't get anybody to take the job because steamboat crews get mean an' nasty and kill whoever stands for sheriff. The citizens like it 'lawless,' is how the paper put it. Well, I'm for law. How about you?" he asked, as if they had just been introduced by their parents at a Sunday social, rather than having just discovered each other on the wild banks of the Mississippi River.

"I'm for law, too," Ada Carter agreed.

That was the first and only lie she ever told.

They were married in Natchez and stayed there three years. A baby was born to them, then died a year later of cholera. It had been a sickly child, prone to coughs and colds. The local physician advised the family the child's only hope for a long life was to take it to a city far from a river. They talked about it, even went so far as to send letters of inquiry about an open sheriff's position in Sedalia.

By the time they learned that job had been filled, the baby had perished. And then it was time to run for re-election and no more had been said about relocating.

Jack Duvall was elected once and re-elected twice before losing his job to Phil Chaney, a local "river rat." Phil was a man who made his living running cargo down the Mississippi on a raft, the remnants of similar crafts Ada Duvall, *nee* Carter, had seen, caught on the outcroppings of brush and bank on her vigil downstream. Phil, and those like him, had all lost their businesses when steam had modernized the river.

Rather than accept change and learn a new trade, the river rats gathered together in packs, making a new living by highway robbery, or by damning the narrow curves in the river, then jumping aboard small craft and taking "ivrythin' what weren't nailed down."

Ada complained bitterly to her husband that Phil Chaney seemed an odd sort to be elected an officer of the law, but Jack was an obliging sort, who admitted the seeming contradiction, then remarked with characteristic optimism, "The law makes strange bedfellows."

When Sheriff Chaney suggested to former Sheriff Duvall that he might do better "somewhere else," Jack had wished him well, informed his wife they were moving, packed the few belongings they had acquired and lit out, as he explained, "for parts unknown."

"Where, exactly, are we going?" Ada asked with an acquired patience, as the stage fell into a rut, striking her head against the side wall.

"We're goin' where ever they need a lawman," Jack informed her.

His vague answer suited the situation, for they tarried in two cities and six towns within the next fifteen years, not counting the six months Jack took off from the law to go fur trapping.

Two more children were born to the Duvalls, neither surviving past infancy. At the graveside of the last, Jack declared that, the way their luck was running, Ada ought to keep a black dress handy. Thereafter, they had no more children.

When the United States marshal's job was offered, Jack Duvall's name was already legend. He was a man known as a white knight, a man whom local authorities brought in to clean up a town. He was, in the parlance, a gunfighter with a law book, a man who talked fast and shot straight. A no-nonsense man who believed in fair play, had no tolerance for fool's mistakes and never wore out his welcome. A Federal position promised him the security he and his wife had never known.

"We'll buy us a house, Ada. No more me bunkin' in the back of the jail, while you keep the home fires burning in a rented room. Buy us some furniture, too, and maybe have us a little garden. With flowers," he had added with a grin. Jack Duvall was a man who loved flowers.

"We'll see," his wife had guardedly agreed, having learned from past promises, that the only two people her husband ever lied to were those bearing the name "Duvall." What she thought, but did not add, was that, even if his predictions were to come true, she would not plant flowers in the garden. To the wife of a lawman, flowers meant only one thing: wilted remembrances dying on a freshly dug grave.

"We get settled, we'll call back the boy," Jack had added, referring to one of a dozen orphan boys the Duvalls had a hand in raising over the years. "He can do some deputing for me. Be good experience."

"Which one did you have in mind?"

"Claw. That boy has lawman blood in him."

"He's good with a gun," she agreed less enthusiastically.

"It takes more than being good with a gun," Jack lectured.

"I know."

"Me and the boys raised him on the Good Book." The "good book," in this case, referring to the Code of Law, rather than some other tome, more commonly acknowledged by that euphemism.

Too many memories. The widow Duvall lay down her pen, wrung her cold hands, then blew on them, as though it were the coldness and not the past which had given her pause.

It was a contradiction, the fact that time pressed upon her, while she had all the time in the world in which to compose the letter.

Looking over at the open window, she noticed the unopened bottle of whisky sitting on the nearby table. Jack had not been much of a drinking man; two shots of red eye and he was under the table. The fact Ada still possessed a bottle of "sweet drinkin' liquor" was testimony to the fact neither sought solace in artificial release. This particular bottle had been a gift, an anniversary present from some man, whose name had been erased by the miles.

"We'll open it to celebrate, when we buy that house," Jack had promised. "We'll sit by our own fireplace, and drink a toast, just you and me. We'll drink it dry."

As dry, Ada had thought, as all the other times, all the other promises Jack had made. As dry as a Kansas summer. As dry as the clods of earth shoveled onto a mound atop of a grave.

As dry as her heart.

She thought about opening the bottle for the sake of perversity. Then she wondered why she still possessed it. Like other items of inestimable value, she could have sold it for a dollar or two.

She wondered why she had taken it out of her worn carpetbag.

Perhaps it was the amber color. Not red, as in "red eye." That referred to the color of a man's eyes when he awoke from too much drink. Not red as in Burgundy red, for it was not grape but grain.

More likely, the color appealed to her because it resembled the stain left in a carpet after the blood had been sopped up.

"I will write that letter!"

The sound of her own voice startled her. She did not recognize it. With new determination, Ada took pen in hand, dipped it into the ink and began.

"Dear Miss --," it started. "Please forgive the impudence of my writing you, but as the widow of a lawman, I think there are things you ought to know. Things *he* will not tell you. Things no one can explain, unless she had lived through them.

"You are young and you are in love. You have considered carefully all the facts as you know them, and you think you can bear the burden of being a lawman's wife. You have thought about the dangers he faces from bank robbers, drifters and drunks; you have faced the reality of sleeping alone at night. Of sleeping alone for many nights.

"You have seen him handle a gun but you are still afraid when a gunfighter calls him out. They say he is the fastest gun alive, but I know there is always someone faster.

You know he is clever, but I have seen low cunning in men not worth the powder to blow them to Kingdom Come. You have seen men play cards and know how luck changes. *He* calls it Lady Luck. But luck is no lady, as both you and I are painfully aware. Luck is neither steadfast nor pure. It is fickle, going not to the worthy but to the fool. He is foolish enough, you grant, so that you think may count on his luck holding.

That is where the fool part comes in. While it is true any man wearing a badge is a fool, it is equally true that she who loves that man is a greater one.

While I do not know you, Miss --, I know him. I would know him well, had I never met him, never prepared his meals, never taught him to read and cipher. I would know him, even if my husband had never taught him to fire a gun."

Ada Duvall paused in her writing to go back and read what she had written. Her lips moved with each word, puckered, compressed, hissed, whispered, until she had finished. It was only then the mistake struck her like a bullet in the back.

"I would know him," she amended, "even if my *late* husband had never taught him to fire a gun."

It was not an easy thing to do, for the inclusion of one single word underscored the fact that Jack Duvall was dead. Dead and buried.

Too late for the family they would never have. Too late for the home they would never buy. Too late to share the bottle of sippin' liquor they would never open.

Too late to confess her lie. Too late to tell that boy with bright blue eyes she was not for the law.

Too late to say good-bye when all she really wanted to do was say hello.

Too late for everything except mourning and warning.

The thought brought a grim smile to her colorless lips.

Mourning. Warning. She was a poet and did not know it. It was an old childhood rhyme.

But then, childhood, too, was dead.

It was always later than one thought.

CHAPTER 2

"I guess it's getting late."

Claw Kiley yawned, carelessly moving a hand to cover his mouth, too late to be of any saving social grace.

"You think?" Cougar Bradburn inquired, stretching her legs underneath the table at which they both sat. Her feet were throbbing, matching beat for beat the thumping in her chest.

Claw nodded, caught her eye and blushed.

"There's a chill in the air," he declared, changing the subject.

"I know where a fella can get himself warmed," she replied, drawing him back to her original invitation.

"I've been up before dawn," he began, looking down into a pile of damp sawdust he had formed with the top of his boot.

"I know," she agreed, more relieved than she cared to admit. She had had a long day herself and her bones were reminding her there were other nights, better times. She stood and walked with him to the swinging doors of the Lowdown saloon.

"Why don't you drop by in the morning?" she invited, her mind already laying itself to sleep in the empty bed upstairs. "We can have breakfast together."

"You? Up for breakfast?" he teased.

"Not from choice. I have to finish taking inventory so I can place an order when Eric comes. He's due in this week."

"Eric?"

She delayed answering him, as the image of a man appeared before her mind's eye.

"Eric Anheiser," she explained finally, fighting to keep her eye lids from drooping. "He and his brother run a saloon supply business out of St. Louie. One of them - usually Eric - delivers the goods by wagon. I'll have to have a list drawn up so he'll know what I need next time."

Claw nodded sleepily.

"How do you know what you're getting this time?"

"He delivers from the list he was given last month. I always have to think days and weeks ahead."

"But you didn't draw up the last list," he protested, moving into the doorway, where he stood, straddled between coming and going.

"No," she agreed. "Bix Bradley did. But I helped him," she added for pride's sake. "There's nothing about this business I don't know."

That seemed to rouse him, for he lifted his head and sought her eyes. When the blue of his met the blue of hers, they held, locked, mated, a merging of youth and jealousy, uncertainty and expectation.

"I'll come by in the morning," he promised, breaking off their eye contact with a willful jerk of his head.

"Good. I'll make you work for your coffee," she promised.

"Counting bottles?"

"That's *my* job. You can carry up empty barrels."

Claw grunted, rolled his eyes then grinned.

"Do I get put on the payroll?"

"I would," she declared, "but I have a suspicion the state of Kansas would consider that a conflict of interest, the marshal working for the lady saloon keeper on the side."

"Who's to tell them?"

"Doctor Fiz Ward."

Which was enough to send him scurrying off to bed.

Claw walked the twenty paces to the United States Marshal's Office, paused outside the door, then, on impulse, moved to the hand-painted sign, nailed to the brick wall. Taking a handkerchief from his pocket, he ran it over the lettering, justifying the action by a silent acknowledgment to the gods watching over fools and lawmen, that the heat and dust of a Kansas summer had made it dirty.

It would not due for a stranger to come to town and be unable to find the marshal because his sign was illegible.

The fact no more than one in two score men could read bore no special significance to him. His action was, after all, just part of the job.

Opening the door which he had not bothered to lock, and would never lock, baring his long absence, Claw Kiley took in a deep breath of tired contentment. He was where he wanted to be, doing what he had always dreamed of doing. It made a man feel at home.

When he caught the movement out of the corner of his eye, Claw moved without thinking. Like a cat, he was ever wary, constantly alert for trouble. Reasoning after the fact, his mind explained what his actions dictated: it was nearing midnight and all the saloons, cathouses and gaming parlors had closed. Working folk were asleep in their beds, while the numerous packs of wild dogs had circled down for the night.

That left very few excuses for either man or beast to be wandering. Only those outside the law were likely to be out and about at this witching hour. If the brief parting of the dark of night were any indication someone or something were amiss, he would know about it.

Stepping lithely to the side of the door, Claw peered out, into the blackness. He counted ten by the steady beating of his heart, then eased the door further open. No sound. No outside motion.

Gun in hand, the lawman, with little more than six months experience as a Federal marshal, darted through the opening, then crouched, cat-like, by the alley at the side of the building.

All quiet.

Feeling foolish, yet not completely convinced he had not seen what he knew he had, Claw holstered his gun and moved into the street. He started to call out, then thought better of it. If there was no one about, there was no good reason to speak. And if there were a man in the gloom, hailing him was more likely to catch him a bullet than a friendly hello.

The longer he stood in the darkness, the more attuned his senses became to the night. He identified the sound of crickets, the faint whistle of the wind, the hum of a flying insect, the barely audible sound of his own breathing. What had been a solid wall of black a moment ago slowly transformed itself into a hitching rail, a pile of horse manure his nose put an six hours fresh, a watering trough in front of the shuttered livery across the street.

For a moment he thought he detected a light beneath the door of the stable, but when he squinted, to narrow his line of vision, it was gone, like the movement of a moment ago.

Glancing to his left, Claw's wise young eyes scanned the Lowdown, more interested than he would admit, seeking reassurance all was well. There were no lights on. The owner, barely as old in her job as he was in his, had apparently gone to bed.

With a slight shake of the head, Claw turned and re-entered his office. Like the lawman and the saloon owner, Hellhole was young, raw, inexperienced. No one was who, or what, they appeared to be; the man in a black coat could be a banker, an undertaker or a gambler. The woman with a Back East dress and a brightly ribboned bonnet could be the dry-grocer's wife, a farmer's daughter or the town's most infamous madam.

The girl with the red hair might own the Lowdown and the boy with a stature as tall as a mountain might be the marshal.

It was not looks or clothes or time on the job which mattered in this rawboned, rough, untamed hider town.

It was determination, courage and luck.

Lady luck.

Grinning at his groundless suspicions, Claw holstered his gun, then unbuckled the belt, swinging it carelessly unto the peg by the door. It had been a long day and he was tired. Time to sleep and save the worrying for the morrow.

It was not until the lamp winked out in the Marshal's Office that the figure moved. Stepping out from the shadows, it looked to the left, then the right, nodded ruefully to itself, then hastened away. The shadow had been patient; more patient than the lawman. For its trouble, it had learned a fact or two.

And knowledge, as they say, is power.

When the screech came, Claw shot bolt upright in bed, a line of sweat frozen to his brow. In one instant his long legs were over the side of the bunk, hand reaching for the pistol, too far away to be of any use.

It was only then, as his fingers grasped empty air, that he put a name and face to the screamer. His hand dropped and his tensed muscles sagged.

Mouse.

"Miss Cougar," he groused, rubbing a hand over his lightly-stubbled cheeks. "Do you know what time it is? Do you have to go hunting when it's dark? Can't you at least wait until dawn?"

For answer, he received the limp, warn carcass of a recently deceased rodent in his lap.

"Thanks a lot," he continued, picking the mouse up by the tail and swinging it away from his body. "But I had something a little more - tasteful - in mind for breakfast. Don't let me stop you, though. Have at it."

So saying, he dropped the mouse at the cat's feet. She eyed him with the grave concern of one whose present had been rejected for no known reason, then whisked her tail and disappeared.

Soundlessly, on cat's paws.

In the morning, on his way to the outhouse, Claw's socked foot landed squarely on the now cold animal, squashing it beyond recognition.

It was scant consolation to the marshal that, for the remainder of the day, no one in Hellhole could guess, by looking at his boots, he was minus one sock.

Collecting his daily ration of one dozen fresh eggs and one pail of milk delivered to his office by ranch children, Claw poured out Miss Cougar's ration, then carried the rest to the Lowdown, a smile in his eyes and a twinkle jumping from one lip to another.

"Morning!" he greeted the lady, also known as his lady, sitting at a rear table. Cougar looked up, took in the size of his gifts, then nodded affably.

"Good morning. Now, you can bring those eggs and that milk over to the Regent."

Claw looked distressed.

"I thought we were going to have breakfast together. Here."

"We are. I've already traded that which you're holding for the same of a cooked nature. The tray ought to be waiting for you."

"You - traded? How did you know what I was bringing? Or that I would bring anything at all?"

She dismissed him with a wave of her hand.

"Our eggs are getting cold. You're late."

When thought of further argument hard-boiled his tongue, Claw turned on his heels and left. With shoulders still slightly rounded, he stomped through the open doors of the restaurant, looked around, then motioned to the waiter with a curt jerk of his head.

"You have a tray for the Lowdown?" he demanded.

"No."

"I was told to pick up a tray of food for Miss Bradburn at the Lowdown. It's supposed to be ready," Claw enunciated carefully, as befit a United States marshal and the bearer of one dozen eggs and a pail of milk.

"There are *two* trays," the waiter informed him, not insensitive to his own position as the dispenser of both food and information.

"Where are they?"

"In the back."

"Go and get them."

The waiter was spared the indignity of further argument by a customer's request.

"More coffee!"

He disappeared with alacrity, leaving Claw to wonder what he had done wrong.

Or if his shirt needed laundering.

Walking into the back, the lawman's keen eyes roved the rear counters, looking for what had been described as "two trays." With a tracker's skill, an Indian's nose and a hungry man's sense of direction, he correctly identified two trays, both of which were covered by the remnants of an old shirt, missing both arms and all its buttons.

Before lifting the cloth, Claw instinctively inspected it for bullet wounds. He did not fancy eating food off a tray protected by the shirt of a coward.

Not only would the hole fail to keep away the numerous black, buzzing horse flies, it would most certainly be bad luck.

It was not that Claw Kiley was superstitious; he simply did not want Miss Bradburn having doubts as to the quality of the food. Or from where the steak liberally spilling over the plates originated.

She was, he thought he remembered, a finicky eater.

Before he could drop the shirt back over the trays, the ever-helpful waiter, to whom Claw was rapidly developing a distaste, passed close by.

"You can't carry both at once. You should have brought help."

"Why don't you offer?" Claw hissed, in good imitation of Miss Cougar. The cat.

Who was, he supposed, not so fussy an eater as her namesake.

"I'm busy."

To prove his point, the waiter sat down and leaned back until his head rested against the wall, while the two airborne front feet of the chair, like a child's gap-toothed mouth, laughed at him thought vacant space.

"You don't look busy to me," the lawman pouted.

"I'm holding up the wall."

For two cents, or two eggs, whichever was handier, Claw would have grabbed the man by his shirt and flung him out the open door, into the alley.

The thought, as it occurred to him, was so appetizing, Claw licked his lips in anticipation.

But he did not wish to appear undignified. Or unlawful. Shoving an insignificant little man down a rat hole was just to the left of upholding the peace.

"Get up," Claw ordered. "And take one of these trays to the Lowdown."

"Why don't you do it?"

"I'm the Marshal."

"Is someone robbing the bank? Is a dirty, rotten hider skinning a shop keeper? Is there a gunfight in the street?" He accepted Claw's silence as a "no." "Then I can't say you're any more busy than I am."

"What's-your-name?" the tall, irate man demanded.

"Claw Kiley. What's yours?"

Claw's mouth moved, but no words came. He was certain a rejoinder lurked just under the tip of his tongue, but his tightly-clamped teeth spoiled his chance at a quick shot.

"I'm going to tell Miss Bradburn," he muttered. It was the worst threat he could think of. Had she known, she would have been surprised, but pleased.

The argument might have continued for another quarter hour, but a voice from beyond brought them both to their toes.

"How long do I have to sit here before someone waits on me?"

The authority in those clear, sharply enunciated tones were enough to bring Claw to the door before he realized what he was doing. With a pout, he stared as the evil little waiter bowed before the customer.

"Good morning, sir. What would you like for breakfast, Doctor Ward?"

"Something just slightly less poisonous than that steak you were serving last night. I saw the steer it was carved from and I wouldn't have fed that meat to a waiter. It's been hanging in the back room for a week."

"The cook is aging it, sir."

"The way that carcass 'aged,' Vernon Trask wouldn't even bury it!"

Vernon Trask was the town furniture maker and undertaker. He never failed to wish the marshal a cheerful "good morning," or a solemn "good night." His politeness did not deceive the lawman. Claw already knew his presence in town was good for business.

"We have fresh eggs today, Doctor. Just brought in. And some fresh milk. Would you like a glass with your coffee?"

"How fresh?"

"Brought in not five minutes gone by."

Fiz waved the man away with an imperious gesture and Claw had the indignity of seeing his milk approved of and consumed by the physician before he, the rightful owner, had taken a drop.

It was obvious to Claw that the waiter was going to be too busy to carry any trays to the Lowdown. With a sigh of resignation, he went about the task himself. Because both trays were filled with irregularly shaped items, placing one atop the other did not seem the recommended method of carrying both simultaneously. However, they were too large and too heavy to be held by one single hand.

Deciding he would be "damned" before making two trips, the marshal lifted his stacked trays and started for the back door.

"I wouldn't go out that way, if I was you," the waiter sneered.

"I wouldn't go on living, if I was you," Claw grumbled.

The waiter shrugged.

"Suit yourself. It's just that..." A tin pie plate injudiciously clattered to the floor, obscuring the man's warning. Claw turned his head, eye lids narrowed.

"It's just that WHAT?" he demanded.

But the little worm was apparently too busy cleaning up the spill to respond. Claw supposed the creature could not clean and speak at the same time.

While he was prying open the rear door with the toe of his boot, the marshal wondered if the waiter owned a gun. Visions of the man hanging, like a side of beef, a small round hole puncturing his "carcass," a metal hook his only visible means of support, filled his mind.

Which led him to wonder if the physician would condescend to eat that meat, or if, like the aged beef, he would pass it off to other, less fussy eaters.

The image of the hanging waiter and the hungry doctor so filled Claw's imagination he did not see the dogs as they came at him. It was a tribute to his powers of reconstruction that he counted six out of perhaps two dozen before pulling back inside, barely saving himself the indignity of feeding the wild canines on Miss Bradburn's breakfast.

"I warned you," the waiter snickered as Claw retreated toward the door leading to the earing parlor.

"Since you seem to know a lot about bank robbers, mule skinners and gunfighters, the next time I put together a posse, you'll be on it," Claw snapped.

"I don't have a gun."

"I'll give you one. Along with one bullet."

"One?"

"No sense wasting the state's money on ammunition. The way I picture it, you'll be the first man on the posse shot."

"Then why give me any bullets at all?"

"Because I've never shot an unarmed man in my life."

Feeling vindicated, Claw marched into the front room. The doctor did not look up from his food. The lawman was almost to the outside door and freedom before being addressed.

"You can bring my dinner up to my office at four o'clock."

The physician, Claw decided, would be the second man he deputized for posse work.

CHAPTER 3

"What took you so long?" Cougar demanded as Claw slipped through the batwing doors, trays in hand.

"Nothing was ready," he declared with a clean conscience. To which Miss Bradburn answered with an extremely unladylike expletive.

"If the Regent wasn't the best restaurant in town, I wouldn't go there," she finished sourly. "Put the trays down here."

"I can't think of any good reason for going there," Claw pouted, doing as ordered. Cougar gave him an odd look.

"You can't?"

"No."

"Then you haven't given the matter much consideration."

"I've given it enough," he grumbled, watching as her flying fingers set out the plates, saucers, cups and bread baskets.

"Have you?" she asked, spreading melted butter over cooling flapjacks. "Maybe you have. I guess you don't have anything to prove. And if you did, you'd prove it on the street. With a gun. I don't have that - dignity; that - ability to impress. I have to do it in other ways.

"What do you suppose people would say if I stopped going to the Regent and started ordering my meals from the Rats Cellar? Or if I dropped into the Hide-on-the-Hoof for a quick bite to eat? The others girls do. The saloon girls; the working girls, in their mended, hand-me-down dresses or their faded, ripped shawls. No one questions why they don't go to the Regent. They know.

"Just like they'd know if I went there. And if I forgot my change purse, the owner wouldn't have to wonder about how I was going to pay for my meal.

"If I walk into the Regent without any money, I'd be allowed the liberty of sending to the Lowdown for the price of a steak and potatoes. If I find myself penniless in one of those other places, they just extract payment from my hide.

"Does that make it a little clearer?"

"Yes, ma'am."

She paused to look at him, read the sadness behind his eyes, and relented.

"I'm sorry. I don't mean to come down hard on you. I know you don't know."

"I want to know," he protested slowly and with feeling. "I want to know everything."

"I doubt that."

"No. I mean it. You teach me."

The flapjacks, eggs, bacon and steak were consumed before she answered his request.

"Why?"

He did not need to be reminded of the subject.

"Because you're my gal."

She blushed and damned herself for it.

"I should think," she declared firmly, "that a Federal marshal could do better than a saloon girl."

"A saloon owner," he corrected her.

She shrugged, as though the differences were slight.

"You about done? I've got work to do."

"What kind of work?"

She arched an eyebrow, hesitated, then nodded with her head to indicate "below."

"I told you: the supply man's due in. I have to inventory what I have, decide how much I'm going to order for next month."

"Eric Anheiser," Claw verbally remembered.

It was not the fact he recalled the name but the way in which he spoke the two words which caught Cougar off guard.

"Yes. You know him?"

"No."

Cougar's relief was palpable. "I didn't think he was on any wanted posters."

Which made Claw wish he were.

"Can I help?"

"Help? Help me?" He grinned.

"Why not?"

"What'll Blade, down at the Wolf's Pelt say? You gonna help him, too?"

"Nope."

She liked his answer. There were few advantages a woman had in business. Being the marshal's "gal," she supposed, was one of them. If Blade did not like it, he was free to vie for Claw's affections.

"All right. Come on."

Taking up a clipboard with a pencil attached to it by cotton string, Cougar lead the way across the saloon, side skirting tables, spittoons and piles of sawdust without ever bothering to look at the floor. Claw, less familiar with the layout, followed at a slower, more careful pace. Without prisoners in the jail, he did not want to be responsible for cleaning up any messes he made.

Descending the dark stairs, Cougar reached the lower level first and had the lamp burning by the time he joined her. Ducking several prodigious cobwebs, Claw straightened, then ran into another, this one spreading from wall to wall. Cougar's grin did nothing to placate him.

"I wipe away the ones which get in my hair," she admitted. "But you're on your own with those higher ones."

"This place could use a good cleaning," he complained.

"Why bother? No one comes down here, unless they're bringing up a barrel of beer or a crate of whisky."

"What about Joshua?" Claw inquired, pointing to a rude bed the deputy had made out of slates suspended over wooden boxes. The lumpy corncob mattress or the moth-eaten grey army issue blanket did nothing to make it look homey. "He sleeps down here. You'd think he'd volunteer to clean it up some."

"I mentioned that to him."

"What'd he say?"

"He ain't one for volunteerin' an' he don't see no spider webs in the dark."

"I'll speak to him about it."

"Don't bother. I'll have Eric clean it up when he gets here."

"Why would 'Eric' clean it up?"

"So he won't get his nice, fancy suit dirty when he traipses up and down stairs, taking away empties and bringing in my new stock."

"Wears a fancy suit, does he?"

"Oh, he's very well dressed."

Claw decided the best way to judge the worth of a man was by the dirt on his clothes.

Cougar interrupted further thought by poking him in the ribs.

"Over there. Those crates - first, be sure they're all filled with empties. If there's empty spaces, put a bottle in it. Each crate holds twenty-four bottles. Then stack the crates over there by the stairs, one on top of another, no more than ten crates high. More than that and they tip."

"He's going to haul these all away?"

"That's right."

"What's he do with 'em? Sell them in St. Louis?"

"He owns a bottling and distillery company. They refill the bottles and deliver them back. I put a deposit on each bottle; five cents. Twenty-four bottles to a crate, that's one dollar and twenty cents. If I return all twenty-four bottles, I don't have to pay deposit on the case he leaves this time. Make sense?"

"Five cents a bottle seems pretty steep."

She shrugged.

"It's structured into the price. A bottle of whisky costs two dollars. I pay seventy-five cents for it, plus the five cent deposit, which I have to figure on losing. The other dollar-twenty is my profit."

"You pay seventy-five cents for a bottle of whisky?" Claw asked, clearly surprised.

"Well, yeah," she agreed, stooping down to check the condition of a dented beer barrel. "But I make up for it in other ways."

Being preoccupied, Cougar failed to catch the expression on his face, or she would have not assumed they were in agreement on profit margins.

"Here," she continued, summoning him over. "I didn't realize the barrel was almost empty. Take it upstairs and fill it with water from the pump. There's one in the back room on the left as you come up the stairs. Only half way," she warned as he wrapped his arms around the wooden-slatted vessel. "Otherwise, it's too heavy."

She meant the admonition as a warning rather than a challenge. It was only after filling the barrel to the top, then trying to lift it, that Claw realized his mistake. Grunting, half from annoyance, half from effort, he managed to inch it to the back door, where he tipped it over, spilling half the contents onto the ground. Making a grand effort not to soak his boots, Claw hoisted the barrel up, then baby-stepped his way down stairs.

"Here it is," he huffed. Then, nothing the empty bottle she held in her hand, added, "Although I think it would be easier to wash the bottles upstairs, rather than down here. There's more light outside and you wouldn't have to carry the water down the steps."

"I'm not going to wash them," Cougar chuckled. "And for what I'm doing, I have all the light I want."

Taking one unopened bottle of whisky, Cougar deftly uncorked it, then poured one third of it off into an empty. Pausing to make a critical determination, she added another drop, then dipped a tin cup into Claw's barrel of water. Before he could protest, she had filled the first whisky bottle to the brim and re-corked it. Placing it back in a nearly full crate, Cougar repeated the procedure. Claw did not utter a sound until she had four filled bottles where before there were three.

"What are you doing?" he finally croaked.

"Stretching my profit margin," she supplied without a thought.

"You're watering down the whisky," he gulped.

She nodded amenably.

"I know what you're going to say."

"You do?"

"I could get away with watering it down more than that and no one would notice and you're probably right. Bix Bradley did. But I want to start off on the right foot."

"The right foot."

Claw started down guiltily at his sockless right foot.

"That's right. God knows, Blade waters his whisky down further than that. Well, I don't really blame him."

"You don't blame him."

"How can I? It doesn't give much of a kick, so men have to buy more of it. And then, too, it takes longer for a man to get drunk. They can drink all night before remembering to tear the place up. Saves a lot on furniture."

"Saves a lot on furniture," Claw repeated.

"No one gives us the bottles and no one gives us the furniture," Cougar seconded. "You know how much chairs are going for these days?"

"No."

"A decent chair costs me four dollars - plus a delivery charge. That's why I save the beat-up ones for Eric. I pay him a little, he repairs them. He says at four dollars a chair there's not much profit in it for him."

"You buy chairs from this Anheiser, too?"

There was a decided edge to his voice.

"He and his brother have a catalogue. They sell all sorts of saloon merchandise. Gaming tables, cards, roulette wheels, chairs, barrels and of course the beer and whisky. And bathtubs, too," she laughed.

She laughed alone.

"You say Blade waters down his whisky?"

It was only then that the skin at the base of her neck prickled. She made a low, hollow noise deep in her throat.

"Did I say that?"

"Yes," he reaffirmed. "You did."

Breathing slowly through her nose, Cougar turned to face the marshal, hands on her hips.

"You mean to tell me you didn't know saloons watered their whisky and beer?"

"And beer?" he demanded.

"Well, not as much," she began, then cut herself off. "Claw, where have you spent our life?"

"Not in the cellar of a saloon," he admitted huffily.

"And you never knew... you never suspected?"

"I never thought about it. I supposed if a bottle were corked, it was - all right."

Cougar's look crossed the boundaries of pity, going well into bemused contempt.

However, she did not voice what she was thinking.

"Well," she began, inspecting the ceiling visually for cracks, "it is all right. There's nothing wrong with watered-down whisky."

"But it's not what a man is paying for."

"He's paying for a bottle, a glass, a seat and a girl to flirt with. If he wants to get drunk in a hurry, he'll buy something else. Brandy," she added. And then quickly, "Brandy bottles come sealed. See?"

Cougar took down a dusty brandy bottle from the shelf, blew away the grey accumulations of time, then displayed it, neck toward him, for his inspection.

"That's proof of - proof," she faltered. "Proof means strength. If you see a band around the cork, that means it's full strength."

"And if I don't -"

"Buy it, anyway," she advised, replacing the rare bottle back in its private catacomb.

"Why should I?" he demanded in his marshal's voice.

"Because that's all you've ever drank. Sit down with a bottle of full-strength whisky and you're eyeballs will be spinning faster than a crocodile."

"What's a crocodile?" he asked in obvious irritation.

"It's a sort of a huge water lizard - a reptile which grows about six feet long. They have a powerful tail and even more powerful jaws. They catch prey in their mouths, then spin around and around in the water to drown their victim. It's not a pretty sight."

Caught between impressed and annoyed at his own ignorance, Claw finally surrendered to his curiosity.

"Ever see one?"

"Sure; around New Orleans," she added evasively.

"Ever see one kill a man?"

"No... but I saw one kill a woman, once."

Claw started to inquire after details, then changed his mind. Had she wished him to know, Cougar would have supplied the details without his having to ask.

"I saw a man's head blown off by a cannon ball," he volunteered, to fill the silence. "The head rolled about twenty feet away from the body.

Perfectly untouched. The eyes opened and closed for a quarter hour. It was the damnedest thing."

"I suppose you boys tried talking to it," she commented, looking down while wiping her hands on her skirt.

"A few of them did, sure," Claw agreed. "The sergeant said he saw him trying to say sumthin', but I didn't see his lips move."

"He was probably asking one of you to put his kepi on," Cougar decided suddenly. "The sun was getting into his eyes. Ever think of that?"

"Nooo," Claw remarked, blowing the word out in a gush of breath.

"Didn't think so."

"Buried him with his hat, though," Claw tried, as though to make amends.

"Men always think of things too late." She dismissed him with a nod of her head. "Go on. Don't you have rounds to make or something?"

"I thought I was going to help you."

"You did. I'm just going to finish counting, then put together a list. I'll be at it the rest of the day," she added.

"Yeah. It'll take that long to water down the rest of the stock," Claw grumbled as he retreated up the stairs. "A man'd think you were raising cattle down here."

He did not hear her laughter, nor would he have appreciated it, if he had.

CHAPTER 4

Claw squinted his eyes into the brightness of the sun, then turned his head just enough to block the rays, thereby staring out of the corner of one eye. The object of his curiosity was a man on horseback. There was nothing significant about the rider. He sat the dirty-white colored horse with easy familiarity, but without the camaraderie a man and beast developed after months of arduous association. His clothes were dusty, his cheeks rusted by a week's growth of reddish stubble.

Perhaps it was the very commonness of his appearance which set him apart. Dismounting at the hitching rail outside the Lowdown, the man removed his hat, beat away a layer of trail grime, then replaced it on his head with a decided downward snap of the brim.

While he did not make a show of staring at his surroundings, the marshal had seen the stranger's eyes flicker as he rode down Main Street. He had never been in Hellhole before, yet did not wish to announce that fact. Stopping at the saloon, brushing away the dirt, patting his horse on the neck before stepping up onto the warped boardwalk were actions calculated to ease suspicion.

Back where I belong, the man's gestures seemed to say. I've been away and now I've returned.

Yet he was not the prodigal son, nor was he a man fresh from prison. Other than those two disclaimers, he might have been anyone. His dress made casual claim toward his being a trail hand, yet the way he rode his mount belied that easy identification. His boots were hand-made and tailored, while his vest was of a dark, brocaded material, giving credence to the fact he might have made his living as a card sharp. Yet his hands betrayed him there, for they were broad and short, with nails broken off from hard manual labor. He might have managed to palm an ace, but marking a card or double-dealing himself a winning hand seemed improbable.

The unknown man wore his pistol low, after the fashion of a gunfighter, yet Claw's knowing eyes could tell, at a glance, the weapon was no more than a cheap six-shooter, the kind a cowboy or a rustler wore. Like the hand-gun, what the lawman could see of the stranger's rifle was nothing special; no engraved stock, no flashy Mexican silver pieces set into the wood. It was a working man's weapon, not the weapon of a man who earned his living working with firepower.

The saddlebags, strapped into place, had a worn, familiar appearance, one side filled enough to carry a change of clothes, while the leather bag opposite was shiny and irregularly shaped, announcing the inclusion of a coffee pot, frying pan and a day or two's worth of flour and bacon.

A rain poncho was carefully wrapped over a blanket, both secured between saddle and bags by a series of leather thongs, the style and material of which might have been found on two dozen horses hitched to rails along Main Street.

Further study revealed a deerskin-sheathed Bowie knife attached to the man's trouser belt, hung on his left side, opposite the gun. The pants pocket on the right showed the faint outline of a farmer's purse; the man's billfold was undoubtedly tucked away in an inside pocket of the short leather jacket.

The reddish hair - that which Claw had seen as the stranger beat away the dust - was close cropped. The man's face was tanned, while the paint-spattered freckles on his nose were nearly obscured by sunburn.

He was a man calculated, by design or accident, to fit into any surroundings; a chameleon, changing color, shape, attitude, in order to pass unnoticed in a crowd. Ten men would have given ten vague descriptions of him, none coming close to pinning a name or an identity to him.

A saloon girl would not have given him a second look, sizing him up as a man who drank alone. A banker would have passed without ever seeing him, determining with prejudice he had no money to deposit, and no collateral for a loan. He was the kind of man a preacher might hold up as a sinner without knowing his background, while an educator would deduce, without ever hearing his voice, he was soft- spoken and versed in his letters.

There was not the discipline about him of the professional soldier, but he could have passed as a civilian, hired by the Army as a scout. He might have been a tinker, a wheeler-and-dealer in patent medicines or tinware, but he lacked the flash and easy smile. He might have passed for a confidence man, had he a gold watch-chain slung across his once high-styled vest.

He might even have been taken for a doctor, had not the aura of death hung round him like a dirty shroud.

With that distinction, he might even have been taken for a lawman, except for the wild abandon of will so carefully hidden behind hooded eyes, and the calculated movements, artfully designed to deceive.

He was Everyman, and therein lay his trouble, for he was about as common as a three dollar bill.

Claw did not have to ask the man his name. He already knew it. The stranger called himself Smith or Jones, Bill or Jim or Tex, but it was a sure bet he was never christened with any of those. He was Somebody, and he had some reason for running and hiding. He was good at the game because he had been playing it for a very long time.

Too long. Perhaps that was the reason he stood out to a practiced eye. He had the kind of weariness men showed after they have been hunted by a posse for two long months. Or the bone-weary tiredness which prompts a murderer to turn himself in to the hangman years after having successfully adopted a new identity and knowing the law had stopped looking for him.

His face was not on any wanted poster Marshal Kiley had ever seen. That did not mean the man was not a fugitive or was free from guilt. It indicated no more than whatever crime he had perpetrated had either gone undetected or had not been committed within the boundaries of the western frontier.

Claw's first instinct was to accost the stranger, introduce himself, flash the erstwhile tin of the badge, breath in the outsider's face. The marshal did not want trouble in Hellhole. If the interloper felt himself watched, suspected, singled out like a calf for branding, he would buy himself a bottle in the saloon, restock his meager supplies at the general store and be gone by nightfall.

Any other lawman would have seized the easy way out, for the rider on the pale horse was trouble. He was Death, with a capital letter. Better to settle for Discontent than face him on the street, confront him in a dark alley, follow his fading tracks with a half dozen deputized townsmen, knowing that behind the next tree He was waiting to greet His followers with a baptism of lead.

One word; any word. A meeting of the eyes; a certain tilt of the head. A snap of the fingers. The wailing of a hungry dog. A child crying "Boo!" Anything would have spooked the man, but the town was quiet, and as still as a churchyard. Not a breath of air, not the slithering of a worm.

The stranger took it all in, absorbed the peace the way a man dying of thirst drew his head into a bucket of water drawn from a dry well, then made a furtive jerking motion, as though undecided where to go, now that he had arrived.

With more courage than the lawman would have given him credit for, the dismounted rider turned his back on the Lowdown and approached the Badge.

"Morning," he said, obscuring his words with a mumbled, sing-song cadence, making his greeting sound long and involved, rather than terse and monosyllabic.

"Good morning," Claw replied, speaking with precise enunciation out of unconscious self-defense.

"I'm looking for a doctor. You have one here?"

He seemed to speak without moving his lips, like a ventriloquist Claw had seen once in Kansas City. The unexpected illusion of himself as the dummy etched itself sharply in the tall man's mind, raising the hairs on the back of his head.

"Run into some trouble, did you?"

The man smiled; it was a facial gesture, a social amenity, no more. An old habit, perhaps; a sense of politeness taught as a child then relearned, with a new meaning and significance, as an adult.

"Burned myself," he said, with a tacit warning not to pursue the subject.

"How'd you do that?"

The stranger smiled again, this time to mitigate the impact of the commandment broken.

"I tried to treat the wound myself - put bacon fat on the blister, wrapped it up, but it hasn't gotten any better. Thought a doc ought to look at it."

The confession told the marshal what he needed to know. The stranger did not want to die and had risked an open confrontation to seek aid. When it came to a showdown, such knowledge might save his life.

"Across the street," Claw pointed. "Past the alley. Shingle hangs outside. Upstairs, second story."

"Is he any good?"

"The best I've ever seen."

The man nodded, tried another smile, but it was thin and forced. For the first time, Claw realized how emaciated the man was; how the skin around his cheekbones was drawn unnaturally taut, as if he had not eaten for days and weeks at a time. Even the stranger's lips were bloodless, making the red of his sunburned nose stand out like a burning sentinel.

"Thanks."

With a nod of his head, almost, but not quite a bow, the wounded man turned, looked around himself to emblazon landmarks in his memory, then set off for Fiz's. Claw remained in the street, so motionless a black fly settled in on his neck to drink his salt-tinged perspiration.

A sixth sense warned the marshal that the stranger was about to look back. This sudden revelation caused Claw to move a half second before Tex or Jim or Bill paused in front of a shop window, ostensively to stare in at a display of lady's hats. What he was actually doing was using the reflective quality of the glass to stare behind his back.

What he saw was nothing. Being thus reassured, he continued his solitary journey.

It was not the knock itself which caused Doctor Ward to look up from his book. It was the sound of flesh against wood, the gentle, almost apologetic, I trust I am not disturbing you, summons.

Removing his thin, wire-framed glasses from his face, Fiz placed a bookmark between the pages, then closed the book, laying it on the desk before him as he spoke.

"Come in."

It was his custom not to acknowledge a patient at the door, honed into a fine old character trait for the simple reason that no one bothered to knock. They simply opened the door, stuck in their head and announced themselves. They had no sense of invading the physician's privacy, no awareness of disturbing him at work. He was the "town doc," and therefore, nothing he could, or might be doing, took precedence over their own needs.

To have someone knock at his door without the preliminary of already being inside the room was a lonely summons to times past, places gone, faces dimmed by necessity rather than years. It was, in its own right, a more glaring intrusion than the more intrusive, "Howdy, Fiz! Got sumthin' here I need you to look at right quick!"

The patient who opened the door did not fit the mental image the healer had rapidly sketched for himself. The man wore no frock coat, bore no dress hat in his hand. There was not the scent of Bay Rum cologne about him, nor the odor of printer's ink or freshly applied boot black.

Yet, there was a familiarity, an appeal of like minds, similar backgrounds. If that were not quite it, then it was something else, more subtle yet equally tangible.

The association should have created a bond between the two men, but did not.

"Doctor?" the man in the door queried, as though afraid he had intruded at the wrong office and disturbed a lawyer or a merchant at most pressing work.

"That's right. Dr. Ward. Come in."

Fiz had the peculiar sensation that if he did not invite the stranger in, the man would back away, turn and be gone, in much the same manner as a the ragged outline of a cloud, resembling an ill-defined human shape, dissipated before one could quite recognize the face.

The man stepped in, politely shutting the door behind him. Removing his hat, he looked around the room, adding further to the reassurance he was in the right place, then turned a set of piercing brown eyes on the master.

"I've burned my arm. I'd like you to take a look at."

The word "please" was implied, without being spoken.

Without breaking eye contact, Fiz nodded toward his examination table. "Over there."

To obey the command, the patient had to avert his eyes. He did so quickly, causing Fiz to feel an almost whip-like sensation at the break.

Laying his sweat-stained hat down on the table, the patient removed his jacket, turned back, without looking, to the coat tree behind the door, hung the worn leather article of clothing on a bare hook, then returned to the bed. Leaving his gunbelt on, the man untucked his shirt, then carelessly popped open the buttons, running his fingers from under the material, bottom to top.

He was slower removing the sleeve from his left arm, drawing it carefully over a gauze bandage, discolored by blood and well soaked with murky drainage.

"When did this happen?" Fiz asked.

"Week ago, thereabouts," came the surprisingly vague reply. Fiz would have guessed the man knew the time, down to the hour. "On the trail," the patient added before he was asked.

"How'd it happen?"

Fiz asked, not because the answer bore any significance to how he would treat the wound, but because he knew the man would lie, and wished to examine the cleverness of the explanation.

What he received for his cleverness was silence.

"How did this happen?" Fiz repeated in almost exactly the same words and precisely the same tone of voice.

"I tried to take care of it myself."

"You didn't get to it right away. Not until after the blistering had started. It's pretty badly infected."

"I know."

"What'd you put on it?"

"Bacon fat."

"By the time you treated it, it was too late for bacon fat to do any good. Clean it off, first?"

"I did what I could."

"Rinse it with water? Soak it in a stream? That would have been your best bet."

No answer. The "I know" was implicit without being verbalized.

"You a doctor?" Fiz inquired bluntly to the unuttered reply.

"No." And then, as a carefully considered afterthought, "I've done some doctoring."

"In the War?"

"No."

"Where, then?"

"Not as a physician. Read up a little on medicine."

"Why?"

"Man who keeps himself company ought to know a little bit about everything."

"I'll have to debride the infected skin. Know what that means?"

"Yes."

"It'll hurt some."

"What is it the Good Book says? No good ever comes without suffering?"

"Not my Good Book. What's your name?"

"Red."

"Red - what?"

"On account of my red hair," the man explained, pretending he had misunderstood Fiz's question.

"The operation'll cost you five dollars if you take a good slug of whisky before I start, and seven if you don't."

The man laughed, which was the last thing Fiz expected. The sound was rusty, like a key turning in a long unused lock.

"What'll it be?" Fiz pursued.

The answer was longer in coming.

"I'll take the whisky and thank you kindly for it."

That was not the man's first thought, nor his second, nor probably his inclination. He knew pain, sought pain as a means of burning away sin. That much the physician understood.

Taking a half empty bottle from his small curio cabinet, Fiz poured a generous amount of the amber liquid into a glass, swished it around so that rivulets of alcohol ran down the sides, then handed it to his patient.

Perhaps mesmerized by the action, the man lifted the glass to his lips, sniffed the contents, then brought it to his mouth. He did not gulp it, as befit a trail hand or a drifter, but sipped it slowly, rolling the flavor over his tongue before swallowing.

"If it's poison you want, I can oblige you for cheaper than it'll cost you to have the arm taken care of." .

"If it were poison I wanted, you would not give it to me," the man replied with a sad, furtive shadow of a smile.

"What makes you say that?" As he spoke, Fiz deliberately turned his back to fuss with his instrument case.

"Because you're a man of healing, not death."

"What makes you think so?"

"What I think, is that your Good Book and mine aren't so far different, after all."

"Suffering is good for the soul?" Fiz inquired, turning back, a wickedly sharp scalpel in his hand. Stillness settled over the room like evening fog. "I'm in the business of alleviating suffering, not causing it," he stated abruptly, rubbing his right hand across the mustache just beginning to show the passage of years with isolated strands of grey.

"I wonder."

"That puts us on opposite sides," Fiz stated, without adding a questioning inflection to his voice.

"I quote scripture, don't preach it."

"Seems to me, you could talk a man to death."

Without waiting for his patient to take another sip of the brandy, Fiz inserted the blade into the swollen, puss-filled flesh of the left arm, made a quick incision, then cut away parts of the once living skin and tissue.

The stranger who called himself "Red" did not flinch. Nor did he make any further attempt to drink. That moment had come and gone. Like opportunity, it had knocked on his door. He had opened it an inch, but not far enough. He would endure, now, without artificial aid.

"Hold this," Fiz ordered, shoving a small basin into the man's good right hand. Without bothering to see his command fulfilled, he turned his eyes back to the now profusely bleeding wound. "Deeper than I thought," he muttered. Then, in a softer shade, "I should have anesthetize you. Put you out."

"I am not a lamp, Doctor Ward. I will not be 'put out.'"

Fiz stopped abruptly, annoyed, or perhaps merely irked, by the audacity of the assertion.

"Oh. I see. You're going to live forever, are you?" Red raised an eyebrow, started to speak, then held his tongue. "If that's the case, I don't know why I'm bothering. Immortal men don't die from burns, or blood poisoning, or infection.

"The kind of man you think you are doesn't take whisky, either. Yet you did. Sort of let yourself down, didn't you?"

If Fiz had not been clasping the wounded arm as tightly as he was, Red would have succeeded in yanking it away from him.

"Mistake," he muttered through clenched teeth.

He did not elaborate on whether his mistake had been in seeking help, drinking the liquor or some other, less defined, but equally costly error.

With an anger often felt but seldom verbalized, Fiz squinted his sharp blue eyes as he searched the stranger's face.

"Who are you?" he demanded. "What are you doing in Hellhole? Who got to you, and who are you running from? We have law here, you know. Damned good law. And I'd just as soon see you die here and now from the poison in this wound, than think of the trouble which clings to your coat tails."

"I don't know what you're talking about!" the loner screamed, spittle flying from his wet mouth. "I told you what happened! There isn't anybody after me. I'm a nothing, a nobody! I'm dead. You hear me?"

"I don't doubt there's a headstone somewhere with your real name on it. Kept them off your trail, didn't it? So what happened - you got homesick and showed your face in the right place at the wrong time? That it?"

"Why do you say that?" Red continued, eyes rimmed with tears. "You're talking nonsense!"

Those were the words, but in his agony, they sounded more like, "Yaw talkin' nun-seence." Too late to stop himself, Red realized the mistake he had made. Taking in a shaky breath, he closed his eyes, forced himself to calmness, then reopened them. In those brief seconds, the caterpillar drew back into its deceiving cocoon, allowing the butterfly to re-emerge.

"I didn't want to come to Hellhole," he said in a perfectly controlled, immaculately enunciated sentence, stripped clean of the tell-tale Southern dialect his outburst had so fleetingly revealed. "I had a bad feeling about it. Didn't know there was a United States marshal here."

"Oh?" Fiz asked, clearly surprised. "You've seen Claw Kiley?"

The man dared smile.

"Asked him directions to your office, as a matter of fact."

"That took courage."

The man nodded again, in the respectful half bow, peculiar to him.

"I'm not planning on staying, Doctor."

"I didn't imagine you were."

"I'm not wanted -"

"- by the law," Fiz finished for him. "But somebody wants you. Bad." Then, surprising himself by the gentleness of his voice, asked, "Want to tell me about it?"

"Now-why-would-I-want-to-do-that, sir?"

"You're gonna have to tell somebody. I'm a better listener than most."

"You're a better observer than most," Red corrected.

"I can hold my tongue."

"No. I don't need to tell my story. Besides," he added, unable to suppress a spasm of pain, "You've already told me more than I needed to know." Prompted by a quizzical twist of Fiz's head, he finished, "About the Law. And the Lawman; Claw Kiley you called him. You bleed for him, doctor. An admirable trait in a preacher, but a bit awkward in a medical man, isn't it?"

"I don't -" Fiz snapped, then abruptly clamped his mouth so tightly shut, the muscles in his jaw jerked. Had he completed the sentence, "I don't bleed for him," Phillip Ward would not only have lied, he would have completed the dance, started the moment Red No-Last-Name-Given stuck his head through the office door.

To cover up their mutual discomfiture, Fiz put a hand on the outcast's chest, pushing him back toward the examination table.

"Lie down," he said. "I've got work to do and I don't want you falling to the floor in a dead faint."

The request was complied with in such a manner as to obfuscate the supposition the Southerner was unaccustomed to obeying orders.

"And drink the rest of that brandy." He added, "You don't finish it, I'll charge you for it, anyway, and pour it back in the bottle."

This time, Red's laugh was good natured.

"You get accused of that often enough, I wager."

"Never."

It was a lie and meant to be taken as such, standing as an acknowledgment there was much left unsaid between the two men.

CHAPTER 5

Protestations to the contrary that he was "not a lamp to be put out," Red slept soundly, once the operation was concluded. He had borne the pain like a Red Man, stoical, quiet, unmoving. It was not until the surgeon's knife had scraped the bone did he groan, and even that noise was muffled, more tortured exhalation than cry.

He had drunk a quarter of the brandy during the procedure, than that much more upon its completion. His eagerness toward the last, as his numbed brain sought release, was pitiful to see, and Fiz busied himself elsewhere until the man's gentle snoring alerted him to the fact his patient had temporarily passed on to greener pastures.

Fiz thought about removing the man's boots, so that his slumber might be more comfortable, then decided against it for no tangible reason. He contemplated removing the gunbelt and had actually started to unbuckle it, when caution stayed his hand. While the sleeping patient was no gunfighter - Fiz drew the same conclusions Claw had - he was dangerous. Fiz did not want him to awake, still groggy from what, in a doctor's hands, was medication, to find he had been stripped of that which he had, and would have, occasion to use.

When Red's respirations were regular and slowed to twenty a minute, and his heart rate lowered to one hundred, Fiz left his office, shutting, then purposely locking the door behind him. He did not fear his patient escaping, but rather shuddered at the idea of some unsuspecting farmer barging in with a toothache or a sprained angle, and receiving a bullet in the face for his trouble.

It was growing dusky by the time Fiz Ward entered the Lowdown Saloon and began his own quiet search for forgetfulness. The stranger had disturbed his ghosts and he did not wish them roaming the streets unchecked. Red eye whisky, he had discovered, reminded them of their place in his past.

Cougar Bradburn made her first appearance of the night at 7 P.M. Walking down the stairs with deliberate slowness, surveying all that she saw with an owner's eyes, she could not help but observe the doctor drinking at a table by himself. Ordinarily, his presence would have proven a welcome invitation for her, but this night she passed him by without a word.

She had been in the business too long not to recognize what a man was thinking, and why. She would leave him alone until the mental kirkyard was full and the bottle half empty.

Marshal Kiley stuck his head through the batwing doors at 9 P.M., waited until he caught her attention, than waved. She smiled and waved back. When he returned an hour later, she was waiting for him at the bar.

"How'd your day go?" she asked, motioning for Steve, the new bartender, to draw him a beer.

"I don't know," he replied, sipping the brew with stilted interest. Then, with a nod of his head, "What's a' matter with our friend?"

Cougar did not have to turn her attention on Fiz to answer Claw's question. Part of her had been watching him all evening.

"I don't know. He came in before seven."

"I saw him earlier," Claw agreed. "He been here since then?" She nodded in the affirmative. "I wanted to speak to him."

"Something wrong?"

"Yeah. Maybe. I don't know." He continued more hesitantly. "Sent a man with a bad burn over to his office this morning. Just wondered how he was doing, that's all."

"It's about time someone broke in on his thoughts. Come on."

Leading the way, Cougar and Claw approached Fiz's table.

"Either Eric's been selling me better whisky than I thought, or you're not too particular tonight," she opened.

It was a verbal card game she played, acting as dealer for the house. Fiz looked up slowly, his eyes red-rimmed from fatigue.

"Sit down," he invited. "Looks like you're busy tonight."

She hesitated before sitting. Her reticence was rewarded by having Claw draw the captain's chair out for her. Nodding her acceptance, she sat, then moved the chair closer to Fiz's.

"Comes and goes. Nothing out of the ordinary."

He looked at her astutely but was unable to read any more into her words than exactly what they implied.

Claw was less subtle, being newer at the game and thus more impatient.

"A man come up to see you?"

"A man? Lots of men come up to see me," Fiz snarled, looking down at his empty glass.

"That's my line," Cougar teased, refilling it for him.

Claw snorted, but Fiz sighed and shook his head.

"What'd you make of him?" he asked.

This time, the delay lay heavily on the marshal's shoulders. He stared down at his interlaced fingers, the beer untouched near his left hand.

"I didn't like him. He's trouble."

"He's not on any wanted posters."

"Why'd you say that? He tell you?"

Fiz shook his head and went back to drinking.

"What man?" Cougar demanded. "The man with the burn? Who is he?"

"Calls himself Red," Fiz explained.

"'bout what I figured," Claw grunted, staring around himself as though sizing up the pot. "Red. He's got red hair," he elaborated unnecessarily for Cougar's sake. "Not your color. Duller. Cut short. Got more freckles than you, though. Face full of 'em."

She could not be sure if he meant that as a positive or a negative character trait.

"How'd he say he got burned?"

"He didn't."

"Look like an accident?"

"No. It was deliberate."

"You mean, he did it to himself?" Cougar inquired, just to keep the game moving.

"It was done on purpose. Someone got to him, and someone else held him down, while a third man shoved his arm into some red-hot embers."

"He told you a lot for not telling you anything," Claw observed.

"I'm a doctor; I've treated more men with burns than you've shot lawbreakers," came the retort from the low calibre weapon. "The flesh wasn't blackened, like it would have been, had he gotten too close to an open blaze - being trapped in a forest fire, for instance. The wound was deep - almost to the bone. Someone held him down a long time. Then let him up."

"Why would they do that?"

It was left up to Fiz which question he chose to answer: why a gang of men would hate another so much they would deliberately roast his arm in burning embers, or why those same men would release their victim after finally having him where they wanted him.

Fiz chose to answer neither.

"I don't know."

"Did this 'Red' say where it happened?"

"No."

"Did he say when it happened?"

"He lied."

Fiz sniffed, wiped his brow with a handkerchief, then summoned Steve. When the bartender moved within earshot, he called for a new bottle.

Neither Claw nor Cougar asked him what was wrong with the one he had not finished.

When the new bottle was delivered, Fiz twisted the cork off, then poured, first to Cougar, then for himself.

Cougar took a drink before speaking.

"What kind of man is he, Fiz?"

"A haunted man."

"Who's after him?" Claw asked, taking up the slack.

"How should I know?"

"I thought with all that talkin' he didn't do, you would have figured it out."

"He didn't do that kind of talking."

"Did you fix him up?"

"I did."

"Where'd he go?"

"He's still up in my office."

While Fiz was speaking, the outside wind came up, banging a hanging lantern against the side of the building. The result was a dull thud, repeated twice more before the wind died down.

Without obvious connection, a drifter came through the double doors, rubbing his hands while blowing on them. Seeing the bar to his right, he sauntered up to it, leaned heavily across the uprights and ordered a drink.

"Looks like it's the day for strangers," Cougar observed.

Beer glass in hand, Claw silently excused himself and walked to the bar.

"Gone flat on me, Steve," he said agreeably, pushing a nickel across the bar. "How 'bout another?"

"Sure thing, Marshal."

Steve drew him another as Claw settled in next to the stranger. The man eyed him with open curiosity.

"Didn't know Hellhole had a U.S. Marshal. My name's Timmons; Hector Timmons. Men call me Heck. Don't get in here much. Got a horse ranch about twenty miles west of here. Run a few cattle, mostly to feed myself and the wife. She'll be glad to know the law's come."

"Pleased to make your acquaintance."

"Buy you another, Marshal -?"

"Claw Kiley. No thanks. Some other time."

"You come out my way, stop in," Heck Timmons invited as Claw discarded his suspicion and moved away.

"Thanks. I will."

"Hey! Marshal!" Claw's head snapped back at the urgency of the summons. "You forgot your beer."

"Thanks."

Returning briefly to the bar, Claw slipped the fingers of his right hand through the glass handle of the mug, shaped like a trigger guard, hefted the weight easily and retraced his steps.

"You know that man?" he whispered, covering the sound of his voice by scraping the chair legs along the wooden-slat floor.

"Not sure. Maybe. He looks familiar," Fiz decided.

"What about you?" Claw asked Cougar.

She glanced over, took in the rancher's profile, then shrugged.

"A lot of men come in here. I might have seen him a time or two. A lot of those small ranchers keep to themselves. They've got wives," she mentioned. "And better things to do with their nickels."

"He doesn't look like trouble to me," Fiz snorted, adding a nightcap to a glass which did not need refilling. "I think he's exactly who and what he says he is."

Before Claw could call the doctor's bluff, Cougar pushed back in her chair.

"And I think I'll close up for the night."

"Little early, isn't it?"

The question came from neither Claw nor Fiz, but from another stranger, this one sitting at an adjoining table.

"It's dull tonight," the mistress decided. "No sense opening up another keg of beer if I'm not going to sell more than a few glasses out of it." Looking across the room, she caught Steve's eyes. He nodded and addressed the room.

"We're closing for the night, boys. Drink up."

Several of the patrons made low, disconsolate noises, but obeyed the order. Within five minutes, the only man remaining, who did not belonging to the small group at the table, was Mr. Timmons.

Slurping down the remainder of his beer, he wiped his mouth on his sleeve, burped, and ambled toward the door in a not altogether convincingly drunken stagger.

"G'night, Marshal," he sang from the double doors. "I'll tell the misses you've gonna stop by one afternoon to pay her a call. She'll be right glad to hear there's law come to Hellhole."

Claw responded by putting a hand to his hat in polite farewell.

"I've got to be getting on, myself," he declared suddenly.

"I didn't mean for you to hurry on."

He shrugged, interlaced his fingers then bent them backwards, as though the digits had stiffened from a long night of double-dealing cards.

"Maybe I'll go up and take a look at your patient, Fiz."

"Now, why would you want to do that? You've already seen him."

"Man looks different when he's sleeping. Just thought I'd like to see him in a different way; maybe jog my memory. Something like that."

"Man looks different when he'd dead, too," Fiz educated him.

"Thanks. I'll keep that in mind."

Fiz waited until Claw was nearly to the outside doors before continuing the conversation.

"The man's got a gun, Claw. He's jumpy as a cat. He hears strange footsteps coming up the stairs, he's liable to shoot first and ask questions second."

The lawman thought to say that if that scenario were enacted out, the physician would have the opportunity of observing his features relaxed in death, but thought better of it.

Not that he was a superstitious man.

"Night."

The wind, which had come up and then died down, began to howl with renewed vigor as the marshal departed the protected confines of the saloon. It was a cold wind, hinting of an early winter. Hunching his shoulders against the unexpected chill, Claw crossed the street, slipping into his own office like a thief in the night.

Miss Cougar, the cat, greeted him with a yowl of recognition.

"You cold, too? Why don't I kick up this fire?"

Without waiting for an answer he knew he would not receive, Claw crossed to the small, pot-bellied stove, opened the door and tossed in several small pieces of wood. They smoked, hissed, spat back bits of boiled sap, then finally caught into a reluctant blaze.

Leaving the hinged stove door open in the hope of warming the room, Claw decided it would be wasteful to burn wood for no better reason than keeping the fur-lined feline comfortable. Settling himself behind his desk, he creaked back in the chair, rocked a moment, then removed his hat and placed it to his left, on the desk.

It was too dark to read without lighting the lamp and once settled, he did not feel like getting up again to take a burning twig out of the stove to use as a match. That left him the option of sitting in the dark or wasting a Lucifer. Opening the top drawer, he removed a loose, sulphur-tipped splinter of wood from the front, struck it against a scrap of sandpaper, then held it to the charred tip of the lamp wick.

The illumination of single candle-power did not appreciatively lighten up his world.

The wanted posters were sitting in a wire basket on top of the desk. Claw could have found them in the dark, read the names and crimes without light, for he had them memorized. There were sixteen in all. Red's face was not among them.

Claw flipped through the heavy-bond papers, searching, not for a face he knew was absent from the gallery, but of face or faces who might be the type to burn a man for sport. Any of the group, he decided, in disgust, fit that bill. Wanted for murder, robbery, assault, suspicion of card sharping, dynamiting railroad tracks, jail break, blackmail or extortion, the faces which stared back into Kiley's blue eyes were lifeless, unblinking.

Dead.

A man in his occupation developed the Gift, if it could be called that, of looking at a face on a wanted poster and making an immediate determination whether that individual were still alive, or if somewhere along the trail he had been ambushed from behind an outcropping of rock, shot in the back from a gunman standing in a blind alley, or pushed over the railing of an upper story brothel.

The men, whose life history he held in his hands, were no longer a threat to him. They would not be discovered breaking into the Hellhole Bank, tearing up the Wolf's Pelt Saloon, or extorting money from an old acquaintance gone straight.

Sixteen wanted posters, sixteen names, sixteen corpses feeding worms or wolves or picked clean by buzzards of the two-legged variety.

The names of Reginald West, Mark Simpson, Harold Birdsong, Art Ledderer, Jerry Drew, better known as Injun Joe Smith, Dead Eye Steve, Cattleman Bob, Daring Dan Diamond, Major Reb, could be consigned to the fire, reissued to other, more or less worthy, but still-warm, compatriots.

None of them deserved to live and probably did not deserve to die in the ways they had. None of them, singly or together, tracked a man for a month or a year, burned the flesh off his arm, then let him go, so they could have the pleasure of tracking him down and performing that operation, or a worse one, again.

Claw Kiley did not know the real name of Red, nor did he know any of the monikers of those shadowing him.

What he did know was a game of cat and mouse when he saw one.

Replacing the wanted posters in his in-basket, the marshal drew the lamp toward his lips, turned down the wick and blew out the flame, killing it with a single blow.

Now the lamp was as dead as those wanted men, no longer sought by law enforcement officials. Their business now, if they had any, was to explain to a higher authority about crimes no longer punishable by mortal man.

In the morning, Claw Kiley would post the flyers outside on his bulletin board. He had no legitimate reason to suppose them dead; for all intense and no practical purposes, they were still wanted criminals. It was his duty to display their names, faces and crimes, and he would do his duty.

Jack Duvall would expect no less.

Jim Bennett and Dan Cord and Jim Carey - all men who had baptized Claw in the nuisances of the Law - would understand.

Duty was a four lettered word.

None of them had ever said it had to make sense.

Replacing his hat on his head, Claw restlessly put a hand on his low-hanging pistol as though to reassure himself it was still there, then walked across the office. He left without remembering to close the door of the pot-bellied stove.

The wind had gotten colder and more bitter. Muttering obscenities to himself about forgetting his jacket, the Law crossed the street and began its rounds.

"'Round and around it goes and when it stops, only the Almighty knows," Jim Carey had joked. He was the preacher of the small, ever-changing group.

Claw had heard those words a very long time ago. Preacher Jim had died from a fall off a horse. Dan Cord had gotten his in Dishwater, Cimarron Territory, so many years past no one remembered how.

Or why.

It was nearing one o'clock in the morning when Claw ended his futile search for shades and ghosts, ending his trek at the foot of Dr. Phillip Ward's stairs. A light was burning in the window.

Making his way up the unevenly spaced, irregularly slanted wooden slates, the marshal tried the knob, found it unlocked and went inside. Fiz sat at his desk, reading, his pair of wire-rimmed spectacles suspended between the base and tip of his nose. The reader glanced up, ascertained the visitor was who he thought he was, and went back to reading.

"I came to see him," Claw announced, failing to identify the patient by name.

"Gone."

Another four letter word.

Something a man of the law was well familiar with.

CHAPTER 6

Eric Anheiser arrived in the morning.

The first inkling Claw had that something was amiss was the large wagon outside the Lowdown. Painted on the side in bold - and to his taste - gaudy red lettering - was the announcement, "Anheiser Brothers." Beneath this banner were the words "Sour Herbs and Branch Water Cures."

The marshal took stern note of the advertisement, deciding that before Eric Anheiser left Hellhole City, he would have cause to take his own medicine.

The sound of Cougar's laughter, ringing as clear as a bell across the entire seven- hundred mile width of Main Street, added to his consternation.

But when he heard Doctor Ward's normally dour chuckling blending into the cacophony, his bad mood would have turned Mr. Anheiser's sour herbs sweet.

Much in the same way spilled ink turned a white shirt black.

With a stiff-legged walk which, in a shorter man, would have made it appear he was traveling on stilts, the marshal crossed the street. Without pausing, as was his custom, to stare into the interior of the Lowdown, looking to see all was well, he marched in, spine erect, arms taut at his sides.

He did not require rubber lifts to increase his height, but he did good service as a wooden soldier.

Claw had planned to greet the threesome with a pleasant and cheerful "Good morning!" make the acquaintance of the dreaded representative from the spirits world, then rush off to prevent a bank robbery, or save a lady in distress. Unfortunately, while waiting for his cue - the sound of gunfire or a shrill scream - Claw's plan fell flat.

"What's this about sour herbs and branch water cures?" he demanded in a pitch nearly equaling his exulted height.

Cougar and Fiz looked across the room at him, started by the petulant tone in his voice, but Eric had a ready answer.

"It's a disguise, Marshal," he explained, as though he and Claw had been drinking buddies in St. Louis long before the later had come to such a place as Hellhole. "If I put 'Beer, Wine and Saloon Accouterments' on the side of the wagon, I make myself a target for everyone, from marauding soldiers to thirsty cattle."

Claw mentally sketched a bullseye over Eric's left brow.

"By proclaiming myself a patent medicine hawker, selling bad-tasting potions and worthless cures, I'm left alone. The only thing worth robbing me of would be my horses, and horse stealing is a hanging offense."

Claw wondered if the hawker had a bill of sale for the animals hitched to his wagon.

"Pretty darned clever, I'd say!" Fiz remarked, slapping his knee in jolly good humor.

"I should think," Claw retorted soberly to the physician, "that you would take offense to having such a wagon, with such a procurement, anywhere in Hellhole."

"Why would that be?" Ward demanded, failing to correct the improper usage of a ten-dollar word.

"It'll take business away from you. I wouldn't be surprised to see townsmen lining up knee deep to invest in good health."

Eric laughed, thinking perhaps, Claw had made a joke.

"They'll be coming in by droves," Cougar agreed. "And I suppose some would call it for their health. Eric always buys a round for everyone wandering in, his first night in Hellhole."

"Never turn down a chance for improving business and good will," the generous man agreed, looking adoringly at Miss Bradburn.

Claw wondered if Mr. Anheiser knew what business he was in, and that too much "good will" could send a man to jail.

"By the way," the newcomer added, standing and extending a hand, "I'm Eric Anheiser."

Claw sized him up for a wrist cuff while shaking.

"Marshal Claw Kiley," he identified himself.

"Heard a lot about you."

"How is that, now?"

"From Cougar and Fiz."

Claw arched an eyebrow, then glared at Fiz, deciding that, in Boston, a man who took liberties by using a casual form of address with a lady and a professional man, would be drowned in tea. He seemed to recall they had Tea Parties there of rather impressive magnitude.

"Eric didn't know a Federal man had come to town," Fiz supplied, apparently misreading Claw's body language.

"I should have taken out a notice on the side of a wagon."

"Sit down and have a cup of coffee," Cougar invited. Claw noted there were no empty chairs anywhere near the table at which they sat.

Nor was there a cup.

He supposed that meant they expected him to squat on the floor while drinking the scalding hot beverage from his hand.

"I-have-to-make-my-rounds."

Meaning, "I have something far more important to do than sit around and chew the fat with you three." As in, "Three's company, four's a crowd."

The lawman decided he would pay a call on Mr. Herbert, president of the Hellhole bank. He had a sneaking suspicion that worthy institution was about to be dynamited.

According to everything he had learned or been told since arriving in Hellhole, such an event was grossly overdue.

Like an unpaid debt.

"I hope you'll come around later, Marshal Kiley," Eric invited, assuming an unwarranted attitude of ownership. "I've brought several bottles of fine French wine. If I known Cougar won the Lowdown from Mr. Bix Bradley, I would have gift-wrapped some champagne."

"I don't like champagne," Claw blurted. "It goes up my nose."

"That's because no one ever taught you how to drink it," Eric offered helpfully. "You sip sparkling wine, you don't gulp it like beer."

Causing Claw to take the Pledge. At least until Mister Anheiser was dead and buried or escorted out of town on a rail, whichever came last.

"Well, I love champagne," Fiz declared in a silence so ominous, a man might have heard a bubble burst.

"Then I'll have to make it two bottles," Eric the Generous offered.

With that declaration, he settled back in his chair. A good kick under his seat would have taken some of the independence out of him.

"I may be busy all day. If I don't see you before you go," Claw began, but Eric waved him off.

"Oh, don't worry about missing me, Marshal. I'll be here all week."

Worrying about missing him had not occurred to Claw.

He was, after all, a dead aim.

"All week?"

"Sure. First, I have to unload the wagon. I've got enough whisky crates and beer barrels under that canvas to restock the new owner for two months."

"Maybe longer," Cougar warned, shaking her head slowly. "What with winter coming on. Men just don't drink that much beer when it's cold."

Claw decided there would be an early winter this year.

"What with the mild summer we've had, I expect a warm winter," Fiz observed, drumming his fingers on the table.

"It will snow before Thanksgiving," Claw announced. Everyone looked at him in tepid surprise.

"You think so?" Eric asked.

Claw would have bet Eric's life on it.

"We don't celebrate Thanksgiving in Hellhole," Cougar educated the United States man. "That's a Yankee holiday."

"We-will-this-year."

Fiz removed a small pocketknife from his vest pocket and amputated a hangnail.

"Might not be a bad idea."

"Why is that?"

"People eat too much, they just might be needing some of those sour herbs of yours, Eric."

Claw laughed, thinking Fiz had made a joke.

"Whatever it takes," Eric agreed.

Claw stopped laughing, feeling the splash of cold water on his face.

"See you later, then." He did not say where he expected to see Eric later.

"Don't forget. I owe you a drink," the beer man called to Claw's back.

Claw left the Lowdown, coming out into the warm, sunny day. Thirteen men had already gathered around the wagon, rubbing their hands in anticipation.

"Get a move on or I'll arrest you all for loitering."

He might as well have saved his breath, for none of the townsmen knew the meaning of the word "loitering."

Mr. Herbert was nowhere to be found. The clerk at the back thought he might be at home, working "on the books." Subsequent investigation revealed that Mrs. Herbert thought her husband was at the bank, preparing a report for the annual stockholders meeting.

"Where is this meeting supposed to take place?" the marshal demanded with ill-disguised annoyance.

"New Orleans."

"New Orleans is in Louisiana," Claw pointed out.

Mrs. Herbert nodded.

"They wanted to hold the meeting in New York City, but some of the major stock holders still find travel there - unsettling."

Claw had the uncomfortable feeling Mr. Herbert considered him "unsettling," as well.

"Where is your husband from?"

"Chicago. That's in Illinois," she added, not completely certain the marshal knew his geography. Claw scowled.

"Illinois is a Northern state. With a claim on President Lincoln," he added dryly.

"President Lincoln is dead."

Claw had an inkling that not only was the bank due for dynamiting, it was long overdue for a tax reassessment. The increased valuation of the improved property put into effect before the demolition, naturally.

All things in the proper order.

He supposed President Lincoln would have agreed.

"When do you expect Mr. Herbert to return?"

"By suppertime, at the latest."

"How long as he been gone?" Claw demanded. He remembered seeing the banker only yesterday.

"Since nine o'clock."

"How can a man get to New Orleans and back between 9 A.M. and suppertime?

"Who said he went to New Orleans?" asked a very huffy woman.

"You did."

"I said no such thing. What I said, sir, was that he was preparing a report for the annual stockholders meeting, to be held in New Orleans."

"To be held - when?"

"Next May, when the Mississippi is free from ice. Everyone knows about freezing."

Claw thanked her for her cooperation and left. Next stop on his road show was at Vernon Trask's Furniture and Undertaking Establishment.

"Good morning, Marshal!" the tall, Ichabod Crane-type man greeted him warmly.

Claw saw nothing good in it.

"How's business?" he asked, trying not to sound too casual.

Vernon licked his lips appreciatively.

"I haven't buried anyone all week, but Fiz's been going out to the Perkins place pretty regular. That's always a good sign."

Claw swallowed, then turned his head away. He had often wondered why a man would go into the funeral business. He decided now he did not want to know.

"How's your inventory? Got several coffins on hand, do you?"

Vernon fairly beamed at the lawman.

"I've got two ready-built; cheap ones, made out of scrub pine and some boards I scrounged from the Furness place after it burned down. That was before your time," he added sadly. "The burn marks don't show, though, and I reinforced some of the weak spots where the wood was thin. I take pride in my work, you know.

"I'm working on a very fine coffin at the moment. When I'm done, it will have shiny brass handles, a silk lining and a matching pillow. The fortunate recipient will need four pall bearers, at least. Maybe six, depending on how heavy the corpse is."

"How much does it sell for?"

"That depends."

"On what?"

Claw had the depressing feeling he was going to get another New Orleans story.

"On a lot of factors," Mr. Trask replied, straightening himself in front of a potential customer. Casually brushing a stray bit of what Claw hoped was sawdust off his black frock coat, the mortician continued. "How much work the body requires. Closed lid ceremonies generally don't require a great deal of - rearrangement. Naturally, I prefer open lid viewing."

Claw cleared his throat.

"Naturally."

"It's so much better for the family. And the spectators. Helps them grieve while they're remembering the deceased the way he was in life."

"Sort of makes you feel as though you're burying a living man, doesn't it?"

Vernon Trask was aghast.

"Oh, never. Not after the embalming."

"I forgot about that," Claw admitted, swallowing his liver.

"And then, of course, price would depend on whether clothing is supplied by the deceased's kin."

"Why wouldn't it be?"

Vernon waxed melancholy.

"You know what they say, Marshal. A dead Injun don't have no friends. It occasionally happens that the wardrobe belonging to the deceased is too fine to bury him in, so the family requests something... a bit more appropriate for the occasion."

"Like what?"

"A sheet. A fine one, though," Vernon added, noting the expression on Claw's face. "Although, now that you mention it, I have had several requests from the family to remove the wardrobe before the final disposition."

Claw did not remember mentioning any such thing.

"And then what do you bury him in?"

"Nothing."

"You mean, you bury him naked?"

Vernon seemed shocked and slightly offended at the marshal's outburst.

"A man comes into this world unclothed," he lectured, underscoring his use of the genteel word, rather than the crude one employed by the marshal, "and you go out the same way. I don't suppose the Lord is overly shocked to receive a gentleman in a state of undress."

"I'll tell you what, Mr. Trask. The next time you get a request from the next of kin to remove the 'deceased's' clothing before burial, you come to me first. I say, if a man is going to be buried buck naked, he ought to be laid out and viewed that way. Just to get him accustomed to being stared at without the dignity of a pair of trousers. Just might be some cold winter night he'll come out of his grave and haunt those who were too cheap to bury him right."

"I couldn't do that, Marshal."

"Why not?"

"It would be a betrayal of my professional discretion. Some men like to take their secrets to the grave. Like the fellow I buried... when was it? About a year ago, I'd say. I was combing his hair all right and proper when I discovered he was wearing a wig. I guess he was a thespian, or a circus performer. I never did say a word about that to anyone. If you'll give me a minute, his name will come back to me...."

Which is more than could be said for the marshal.

If the undertaker could offer no solace in his quest, Claw decided to go in a different direction. While the former worked with the dead, his next journey took him to a man who worked with those who wanted to get dead - dead drunk.

"Blade!"

The small, square-shouldered man so-called emerged from the back room, wiping his hands on a towel. When he saw who the summoner was, he gave the tall man a grin.

"What'll it be, Marshal Kiley? Beer's on the house."

Remembering Cougar's warning that Blade watered his beer more than she did, Claw decided it was too early for a drink.

"I see the beer man is in town. I expect you'll be buying stock from him?"

"Not this time."

His interest was piqued.

"Why not? Prices too high? Whisky no good?"

"Don't need any, is all. Besides, he'll be back again before winter."

"That's not what I understood from talking to him."

"He was probably talkin' about resupplyin' the Lowdown. He'll come through at least once more before it snows to bring me my order. And sell kegs of beer to the other watering holes around town."

"Why does he come through so often?"

"Can't carry it all in one load. Besides, the Lowdown and I don't buy the same type of beer."

"So I understand," replied the worldly lawman. "What do you know about him?"

"About Eric?" Claw flinched. He had expected more decorum from the proprietor of the Wolf's Pelt. "He's all right. Friendly. Everyone likes him."

Claw looked around the saloon for fire law violations.

"Ever been known to short-change a customer?"

Welsh on a bet? Spit on the street?

"Don't suppose he has to. He and his brother make a damn good livin' doin' what they do. They sell all over the state; even into the Cimarron, if I ain't mistook."

It was the "miss" and the "took" which narrowed Claw's eyes.

"They got a huge warehouse in St. Louie. Seen it once when I was passin' through. My brother was gettin' hanged in Galena. Wanted to see him one last time. Seems he robbed a steamboat. I don't know why; I a'ways said I'd send him money. Anyway, them Anheiser brothers got a big distillery. I hear they're openin' a brewery, too. Wish I owned a piece of it."

Claw wished he had a piece of it too, but not the same piece Blade had in mind.

"Thanks for the information."

He was sorry he had asked.

"He do sumthin' wrong, Marshal?"

"Why do you ask that?"

"You seem mighty interested in him, is all."

"Just never heard of him. If he's doing a lot of business here in Hellhole, I thought I'd check him out."

Blade scratched his chin thoughtfully.

"There is a guy knows a heap more about them St. Louie Anheisers than I do. You might ask him."

"Who is he?"

"Think his name is Bill Smith."

"Bill Smith?" Claw demanded, hands akimbo. Here was another suspicious-sounding name, this time, linked to someone Claw would very much like to pin a crime on.

"What relation is this Bill Smith fella to the Anheisers?"

"Second cousins, or sunthin'. Heard Eric talk about him last time he was through."

"Where can I find him?"

"In Washington, I 'spect. He's some sort of U.S. senator, or Secretary of War or some such."

Claw left without thanking his informant. He was almost certain "Bill Smith" was not the Secretary of War's name, but he could not have listed one singe senator, had he tried.

For that matter, he did not know the name of the vice president.

Or even if there were one.

Which gave Claw Kiley something else in common with Abraham Lincoln.

CHAPTER 7

The man called Red grimaced in pain as he gripped his wounded left arm with his right. It was a poor man's way of alleviating pain, something he had learned a long time ago, when proper medical care was hard to come by.

If a man pressed hard enough, he slowed circulation to the effected part, thus temporarily easing the agonized throbbing, much in the same way a tourniquet stopped the bleeding before an amputation.

Red was not a doctor, had never given the occupation much thought. What he had explained to Fiz Ward had been the truth, for he was - or had been - an honest man, and lying came hard.

Not as hard as it used to.

But then, there had been a time when eating maggot-ridden meat had been an impossibility. Now, he would have paid five dollars for the privilege.

He should have stopped at the General Store to refill his depleted saddlebags.

He should have gone into one of the watering holes and bought himself a bottle.

Should have, would have. The best laid schemes o' mice an' men.

Only a well-educated man would have known the author of that quote. Once-upon-a-time, Red, under a different name and a markedly different personality, had been proud of his accomplishments as a scholar. Nothing had seemed more important than widening his universe through formal education.

What was the expression? A gentleman and a scholar.

He laughed bitterly.

What good was his book learning now? Of less use to him than his former title.

He groaned aloud, then bit his lip, drawing blood from the shame of his weakness. A gentleman did not show suffering, never revealed the depths of his emotions, no matter how tender or how acute. A gentleman maintained his decorum, never forgetting who he was, and from what blue blood he had sprung.

A gentleman wore white gloves, spoke with a soft, refined manner, never employing an uncouth word or tending an unclean thought. A gentleman walked with his head held high and his face to the wind, relishing the challenges of the hunt with equal vigor to those of the business world.

A gentleman was never the hunted.

A gentleman never ran from --

He chewed the word off, preventing himself, even now, from thinking the crude, though not uncommon, everyday expression.

A gentleman he was born and a gentleman he would die.

Sooner, he expected, than later.

Doctor Ward had treated his wound, staving off the inevitable killing infection. That gave him a week, perhaps a month, if he were lucky.

Lucky. Another word from his past. He had heard it said a gentleman was lucky because he was born with a silver spoon in his mouth. His father, God rest his soul, had always answered that a gentleman need make no excuses for his birthright. It was neither chance nor luck which brought a man into the world: it was a conscious act between a man and a woman, with the blessings of the Almighty.

A man of breeding was superior because he was born into a proper, aristocratic family. A lowborn man was created inferior because he was born into the working class.

Everything was white and black to his father.

In the course of his own lifetime, Red had learned that gradations of light and dark held more prominence than his father would ever have acknowledged.

A dog howled in the distance, sending a shiver of fear through Red's wracked body. He jumped, darted to his right, had on his gun, and waited. Gentleman seldom had to wait for anything.

Red was used to waiting. Patience had become ingrained in his otherwise tumultuous nature.

His father would never had agreed with the expression, "All good things come to he who waits." His father believed it was his God-given right to have what he wanted, when he wanted it. Patience was not a virtue of the New World nobility.

When the cry was not repeated, Red forced his cramped muscles to relax. Slowly, with the stealth of a rattle snake, he unwound himself from the defensive posture he had naturally fallen into and returned to his fire. The cold fear of detection was so strong upon him however, he kicked the few burning twigs into an early grave.

No sense taking chances. A careful man lived to run another day.

Red did not know why, exactly, he wanted to live. His life for the present, the foreseeable future and the recent past, was unmitigated hell. He had suffered beatings, exposure, near starvation, thirst, acute loneliness and finally a nearly fatal burning. He could look forward to more than the same, until time caught up with him, in the guise of the living shadows of night.

His end would finally come when their patience ran out; when they tired of the children's game of hide and seek. Then, and only then, unless he had the good fortune of falling down a well or shooting himsef in the head, would the final act in this horrible drama be played out.

He smiled to himself. Not a kind smile, not a wistful remembrance of gentler times, but a bitter recollection of a world which no longer acknowledged him. He had been good at charades, once. No one was better in disguising himself at the dressing box than he; not one of his cousins, his boyhood friends or visitors from abroad could pantomime the title of a novel, or wordlessly get across a famous quote, with more dispatch than he.

But those incidents were long ago, and what had been amusing as a game was demonically transformed, by dire necessity, into a living hell. Disguises now were not the dictate of pastime but donned for the purpose of prolonging life. Wordless communication in Red's present was the dictate of caution, rather than farce.

No one had told him when he was twenty that the rules of the game would change. No one warned him that innocence died an ugly death.

For lack of anything better to do, the fugitive drew his saddlebags toward him. Flipping open the leather flap with a casualness he did not feel, his weary fingers sought what he knew was not there. Aside from a half pound of dried navy beans and five coffee beans, he had no food. Water, which should have been less of a problem was tantalizingly far away, for he had no strength to walk to the cheerful bubbling creek two hundred yards from his camp.

Even the luxury of a fire was denied him. They were out there. Red could feel them, hear them, smell them, touch the electricity of their ever-present thoughts. Like a mouse or a rabbit or a prairie dog, his were the senses of the hunted. Ignore a change in the wind, disregard the flutter-like noise of a leaf falling from a tree, pause in his ever-vigilant backtracking, and he too would fall prey to the men in wolf's clothing.

Tossing the saddlebag aside in uncharacteristic abandon, he lay down on the grave-cold earth, head propped up against his saddle. In the morning, he would have to make a decision. A man might go hungry and understand why, but a horse lacked the ability to justify its aching innards. He would have to find a ranch or a squatter's shack or a barn and feed the animal.

Failing in that, Red No-Last-Name-Given, would have to release it. Left to its own resources, the horse would make its way back to Hellhole where someone would take pity on it and feed it.

An animal, Red had learned, was accorded more sympathy than a man.

Miss Cougar was restless. Flicking her tail in feline annoyance, she jumped down from her warm perch atop the marshal's bunk, made the circuit of the outside office, then scratched at the back door. Claw, who was not asleep, rose noiselessly from the bed and tiptoed across the cold floor. Turning the brass knob which he had oiled only this evening, he pushed open the door just wide enough for the cat to escape.

He was weary but not sleepy. His bones ached yet his mind was active. His warring body was too caught up in the conflict to allow him to rest. With a sigh of resignation, the lawman backtracked to his bed, pulled on his boots, then strapped the gunbelt around his middle.

The hours of darkness were no friends to the hunted or the peacekeeper. They concealed the predator with a cloak of invisibility, while taunting the rest by assurances that all was well.

Hellhole was quiet but all was not as it should be. There were forces afoot he did not understand. No sleep would come until he was certain he had done all that was humanly possible to allay the danger.

He could have walked the streets of Hellhole blindfolded and found his way, but tonight Claw Kiley did not blink. It was not a time for a child's game of blind man's bluff, but rather one of vigilance. Whomever or whatever was stirring this night was prowling for something. By dawn, he would know what, or he would be dead and past caring.

At least, that was what Jim Carey had always said. He was the itinerant preacher man in the uneasy mixture of lawmen, hiders, trappers and drifters with whom Claw had grown to manhood. Part father, part saint, part devil, Jim Carey knew his Bible almost as well as he knew his gun. He was a great one for talking and the tall, lanky boy these men adopted was a good listener.

"Death, Claudius," Jim had said, "is only a passageway into another life."

"What kind of life?" the youth had demanded, oblivious to the stares and winks of those others, less attentive, or perhaps just more jaded than he.

"Can't say for certain," Jim lectured, running a cleaning rag through the barrel of his black-powder rifled musket. "No one's ever come back to describe it."

"Then how do you know there is another life?" Claw demanded, squatting on his haunches, nose nearly pressed into the older man's face.

"Faith, boy. A man knows here," he demonstrated, pointing to his heart, "what he don't know here," he concluded, tapping his temple with the end of the rifle.

"Faith," his disciple repeated with an uncomprehending frown. "How do I know if I have it?"

"You're born with it."

"Then I guess I ain't got it," Claw declared solemnly. "I was born without parents and I was born without faith."

Jim Carey had paused from his task, shaking his head slowly.

"No man's born without a mother and a father, boy," he declared. "Maybe you never knew yours, but you had 'em. Just like you have faith."

"Then how do I find them?" the pupil inquired innocently.

"You look."

"Where?"

"All around you."

Claw rose slowly to his feet, eyes searching the small group of misfits gathered around the fire.

"Are one of you here my father or my mother?" he asked.

"You've got to look beyond what your eyes can see, son," Dan Cord had replied. "I think that's what Jim is saying."

"How can I look beyond what I can see?"

None of the men had a ready answer and the conversation died down.

Walking around the perimeter of the camp, as he now paced the ill-defined edges of his town, the words of those men came back to him with the clarity of a dream. They had spoken in parables which, to his child's mind, were nearly incomprehensible. Coming back to him now, he was still uncertain what they meant.

Seeing what he could not see; feeling what he could not feel; passing from the known to the unknown. Ethereal words translated poorly into stark reality. Mysteries men whispered to one another in the darkness, afraid to carry on the discussion into the light of morning.

With the coming of dawn, all things changed. The world turned from upside down to right side up. Shadows gave way to substance, while unanswered questions lost their edge of urgency.

Predators retreated into the background, the owl to sleep, the murdering shade to resume the guise of a man.

Faith. Jim Carey told Claw he was born with it. Tonight, as his right hand fingered the cold, unyielding, insensitive butt of his pistol, Claw Kiley was not so sure. He had an inkling - call it a lack of faith - that no gun, no posse, no preacherman was enough to ward away the evil lurking in the night.

Tonight, Claw did not even believe his badge would protect the innocent.

That realization was far stronger than any belief or doubt. It was hell on earth. It was the beginning of the end, the fading of bright red to dull rust, the odor transmuting from a sharp iron smell to one of sickly copper. It was the clear whites clouding over with the cataracts of death, the rattle of trapped air inside unmoving lungs, the agony of pain slipping away into nothingness.

He remembered Vernon Trask, the scarecrow man who worked in wood and corpses. He was making a coffin, a fine one with silver handles.

Silver bullets, Claw had heard, were used to fend off the powers of darkness.

He had never been wealthy enough to buy any, nor had he known any man who had.

Godliness, he supposed, would have to be enforced with lead.

It was not a movement he saw, but rather, a lack of movement. Turning with exaggerated casualness, he held his breath to listen, narrowed his eyes to see.

Over at the doctor's office, there had been a displacement of night. Someone or something had gone up the stairs.

With an anger so acute it almost choked him, the lawman crossed the street in long, determined strides. God damn that doctor, anyway. He never locked his door. Anyone with a mind to it, could slip in, unnoticed, slit his throat, steal whatever valuables came within easy reach, and be gone before Fiz's spirit reached the Pearly Gates.

Up the steps, two, three at a time, fingers of the left hand curling around the cold brass knob, turning it as the shoulder forced open the unresisting door. Pistol out and drawn, lips compressed into skull-like whiteness, legs slightly apart to absorb the repercussion from blow or recoil, Claw Kiley entered the office, a soldier defending the weak point in a battle line.

One second, two, before his eyes adjusted to the thin yellow light cast from the lamp with the wick turned low.

"Put the gun down," came the simply expressed order. Claw froze, unable to comply with the words. "Put the gun down," they came again, this time softer and with less command.

"I heard something," Claw explained, unconvinced. "Saw something. Felt something. On the stairs."

"So did I," Fiz said. He was seated in his rocking chair, not in its usual place by the desk, but pulled away and centered, so the sitter could face the door. His hands appeared folded, hidden underneath a small, hand-knit blanket Claw had never seen before.

"No one came up?"

"No."

"You're sure? You couldn't have missed him?"

"No."

Claw's eyes met Fiz's, silently questioning him, least the older man's words were no more than a smokescreen, dictated by an unseen foe hiding in another room.

"I'm alone," Fiz said, without the total reassurance such a statement should have brought to both of them.

Claw did not relax, nor did Fiz remove his hands from beneath the woolen cover, which now appeared to be a comforter or perhaps a receiving blanket, made from brightly colored squares of yarn, sewn together into a whole.

"I couldn't have been mistaken."

"I didn't say you were."

"Then where did he go?"

"Jumped off the stairs. If it were a man. I heard it land. Couldn't be certain. Went off into the alley. If there was anything there."

"You shouldn't be sitting here like this, Fiz. You're not safe."

Fiz hesitated a long time before slowly drawing back the blanket. Beneath it, his right hand was wrapped around a pistol so diminutive, it might have been a woman's derringer. But was not.

"That won't protect you. It's not enough."

"It's all I have. That, and -" Claw almost drew his hands over his ears, so as not to hear the rest. "Faith."

Too late.

"What are you going to do? Throw a Bible at him?" Claw retorted angrily, aware, for the first time, of his heart beating madly in his chest.

"It's better than nothing."

Which was no comfort at all to the marshal. "Better than" and "nothing" had one common denominator: death.

"You can't stay here tonight."

"Yes, I can."

"Take a room at the Hellhole House. Or ask Cougar to put you up."

"No."

"Then, I'll lock you up for your own good."

"Protective custody?" Fiz asked. "What makes you think your office is safe from whatever it is out there?"

"I don't. But it's better than waiting here. All alone."

"I've been alone a good deal of my life. I'm not afraid to be alone."

"I didn't say you were."

"I've been thinking."

It was an invitation.

"About what?"

"About death."

"Your own?"

"I've already thought about that. There's nothing in my own death which interests me... except maybe the time."

Claw swallowed.

"About whose death, then?"

"A lot of people's death. About some who are already dead. About others, who will die."

"We all die."

"Not yours."

Claw did not mean to feel relieved, but he was.

"Who, then?"

Fiz started to shake his head, stopped, then looked away. He did not want to lie. Silence was neither truth nor untruth.

"Whose death, then?" Claw persisted. Then, accusingly, "You're not God."

"No. I'm not God."

"Whose death?"

"Ask God."

"Damn you."

The doctor looked up sharply, squinted away a stinging retort, then sighed.

"Damn me, then. I've been damned before. Doesn't make any difference. I don't suppose God listens to the idle cursings of men."

Claw broke eye contact with his friend, looking down at his boots, then up, over Fiz's shoulder to a daguerreotype hanging on the wall. It was a photograph of two men standing outside a tent. Both wore uniforms.

Grey uniforms.

Fiz knew what Claw was staring at without having to turn back.

"It's not a statement," he said softly.

Claw should have replied, "I know," for indeed, he did know. Instead, his youthfulness answered for his wisdom.

"What is it, then?"

"Just a remembrance."

"Of a Lost Cause?"

"I never fought for any Cause, Lost or otherwise. I fought for..."

What could he say? I fought to die and had the audacity to live? I supported the side I thought most likely to get me blown apart? I am a Southerner, damn you, and I went with my State?

"I fought to save lives."

The statement came out sounding like a lie, which it was not.

"Just the same as I'm fighting, right now, to save yours," came the stubborn retort.

Fiz flinched, not because Claw had a better answer, but because he loved him.

Testimony to the contrary, love always hurt more than hate.

"My life is not in danger."

"I say it is."

"From what?"

A challenge.

"I don't know. Something hateful. I felt it on your stairs. Come with me. Back to my office."

"I can't do that."

"Why not?"

"Because I won't run. Because someone - innocent - might need me during the night and not be able to find me."

Because if something that hateful wants me, it will find me.

"Then let me stay up here with you. I can sleep -" Claw looked around the small examination room, trying to locate a place of safety. "In your chair. You can go to the back room, sleep in your own bed."

"No."

"Why not?" More exasperation now.

"Because someone innocent might need you during the night, and not know where to find you."

"All they'll have to do is start shouting. Or fire off their gun. I'll hear it and come running."

Fiz hesitated, running over the scenario over in his mind. It sounded like fine wine but tasted of vinegar.

"I don't need protection."

But maybe you do, the physician thought suddenly. Maybe I'm being selfish; maybe the unknown force out there isn't after me, doesn't want me, but instead, is seeking the marshal. He swallowed, his Adam's apple bobbing down, then up.

"All right. You can sleep here. But not in my chair. In the side room. On the bed."

Too late. He had taken too long, thought too loudly. For a second, the room had a decidedly acidic smell to it.

More like brimstone than soured grapes.

"I'll see you in the morning, Fiz. Maybe we can have breakfast together. At the Regent."

"You can't afford it."

"Well, then, you can buy."

Fiz snuffled, took out a cotton handkerchief from his pocket and brushed it under his nose.

"Don't want to be seen in your company. Makes it look like I'm drumming up business."

"You don't mind drinking with me in the Lowdown."

"That's different."

"Why?"

"Because I say so. Leave me alone. I'm tired."

He was tired. Bone weary. It required almost more energy than he possessed to keep his eyelids half open.

"Good night, Fiz."

"Good night, Claw."

The youth, who had not fought for the Lost Cause, tipped his hat respectfully, and slipped away into the night which was neither blue nor grey, but merely black, which was the absence of color.

As soon as the door shut behind him, Fiz regretted letting him go.

Like the Marshal, he, too, knew Vernon Trask was building a fancy coffin.

CHAPTER 8

As Claw walked down the steps from the doctor's office, it began to rain. Huge, cold, wet, fat drops poured down from the angry sky, soaking him by the time he reached the ground.

Pulling his Stetson lower on his brow, Claw turned into the onslaught, struggling against the wind. Twice he stopped, thinking he heard his name shouted, but in neither case could he be certain. With a resignation which disturbed him, he made his way down, then across the street, breaking into his own office with a vicious shoulder to the water-swollen door.

Inside, it was cold and damp and pitch black. Ordinarily, such blackness would not have bothered him, but tonight, the inky obscurity was a threat. Shaking himself like a dog to rid his body of excess water, Claw slapped his hat onto the peg by the left side of the door, then squish-squashed across the room to his desk.

Feeling his way by touch, he located the lamp, pulled up the blackened globe, struck a match and lit the wick. It sputtered, then died. With an annoyed curse, he struck another, this time holding it to the wick until the wood burned down to his fingertips.

Thus assured the lamp would stay lit, he lowered the globe, incidentally cutting off half its brightness. He made a note he knew he would not keep, to clean the glass in the morning.

Turning around, lamp in hand, he froze as he saw an object lying on the floor. His first thought was that the dead animal was a mouse, left by Miss Cougar as a welcome home.

No. That was not entirely true. His absolute first thought had been that the body deposited dead center was that of a man. But that could not be true, inasmuch as the dead creature was far too small to have been an adult male.

His first rational identification was of the mouse. But the carcass was not a mouse. Inasmuch as it was too small to be a man, it was equally too large to be a rodent.

Closer observation proved the object to be a rabbit. A big brown buck, it's hind legs stiff and straight in rigor mortis.

His cat had been out hunting. Since he had spurned her offering of a mouse, she had gone after bigger game in hope of pleasing him.

Only slowly did realization come that cats did not bring down rabbits.

Nor did they slice their throats open with a knife.

The dead rabbit was not a gift from Miss Cougar; it had been left by a two-legged beast, as a warning.

A warning of what, and by whom?

Gritting his teeth, more from disgust than revulsion, Claw stooped down to pick up the dead animal. I was only after he felt the still-warm rabbit in his hand that he noticed an ear had been sliced off. With tears running from his eyes at the desecration of the helpless, innocent animal, Claw hurried out back with it, looked around in wild abandon, then heaved the carcass into the night.

He heard it land with a dull thud a second before he reentered the office, slamming the door shut behind him. In a moment, no more, a growling pack of half-domesticated dogs tore it apart, grateful for the gift from the unseen stranger.

Reflecting on the cruel irony of the dead rabbit, meant to serve as a dire warning to a man, ending up as a meal for starving dogs, Claw washed the blood from his hands. After wiping them on his trousers, he angrily went to his front door and heaved the pinkish water into the rain-soaked street.

He decided he did not need to know what kind of man or men mutilated a harmless animal; all he wanted to see were their faces.

Suspended from a hempen rope.

Replacing the bowl, Claw's initial anger subsided into more reflective thought. Men were not hanged for such deeds, nor should he wish them to be. Every boy in Hellhole had a knife in one pocket and a lucky rabbit's foot in the other. While the superstition had never appealed to him, the connection between death and luck being a perverse one, Dan Cord had explained, once, a long time ago.

"That's just it, boy," he had said, flipping a coin in the air and then letting it drop onto the ground. "No man wants to die. Call it a sacrifice. The rabbit giving its life so the bearer of its foot can live. That make it any clearer?"

"The noble savage, now," Jim Bennett had added in another discussion at another time, "always says a prayer to the spirit of the deceased animal, thanking it for providing nourishment for himself an' his family. That's the right way of doing things, to my mind. This is the way the Lord set up the world, Claw. One critter eats another to survive. The only sin comes when the beast doing the killing don't eat what he kills. That makes it murder in my Book."

Whoever had killed the rabbit did not eat it. Therefore, according to the Gospel of St. Jim, he had perpetrated a crime worthy of hanging, thus justifying the marshal's initial thought.

Further deliberation brought the face of Fiz's patient - the man with the burn – to his mind's eye. There lurked in Red's eyes that type of wildness which might have driven him to such an act. That being the case, he was not only senselessly violent, he was most probably out of his mind.

Claw had shot mad dogs for less cause.

Growling angrily, the marshal threw himself down on his cot, burying his face in his pillow. Before there was the slightest thought of rest, however, his cheek touched something stiff and cold. With a groan of anger, he jerked back and fumbled in the gloom for the alien object.

Recognition was immediate. The dead rabbit's missing ear.

His first instinct was to toss it out with the rest of the body, but that gesture seemed too inhuman, too uncaring. He thought, then, to bury it, as a silent tribute to slaughtered innocence.

His last, and final determination, was stepchild to neither thought. Getting up, ear clutched firmly in hand, he walked to his desk and placed the bloodless, amputated appendage into the left side drawer of his desk.

Evidence.

He was nothing, if not a lawman.

Claw knew it was morning when the slight tap on his door alerted him the milk boy or the egg girl had delivered his daily provisions. Not feeling well enough to greet either child, he waited until he was sure they were gone before getting up and retrieving the food.

Seeing both the eggs and the pail of milk tucked close to the door in a futile attempt to shield them from the cold, still sleeting rain, Claw brought them inside. He was not hungry, but had an instinctive awareness the mechanical preparations of fixing breakfast would occupy his racing thoughts.

Working with a determined diligence, he scrambled half a dozen eggs, hard boiling the remainder for lunch. The milk he drank straight from the pail, pausing for breath only twice before finishing his ration. Not until putting the pail down did he remember he should have saved some for the cat.

Feeling acutely sensitive for his omission, he determined to walk to the Regent and buy her a bowlful of milk, when he heard a scratching at the back door. Despite the fact his thoughts were on the cat, Claw's jangled nerves misinterpreted the sound, making him believe it was the dead rabbit, come back to life. The idea of the one-eared animal so unnerved him, he did not move until Miss Cougar meowed, asking a second, and more insistent time, to be let in.

It was not without trepidation that he obeyed the summons.

The feline, tail curled around her two good ears for protection from the wet, walked into the office with an owner's offhandedness, then looked up at her companion, waiting for him to close the door behind her. Not until he had completed the task did she go to her bowl, in search of her morning refreshment.

"The milk boy hasn't come, yet," Claw lied, then blushed from the untruth the cat had not accused him of. Unable to admit his culpability in drinking all the milk, Claw threw his rain cape over his shoulders and ran out into the storm.

The restaurant was just opening as he entered. Tossing a coin into the astonished waiter's hand, he marched into the back, poured milk into a glass and left the way he had come, oblivious to the man's shouted warning that he return the glass "forthwith."

"Here, Cougar, Cougar, Cougar," Claw purred as he entered the office, summoning the cat by the repetition of her pet name. Like death, his chant came, uncalculated, by threes.

If a man saw one shooting star, he was assured of seeing two more.

If he made the acquaintance of one new friend, he would gain a pair to go with the first, within a short while.

If he found a penny in the street, he would be three cents richer by the end of the day.

Men died in threes.

Claw knew, without ever once broaching the subject, that Vernon Trask would not be content to make just one fancy coffin. Knowing what the Marshal did, he was, without doubt, working on coffin number two at the present moment.

Claw could think of three people he did not want to die:

Cougar Bradburn.

Fiz Ward.

Joshua Jackson.

Three friends, all of whom he had met since arriving in Hellhole.

He might have added his own name to the list, for he did not want to die, either. But people he wished to save, and men not wanting to die, constituted a separate category. He was one. The interloper, Red, was the second. And the group of men trailing Red made three.

Three was a holy number, signifying the Trinity: the Father, the Son and the Holy Ghost.

Ask a man in the street to name the first number that came into his head, and nine times out of ten he would pronounce the number three. That was a lesson he had learned as a youth, by watching a card sharper play tricks to pass the time. Later in life, it had also earned him two bits for every bet he won guessing the "mystery number" strangers were thinking.

Claw had never been especially fond of the number three.

His favorite number was one. If a man had to choose one numeral over another, he ought to pick the highest.

Or lowest, depending on one's point of view.

The morning was drizzly, but not as bad as he had anticipated from the look of the sky the night before. Finishing up his morning toilet, Claw stared at his reflection in the small looking glass nailed to the wall opposite his bunk, declared himself "fine," and went out to face the day.

He had not planned on stopping by the Lowdown, but noting the swinging doors propped open, he stuck his head in for a look-see.

"Morning, Marshal!" Steve called, waving him a friendly hello.

"What's going on? Someone moving out?" he asked with a well-calculated tease to his otherwise suspicious voice.

"More like someone's moving in," Steve joked back, failing to note the stern rebuke in the lawman's face.

"Oh?"

"It's Eric. He's moving the whisky and beer barrels from his wagon into the cellar."

"Tell him not to trip," Claw warned. "The stairs are rickety and dark."

He was not worried about Mr. Anheiser falling and breaking his neck. That would not only solve Mr. Trask's dilemma as to who would fill his first coffin, it would be one name Claw could chalk off the top of his list of threes. Rather, he was concerned that Eric would only break a leg and have to be housed *somewhere* in Hellhole until he was well enough to travel back to St. Louis.

"Don't worry, Marshal!" hailed a cheery voice from beyond. "I have cat's feet."

"I-doubt-that," came the annoyed response.

Looking beyond the barkeep, Claw caught a glimpse of Eric's head disappearing down the back stairs of the saloon. He thought he might offer his services to the lady owner in the hope of shaving off a day from Eric's stay in Hellhole, then changed his mind as he saw Joshua, arms around a keg, stagger in from the rear alley.

"Mornin', Marshal!"

Thus adding to the growing list, three cheerful faces. To the Marshal, that sounded like an ill omen.

Crossing through the front of the Lowdown, Claw stood by the head of the steps, thumbs tucked into his gunbelt, neck extended as he stared into the depths.

"Joshua!"

"Right up, sir."

In a moment his deputy reappeared, stray bits of straw clinging comically to his shirt and hat.

"What are you doing?"

"He'pin' ol' Eric out. He's got a whole mess'a crates and kegs to git took off his wagon and brung down -"

"I know. He'll have to do the hard work by himsef. I want you to ride out to a ranch run by a man named Timmons. Introduce yourself to him and his wife. They don't know law has come to Hellhole. Might do them good to make your acquaintance."

"Yes, sir." Joshua hesitated, then looked wistfully outside. "Sure is a lot o' work to be done here, though, an' I tolt him -"

"That's how the law is, Joshua. It waits for no man."

"Where exactly does this fella, Timmons, live?"

"Can't say for sure. Out there." Claw waved his hand in the vague direction of the moon. "And while you're at it, you might get the name of three or four other ranchers from Bark down at the livery: those who have set up homesteading outside Hellhole. Go and see them, too. Take your time. If they have any chores need doing and they offer you a bit for your trouble, then I don't see any reason why you shouldn't help out.

"I won't look for you for, say, a week."

The deputy grinned, wiped his brow with the back of his hand, then nodded wisely.

"I'll be seein' you, then, Marshal."

"Yeah."

With a hop and a whistle, Joshua disappeared.

"Spreading the good news?"

Claw did not turn around until he felt the blood in his ears drain.

"Never hurts," he admitted, nodding to Miss Bradburn. "I got to thinking about what Timmons said -"

"I know what you were thinking," she acknowledged. "Wouldn't want to help yourself, would you?"

"Wish I could."

"I bet."

"Seen Fiz this morning?"

"No. Why? You suspect him of helping Eric, too?"

"No. I... wanted to ask him a question."

"He'll charge you."

"Not a medical question," Claw pouted.

"Oh. I thought maybe you were feeling poorly. You look kind of peaked."

Which was an acceptable lie, under the new category, "All's fair in...."

"A professional question - about something else."

"Anything I can help you with?" Which was more innocent than it sounded.

Claw hesitated, shifted his weight from one foot to the other, then hunched his shoulders.

"I don't know. I need to ask someone -" He stopped himself, unhooked his thumbs and stared down at his hands.

"Older?" she guessed. He shook his head. "Wiser?" No, again. "A man?"

He waited for her to add another, then kicked out with his boot as she stopped at three.

"Southern," he blurted finally.

"In case you don't know, Louisiana is a Southern state. I hail from thereabouts." He gave no indication of hearing. "Fiz's from Maryland. That's only a border state."

"Someone in the War, then."

"Why didn't you ask Joshua?"

The thought had not occurred to him.

"I don't think of him that way," he confessed slowly. Then, defensively, "I don't think he'd know what I want to find out."

"And I wouldn't know, either?"

"Maybe it's nothing."

"Maybe it's not," she agreed.

Taking the lead, Cougar walked to the bar. He followed. When they were thus on different ground, he leaned forward against the counter top and averted his eyes.

"What does a dead rabbit mean to you?"

She might have answered "stew," for that was her first thought, but did not.

"It could mean a lot of things. Go on."

"What does a dead rabbit with its throat slit and an ear missing mean to you?"

"What does it mean to you?" she guardedly inquired.

"Not a hell of a lot. Other than it's a warning of some sort."

"Where did you find this rabbit?"

"On the floor of my office. Last night."

As a word was forming on her lips, Eric's happy voice hailed them from the stairs.

"I think I'm going to do some cleaning down here, Cougar, before I bring in any more stock. Bix Bradley had a head for business but he wasn't one for any sort of order."

She waved an offhand agreement, then changed her mind about answering Claw.

"Go ask Fiz."

"I will. And Cougar -" She stared up at him quizzically. "Thanks."

"For what?"

He left without replying, letting her question stand as the second unanswered interrogative of the morning, making them even at one apiece.

Fiz was not in his office, compelling the marshal to wait until afternoon to ask his question. When he finally tracked down the elusive physician, his patience was nearly at an end.

"I found a dead rabbit in my office last night," Claw announced unceremoniously. "With its throat slit. I found this under my pillow."

Removing the rabbit's ear from his pocket where he had kept it warm all morning, Claw tossed it to Fiz. The healer caught it with a deftness honed from the long use of his hands as tools.

Fiz stared at the severed appendage a long beat before looking back up at his friend.

"Where was the rabbit?"

"On the floor."

"Still warm?"

"That's right."

"Then whomever left this for you had just been in your office. On a cold night, the carcass would have cooled off quickly."

"I know that," Claw snarled with annoyance. "I'm not a fool, you know."

"No," Fiz agreed, slowly running his fingers over the rough incision which had severed the flesh. Then, with a self-conscious jerk of his hand, he smoothed the fur, too late to do any good for the physical component of the dead mammal, but never past soothing the spirit. "I never said you were. What does this mean to you?"

Exasperated, Claw stomped his foot.

"That's what I came here to ask you."

"Why me?"

"Because you're -" He was going to say "Southerner," then remembering Cougar's words, changed his mind and finished, "a physician."

Accused of being a physician, Fiz responded as such.

"The surgery was crude; performed with a hunting knife, not a scalpel. Someone did it in a hurry, without taking much care."

Which was not what Claw wanted to know and both men knew it.

"I think he did it - that man. Your patient." The "your" standing as an accusation.

"No. It wasn't Red who left this for you."

The answer came as a tacit acceptance of Fiz's responsibility.

"What makes you say that?"

"Because I know who left it."

Suddenly, Claw did not want to pursue the subject. With a dry mouth, he opened, then pursed his lips. He was a long time debating Fiz's extraordinary statement.

"You? It was you who left it?"

Fiz blinked three times, then shook his head.

"Did I say I left it? No. I said I know who left it."

Leaving Claw to wonder which way he would have been better off.

"Are you going to tell me?"

"The men who are after Red. The men who know who he really is. What his name is." He did not include in his sentence, What he did to make them hunt him.

"You - know these men?"

"Not personally."

"You've seen them? Here in Hellhole? You've spoken to them?"

"No."

"No? No to what?"

"No, I have not seen them. No, I have not spoken to them."

"Then how do you know who they are? And what they want?"

Still clutching the dead rabbit's ear, Fiz rose from his chair, deliberately turning his back on the lawman. Walking to the window overlooking the stairs, he drew back the curtain and stared out into the gloom of a grey overcast sky.

"Last night. Remember?" he asked. "You thought you saw someone outside my office. I felt someone there, too. That same someone - or one of his companions - left this for you."

"Why didn't you tell me that last night?"

"Because it hadn't happened last night when we were talking."

"What hadn't happened last night?"

"They hadn't killed the rabbit; they hadn't yet decided whether or not to leave a warning. Something changed their minds."

"What?"

"I don't know."

"You seem to know a hell of a lot, without knowing anything."

Fiz turned back and held out the ear for Claw to take. He accepted the gift without hesitation.

"Let's just say I suspected as much from the beginning; from the first time I saw that man with the burn."

Claw noted the patient was no longer "Red," but "that man with the burn."

"Tell me."

"You noted he was running from a terrible danger; you saw he was scared. He has a right to be." Fiz took in a deep breath, shaking his head over his not so deeply buried memories. "He didn't talk much to you, did he?" Claw indicated that were true. "He didn't dare. He didn't want to give himself away."

"He thought I'd recognize his voice?"

"Not his voice. His dialect. His... cultural background. He's a South Carolina man. The Low Country. You know what that means?"

"Tell me."

"He is - or, rather, he was - a man with money. Either a plantation owner or the son of a plantation owner. Probably both. Whatever his name is, anyone from Charleston would immediately recognize it. This man - 'Red' - was a slave holder, Claw. Not one of those scratch cotton planters who owned half a dozen Negroes, but a man who owned hundreds.

"That's where he got his medical training; out in the fields." Fiz shrugged. "Or in the slave compounds. Most planters didn't bother calling a medical doctor when a black fell ill; they treated the injury themselves. The fact my patient bothered to learn medicine indicates to me he had quite a pecuniary interest in keeping his workers in good health."

"What does that have to do with anything?"

"I'm just telling you," Fiz snapped. "I thought you wanted to know."

"I do," Claw replied, holding up his hands in surrender.

"He was wealthy, he was well educated and he was utterly loathed. By his niggers."

"Go on."

"I don't have any specifics. The War came. Whether he fought or not is irrelevant. Charleston and the Low Country didn't fall until late in the conflict. I imagine this man's plantation stood pretty much untouched until right near the end, when Federal troops came and liberated those black men and women still held in bondage."

"Are you saying the men who left this warning - the men who are hunting this Red character of yours - are his former slaves?"

"That's what I'm saying."

"Why?"

"I told you. Whoever or whatever 'Red' was, he was hated by his slaves. Once they were freed, they went after him."

"The War's been over three years."

"Three years, three hundred years. Time won't change how his pursuers feel. Maybe he was a cruel master. Maybe he was a devil. Obviously, some men think so. He owes them. They're going to make him pay."

"And the rabbit?"

"Have you ever seen a black man with an ear cut off?"

"I might have."

"Ever wonder why?"

"Yeah."

"Ever ask?"

"No."

"When a slave escaped from a plantation, he was hunted down by dogs. When he was caught, he was jailed and usually branded on the forehead or the cheek. That marked him as a troublemaker. If he didn't learn his lesson - if he escaped again and was caught - he had his ear cut off. A man might find some way of hiding a brand, but he can't hide a missing ear."

"Then why not cut off his ear the first time?"

"It ruins his value," Fiz replied matter-of-factly. "A plantation owner could still sell a slave with a brand, promising the prospective buyer the slave had learned his lesson. But he couldn't sell one without an ear. A black man with only one ear meant trouble. He's dangerous. And consequently, the owner had to keep him. Or sell him as a scrub, for a tenth of his value.

"Like a horse," Fiz added, narrowing his eyes. "You own a bad horse - one that can't be broken - he's no good to you. You sell him as a good horse and the man who buys him comes back, demanding the return of his money. Same with a slave. No one wants to buy a slave who's constantly trying to escape. He's more trouble than he's worth."

"You make it sound so cold."

"I'm just telling you how it was. Do you want to hear it, or not?"

He did, but suddenly, not from Fiz's lips.

"Did you ever own a slave?" he blurted, despite his misgivings.

"That ear under your pillow was a warning to stay out of it. Those men - the ones after 'Red' - they want him. Bad. Bad enough to tell you - the law - it's none of your business. If you stick your nose into their affair, they'll kill you, too."

"There'll be no killing in my county."

"Leave them alone, Claw. It has nothing to do with you."

"You can say that - to me?"

"You can't stop them." Implicit in that threat was the unspoken, Maybe you shouldn't stop them.

"I'm here to uphold the law. The law guarantees every man suspected of a crime to be legally charged, the right to council and the right to a fair trial. What you're doing is condoning murder."

"Maybe I am."

Claw was stunned. While the pinion wheels spun in his reeling brain, he crossed to the stove and poured himself a cup of coffee from the perpetually half-filled pot. Only after he had blown a stream of air over the simmering liquid and taken a sip was he ready to face the man who had become his friend, and then transformed back into a stranger.

"No." And then, after another pause to sip Fiz's coffee, "No," again. "That's what you want me to believe. It won't work, Fiz."

This time, it was the physician's turn to play obtuse.

"I don't know what you're talking about."

"First of all," Claw began, hitching himself carefully into a sitting position on Fiz's examination table. "There's something about that man - that Red character. I saw it in your eyes."

"What - something?" Fiz snorted, going himself to the coffee pot. Instead of pouring himself a cup, however, he opened the outside door and tossed the dark, boiled-down liquid over the railing. "He's a patient. Not even that," he pursued, slamming the empty pot back on the hot burner. "He didn't pay me."

"All right," Claw agreed. "So, he owes you."

"I didn't say that! He doesn't owe me anything. A man can't pay, I don't hound him to death like some people. Like you, I mean," Fiz continued, realizing his error by omission.

"I don't hound people to death, either, Fiz," Claw pursued easily. "I bring them in alive. When I can. And no one 'owes' me anything... except perhaps a respect for the law. The same law you respect."

"You're talking me to death."

The few remaining drops of coffee left clinging to the side of the pot sputtered, then evaporated, as the heat broke them down into steam.

"You advise me to leave these black men alone - you tell me what they have in mind is none of my business. You know that isn't true. It's every man's business."

The black, speckled enamel on the coffee pot crackled, sending a tiny chard flying off into the empty space of the office.

"I'm too busy to worry about every man's business, much less yours. I gave you a good piece of advice. Follow it or not as you will. Now leave me alone. I have work to do."

"What work?"

"Doctor work. Unless you want to help. There are three thousand things around here you can do. Sweep the floor. Wash out my basins. Clean the instruments. Roll bandages. Make the bed which you're sitting on."

"It won't work."

"What won't work, for Heaven's sake?"

"This fear you're building up. You can' be afraid for me, Fiz. Neither of us can live that way. You're a physician; you understand contagion. Fear is contagious. I'm not immune from it."

"I wasn't trying to -"

"I've seen enough fear in my life, Fiz - seen brave men shake in their boots - men I admire. Men I've watched stand up to a dozen robbers without a thought for their own life. But put that same man in a situation where his friend, or his wife or his town is scared for him, and he gets frightened, too. He feels the hot sting of those bullets ripping through his flesh; hears his own life's breath gushing out of some hole blown in his chest; smells his own blood spurting from a severed artery.

"Don't do that to me."

The red-hot bottom of the coffee pot suddenly warped from the excessive temperature of the burner, propelling it into the air. Both men jumped from the unexpected noise, though neither relaxed when ascertaining the cause.

With an annoyed invective, Fiz went to grab the handle, remembered almost too late it would burn his fingers, and quickly drew a pocket linen from his trouser pocket. Using that as protection, he lifted up the pot, looked around for somewhere to put it, then slapped it down on the window sill. The paint on the wood immediately bubbled.

"You've got me all wrong," Fiz insisted, stuffing the burned rag back into his pocket.

"Have I?"

"I'm not worried about you. I stopped worrying about - about anybody - a long time ago. I do my job; I do what's required of me. That's all anybody has a right to ask. I was referring to justice."

"Is it justice to let men take the law into their own hands?"

"It can be."

"So, you've tried this 'Red' - judged him, found him guilty, without ever hearing his side of it?"

"That's right."

"No, Fiz. That's wrong. But if that's all it was, I'd let it drop right here."

"Why is that?"

"I could understand your feelings."

"Then let it drop."

"I can't. You're not a judge and jury. Neither am I. And no one - no one, Fiz - deserves to be hounded like a dog, caught, shook around, scared out of his mind, bitten and let go, so others - no matter how righteous their cause - can do it to him, again and again.

"No one man, Fiz, ought to be held responsible for the sins of many."

"What do you think Jesus Christ did?"

"We're not talking about Christ. We're talking about -"

"I know who we're talking about!" Fiz cried. Then added defensively, "You don't understand hatred."

Claw smiled, but the facial gesture betrayed no humor.

"I understand vengeance. I saw a man I loved more than anyone else on earth shot dead by a gunfighter looking for nothing more than a reputation. It was the most God-damned senseless killing I ever hope to witness. I wanted to tear that son of a bitch apart with my bare hands. I wanted to make him suffer. I killed him, Fiz - but in a fair fight. And if there's a hell, that's where I sent him. But I didn't play cat and mouse with him. I'm not God. And neither are those former slaves."

"I'm going to make more coffee. You want some?"

"No." Claw slid off the bed, flexed his cramped leg muscles, then moved toward the door. "And Fiz - thanks."

"For what?"

This time, Claw had an answer.

"For sacrificing your principles."

He left only a second before the coffee pot hit the closing door.

CHAPTER 9

The rain had begun again, not in the torrents of the night, but steady enough to make miserable a man caught outside. Abandoning all hope of drying his jacket, Red took the heavily sodden leather from off his makeshift drying rack and put it on, forcing his injured arm through, what seemed to him, an ever-narrowing opening.

He was cold, chilled to the bone, yet the idea of increasing the small blaze he had dared rekindle frightened him more than the threat of chest congestion. They were out there, watching, waiting, biding their time.

A wisp of smoke, the unmistakable smell of a wood fire, was an open invitation.

Come and get me.

Not that they needed an invitation. They would come, whether or not they were asked.

They were not, Red thought dryly, gentleman. Certainly not in his father's or his grandfather's sense of the word.

But their time was over. Dead and gone. Their principles had fought a great civil war and lost.

Red sneezed, then struggled to stave off another, biting his tongue in the process. With a savage jerk of his head, he stifled the terrible pain brought on by so little a wound.

He had suffered whippings, beatings, burnings and a near hanging without more than a whimper, yet the self-inflicted hurt from biting his own tongue wracked his frame with torment. Such was his misery that the smallest hurt, heaped on top of the greatest, was what finally broke the spirit.

The rain came down harder, in sheets of sleet this time, striking and stinging his face like blows from a backhand. It was too cold for September. He remembered other Septembers, when the days were warm and the evenings just chill enough for a light coat. Where the scent of jasmine and magnolia lingered in the air, while the hanging vines, clutched so firmly around the trunks of trees, had not yet begun to lose their grip.

September was a time of harvest and revelry; to assess the well-filled cupboards, lay in the cords of firewood and prepare for a winter still six weeks away. It was a time when boys went back to school and girls tried on the new dresses they would wear to holiday parties. It was the month for finalizing the old and preparing for the new; hectic, lazy, conflicting days and nights of change and expectation.

It was not a time for frozen rain, sheering winds, hopeless desperation.

In his past, there had been no time for those physical and mental torments.

"No time," he mused ironically, "like the present."

October was the month for spooks and spirits and haints to wander abroad. That was when the weather turned cold and the faded colors of the brightly painted autumn leaves fell from the trees. Time when a boy drank hot cider and a man sipped warm brandy beside a roaring fire, each curled up by the hearth in his own peculiar way, to meet the coming of winter.

With his head nodding on his chest, weighed down by memories, the man named Red closed his eyes, lulling himself into a trance by the willful summoning of the days gone by.

***

"It was cold and rainy outside, just like it is now," Grandfather McKinnon began, his words crackling from withered lips like dried twigs stepped on by youthful toes. "I was your age, Kenneth, not a day more; nine years old and thinking myself a great man of advanced years."

The teasing in the old man's voice made the boy wince. If was difficult to imagine his father's father ever young; much harder to believe than the stories he told of goblins and witches, which always held the ring of truth in them.

Harder, even, than to imagine himself grown up, although, at nine, he had already assumed many of the duties he would carry throughout his adulthood.

"I was coming home from school, on foot," grandfather added, "for in my time, a boy walked to his lessons and didn't have his own pony to ride."

"I know," the child acknowledged solemnly. "Those were the days when every horse was needed for the war."

"The War For Independence," the old man stressed. "It wasn't a year later, when I was ten, that I joined the army. I was big for my age - bigger than you will be, son. I passed for a man of sixteen."

Kenneth sat straighter and stretched his legs out to their full length, attempting, by demonstration, to belie the elder's prediction. His efforts did not go unnoticed by his father, who exchanged a wink with the assemblage.

"I lost my way when the storm clouds covered the moon," the old man continued, sipping his drink. "I won't say I was afraid - and I won't say I wasn't afraid. But I was in a big hurry to get home, and so started running. I ran so fast and so far, by the time I stopped to catch my breath, I was lost.

"I found myself in a woods, deep and dark, without a star or the moon to light my path. I got myself so turned around, I didn't know up from down. I twisted this way and that, tried looking for my footprints so as not to go back the way I'd come, but they were lost in the mud and the brambles.

"Now, I'd heard about what happens to a boy caught out alone on such a night - a pitch black night when the rain came down and the wind was howling - but it wasn't until the thunder rumbled and the lightning flashed that it came back to me - what my own grandfather McKinnon had said.

"He had told me that the thunder was caused by the gods in the Parthenon, warning those down on earth they were displeased about something. The lightning was their way of opening up the sky so they could peer down to see us mortals better. That had this game, he said, whereby they'd hurtle a bolt of lightning down and strike the ground with it. If it happened to hit a grave of some long-dead fellow, why, that man would rise again.

"Only he wouldn't be like he was in life. No, sir. He'd be exactly what he was in death - all rotten and decayed, or maybe just a set of animated bones. Oh, he'd be able to think, all right, and he'd sure have the feelings of a living soul, but he wouldn't have the warmth of his blood cursing through his veins.

"Now, I had that knowledge in my mind as I walked, hoping and praying it wouldn't start thunder and lightning, but, of course, it did. As I said, it was that kind of night and there I was, alone and lost and wishing I wasn't.

"I walked and walked and walked, must have been miles out of my way, for after a while, I started hearing another sound, not the wild elements and the tree branches striking one another. I hurried ahead, thinking I'd come out at a house or a clearing, but instead I emerged from that deep, dark wood at the river.

"Now, there wasn't any boy knew that land better than I, and I knew there wasn't any river nearby. So I bent down on the bank and plunged my hand in, just to prove to myself it wasn't there. But it was. My hand came back wet and dripping with that kind of slimy vegetation which clings to the sides of river banks and rots.

"There wasn't any way for me to be sure, but what I held in my hand didn't exactly feel like leaves and river weeds a'tall. As I brought it up to my nose, I had the uncomfortable feeling it didn't smell quite like that, either. It smelled like -

"But I'm getting ahead of myself. Tossing the mess back into the water, I stood up real fast and thought to run away, but something held me there - call it a power. Like I was in a trap and couldn't move. No matter how hard I struggled, I couldn't lift my feet from the mud.

"You know and I know there's many a backwoods swamp that's swallowed a wild hog, or a lost boy, and I was sinking fast, up to my knees, when I saw the light. Just a wink, out there on the river, no more. Like the blinking of a giant's eye. Seeing as I was in no ways particular as to who helped me out of that bog, I raised my hand and hailed the stranger, out there on the water.

"'Help!' I cried. 'Help me, I'm bein' pulled into the mud!'

"In a moment, I heard the rowing of oars and the sound of a small row boat pullin' against the current. My breathin' came pretty jagged, I can tell you, for I could see something - or someone - all dressed, as I thought, in white - drawing close to me.

"'Ah'll he'p yuh, boy! Hang on,' this man called out to me, but his words wasn't as clear as I'm saying them to you now. They were garbled, like a man talkin' without movin' his lips. But, as I said, I wasn't in any position to refuse.

It took him a good long time to come up to me. By the time that old row boat came close to shore, I was in that slime up to my waist.

"'Take mah hand," the creature ordered, scratching out that long arm of his. I took it, and, so help me, God, came close to screaming, as my cold fingers wrapped around fleshless bone.

"It was pretty clear the man himself - if you can call him that - didn't see anything wrong with his condition. Or at least I thought that at the time. He just wrapped those bony fingers around my child's wrist with one hand and pulled me aboard, as though it were flesh and muscles covering his bones and not..."

Here Grandfather McKinnon paused to let the horror of his tale sink into the minds his listeners. No one moved, their once-warm drinks cooled to room temperature; the same degree of coldness a body would assume after death.

"As soon as my feet touched the wooden floor of his row boat, this man, or more rightfully, this skeleton, resumed his seat and began working the oars. I determined not to sit, but the ride was uncommonly rough, and I was soon compelled to drop down, or be thrown overboard.

"If you'll take me home, my father will reward you well," I stuttered, hardly knowing where my cloven tongue found the ability to articulate. My companion did not answer for what seemed an eternity. When he finally did speak, I had to bend forward to hear his words, for his voice was stretched thin and indistinct.

"'What reward fo' a dead man?" he asked, making me sorry I had spoken. He rowed, by my reckoning, for half an hour before resuming our conversation.

"'Yuh goin' on a journey,' he announced. This time, while closely observing his face, I thought I could make out the faintest movement of tongue inside his nearly clamped teeth. Then, as the clouds parted from the moon, I was enabled to observe him with closer scrutiny.

"There was no color about him anywhere, just the whiteness of bone. There was, however, as I determined, small patches of skin still adhering to his cheeks, and several small tufts of hair, which I presumed to once have been a fine black beard. He was - or had been - a man of middle height -

once broad-shouldered and muscular, if the spread of his shoulders told the truth.

"I could not tell the color of his eyes, of course, for he had none. How he saw, I did not inquire. But that he could see I determined by his occasional glancing up at the sky, or his studied look at my own countenance.

"After we had traveled in this manner one hour, I ventured again to draw him into conversation.

"I live at the plantation known as Flowering Tree," I stated boldly, and a bit too loudly, for he averted his head to lessen the effect of my shouted sentence. "I should very much like to be taken there. I am already late for supper." When he gave no other indication of hearing, I tried again. "I shall be missed," I warned. "When I do not arrive home, a search party will be gotten up."

This time, I thought I saw him smile, although upon reflection, I do not know how I received that impression, as he had no lips, nor any eyebrows with which to convey that emotion.

"Dey be gittin' out da dogs?" he inquired in so friendly a tone, I thought perhaps he knew - or had known me - in life.

"They will most certainly get out the dogs," I assured him, shuddering from a sudden uptake of the wind against my bare cheeks.

"'Fine, blue-blooded hounds?' I nodded agreement. 'Ah know how it be done,' he pursued familiarly. 'Dey will take an article of yuhr clothin' an' bring it to da kennel. There, da hound masta will hold it out fo' da dogs to sniff. Once dey habe taken yuhr scent, dey will be set off, bayin' loud 'nough to raise the dead.'

"He laughed at his own joke, though I saw no humor in it.

"'Dose dogs - so bery valuable - will go running through the woods, will dey not? An' da men will follow, some on horseback, others on foot. The dogs will be far ahead, but da men will follow them by sound. A good dog-man knows how to read the sound ob his animals; how they yip an' bark when dey are on the scent, how dey whine an' whimper when dey lose der prey. Ain't day so?' he inquired of me, as though I were a full-grown man and not a boy.

"I swelled with the importance he seemed to place upon my shoulders.

"'That is so,' I agreed, nodding my head. 'Are you - I mean to say, sir - were you a dog man?'

"'Ah know somethin' 'bout dem,' he admitted, then resumed his strenuous task.

"I marveled at the power with which he rowed, back and forth, back and forth, never a break in his rhythm.

"As the night grew on and the temperature dropped, I shivered, drawing my coat closer around my shoulders. This action seemed to wake him from his repetitious motion at the oars, for he looked over at me.

"'Yuh be chill, boy?' he asked. This time, I bristled at the word, for I had ceased to think of myself as a 'boy,' and rather considered myself a man.

"'It is cold, sir,' I acknowledged. 'But I find little comfort in my coat, as it is wet. I fear I may catch cold, if we do not come to land soon, and I be placed in front of a warming fire.'

"'So much da pity,' he commiserated, giving me the unsettling impression he had no pity to spare for any but himself. I resolved, therefore, to speak no further. But that was not his idea, as he continued. 'What yuhr name, boy?' he asked, placing an emphasis on the word, as I supposed, to irk me.

"'James McKinnon.'

"'James McKinnon,' he repeated in such a manner as to bring a tone of familiarity to it.

"'Do you know me, sir? Or my father?'

"'Say, perhaps, Ah know *of* yuh,' he replied. 'You ob Flowering Tree.'

"To speak truth, I did not know whether he was mocking me or speaking truth. Inasmuch as I had spoken the name of my ancestral home, he might have divined the name from our conversation, and not from some previous knowledge. I resolved, therefore, to continue my interrogation.

"'Did you live hereabouts?'

"'Where is hereabouts?' he inquired.

"'In the Low Country; Or in Charleston? My father has a townhouse in the city. It is a very fine one,' I bragged. 'We spend time there when the season is unhealthy to be at our mansion.'

"'Da miasma,' he agreed. 'It can bring on da fever.'

"'Is that what took you off?' I blurted, as only a child can in such a situation. My companion stared oddly at me a moment, then seemed to laugh.

"'Ah was not prone to sech diseases,' he confessed. Then, more strongly, 'No. Dat is not what took me off.'

"'What, then?' I demanded.

"'Da little masta knows how to speak to underlings,' he observed, raising my ire. 'But who is master now? Who holds yuhr life in his hands?'

"So saying, he removed his skeletal hands from the oars and held them out to me. Peculiar to say, the oars kept moving, just as though he were still rowing.

"'My life is in the hands of God, as is the life of all true Christian soldiers,' I retorted stubbornly, refusing to give him an inch. He considered my words carefully before speaking.

"'Would yuh say,' he said, 'dat God watches out fo' all His childr'n equal, or are dere some who merit special attention?'

"'I would say, He watches over all and protects those who do His bidding.'

"'And do yuh do His biddin'?'

"'I try to,' I humbly acknowledged, which caused him to have a fit of laughing. "'Why do you find amusement in my statement?' I demanded, suddenly frightened to think that perhaps he were some messenger from Beyond, come to take me away for transgressions so small I had not marked them as such.

His attitude did nothing to dispel my fears.

"'What river is this?' I asked, beginning to shake like a babe deprived of its mother's milk. 'I do not remember a river here.'

"'Dis be da Riber Styx,' he informed me. When my recognition was not immediate, he added, 'Da riber across which da dead mus' pass.'

"'But I am not dead,' I protested, weak from mounting terror.

"'How yuh know? Perhaps yuh are an' simply don' know it. Perhaps yuh fell in da swamp an' was sucked under. Or mebbe yuh was lost in dat wood an' da men wid dogs didn't find yuh in time.'

I considered his words carefully, then held out a hand. Flexing my fingers, I put them to my face, where they were yet warm to the touch.

"'I live,' I avowed sincerely. 'It is you who are dead.'

"He shuddered, as though my words were unwelcome to hear.

"'But yud be speakin' to me an' Ah to yuh,' he pointed out. 'How can a livin' soul talk to a dead one?'

"It was a good question and one for which I did not have a ready answer. I therefore determined to change the subject.

"'Where are you taking me?'

"'Ah takin' yuh to da other side.'

"'The other side of the River Styx? You are taking me to the Land of the Dead?' I cried, now seriously frightened. 'I do not wish to go there. Turn around immediately and return me to shore!'

"'How well yuh gibe orders, little masta. But Ah am no longer required to obey dem.'

"In the far distance I thought I heard the sound of hounds baying. I eagerly craned my neck, hoping to catch a glimpse of so welcome a sight as my father's dogs.

"The sound had the opposite effect on my companion. With a low snarl of discontent, he took hold once again of the wooden oars and began rowing with renewed vigor.

"'That is my father,' I tried, softening my voice so as not to offend him. 'He is out looking for me.'

"'What be good fo' da goose be bad fo' da gander,' he answered, confusing me with his sentiment.

"'Please,' I begged, shimmering closer to him and placing my small hand on the bony protrusion of his knee. 'Take me to shore. My father will pay you well.'

"'Pay me well?' he demanded. 'Wid what he pay me?'

"'With gold and silver,' I replied.

He shook his head sadly.

"'Dat ob no worldly good to me.'

"'What, then?'

"'Ah wish...' he began, then hesitated. 'Ah wish fo' rosemary and sage.'

"'You wish for herbs?' I asked with some skepticism. 'Who would want herbs when he might have money?'

He choose not to answer me.

"'Hab yuh sech t'ings in yuhr home?' he demanded.

"'Yes,' I assured him, thinking him the fool. 'We have such herbs. Ask and you shall receive whatever it is you want.'

"'An' will yuh git sech t'ings fo' me yuhrse'f?'

"'I will.'

"'Swear to me.'

"'I swear.'

"Now you won't believe this," my grandfather added, feeling the full effect of all eyes upon him. "But the next moment, I found myself in the kitchen of my own home."

"'Of Flowering Tree?' the boy named Kenneth asked in dumb astonishment.

"'The very place. In fact,' he continued, pointing with a crippled finger, nearly devoid of flesh from his advanced age. 'It was at that very spot where you stand now that I paused after emerging from the kitchen, pockets full of rosemary and sage.'

"'But how?' Kenneth demanded, moving a step off the "spot." 'How could you be in a boat upon an unknown river one moment, and in the kitchen of Flowering Tree the next?'

"'That,' Grandfather McKinnon remarked, stroking the thinning tufts of white beard, 'is a mystery for which I have no answer.' The child started to interrupt when the elder resumed his unfinished sentence. 'No answer explainable by learned men. No answer acceptable to the Christian Church.'

"'Come,' the boy's father interrupted. 'Never mind the inexplicable. What happened next?'

The elderly patriarch smiled wisely.

"Before I left the boat, my unearthly savior had given me instructions. Once I had the requisite herbs filling my pockets, I was to hold both hands in the air, high over my head –" He demonstrated by reenacting the scene. "Close my eyes, hold my breath, and turn around – once clockwise and twice counter-clockwise. Making three turns in all."

Standing up with considerable difficulty, the old man patted his pockets, sucked in a mouthful of air through nearly compressed lips, closed his eyes and made the circles, counting as he performed the act.

"One. Two. Three."

Not a soul stirred until he had completed the circuit. Only when convinced he would not disappear did his son speak.

"What happened?" he whispered, though Kenneth had an awareness his father had heard the story numerous times before.

"I was cloaked in a puff of smoke and whirled back to the tiny row boat on the river. Immediately upon my arrival, the skeleton-man clutched at me, fingers probing my pockets for his treasure. Not until his hands were full did he appear satisfied."

"What did he do with the herbs?" Kenneth blurted, barely able to contain himself.

"Do? What did he do with the herbs?" James McKinnon smiled darkly. "Why, he traded them, of course."

"To whom did he trade them?"

The grandfather shook his head.

"The next thing I know, I was lying in the woods, my father holding me in his arms. 'Wake up, child, wake up!' he was crying. When he saw my eyes flutter open, he gave a shout of thanksgiving, praising God for my safe return from the dead."

"You mean, your safe return from the boat - and the queer rower?" the boy corrected.

"No such thing. For you see, no one believed my story. When I was able to catch my breath and steady my nerves, I told my father of my strange experience. He said it was no more than delirium - that I had gotten lost on my way home from school, fallen victim to the harsh weather and fainted. By the time he and his overseer found me, I was near death from exposure."

"But," Kenneth exploded, "you did not believe it was all a dream?"

"I came to believe it was a dream," he sighed. "I had to, for how could it be otherwise? As I lay in my bed, recovering from congestion of the lungs I contracted from my ill-fated journey, I thought no more about it for a fortnight. It was not until I was well enough to go downstairs and resume a semblance of my normal activities that I heard of another adventure. One which had taken place the very same night I had gotten lost.

"It appears a slave had escaped from a neighboring plantation. He was very valuable property and there was much excitement over his disappearance. His owner called out the dogs to hunt for him, but when my father sent 'round word of my disappearance, requesting the use of his tracking hounds, that altered the situation.

"Coming from my father, such a request was not to be disregarded. The neighbor and his dog master met him at the edge of the wood and together they went in search of me. Had he not heeded my father's request and come as quickly as he had, I surely would have perished.

"Once I was safely put to bed, the men, my father included, went in search of the missing slave."

"Did they find him?"

"They trailed him through the wood, finally coming out miles away, and in the opposite direction from where I was discovered. There they saw the runaway on the river, rowing a boat he had apparently stolen from one of the sharecroppers. The men pursued and eventually caught up with the boat. There was nothing in it but... the skeleton of a long dead man."

"How could that be?" inquired the boy's maternal uncle, who sat opposite him in one of the fine old family heirloom chairs brought over from England. "How could a dead man row a boat?"

"There never was a satisfactory explanation given," the grandfather acknowledged. "And no one could explain the presence of rosemary and sage found at the bottom of that boat."

"You could," the boy pointed out with childlike belief.

The older, wiser men ignored the impertinent interruption.

"It was my mammy, the old house servant who had raised me from a babe, who took me aside and finished the story. 'Rosemary an' sage,' she said, 'be magic herbs. Wid dem, someone wid da power - someone old an' wise in da ways ob da black Af-rican arts - a witch, yuhs preachers say - could take a man's soul an' mobe it from one body to anodder.

"Wid a few flakes o' sech common seasonin's, dis Ancient One could perform da feat only ha'f way; not into da body ob a anudder libin' man, but jest into that ob a dead one."

"And so I finally understood that the skeleton in the row boat - my savior, for thus I truly believed him to be - was that escaped slave. He had gone to the Wise One and pleaded for help. Being slaves, having little access to the rosemary and sage found so plentifully in our pantries, he had done what he could for his Brother. He had taken his soul and placed it in another body - the remains of a long-dead man - in order to disguise him from his pursuers.

"That slave - his name is lost to memory - found me in the wood and drew me into his boat. Seeing me as a means of his escape, he made the bargain which I have just related. With all the magic contained in those herbs, he was then able to move from the skeletal frame into one of flesh and blood, leaving the bones of the first transfer behind."

"And he was never found? This slave?' Uncle Jasper Hawkins inquired, motioning for a servant to come and refill his glass.

"Never. Out of obligation for the use of his hounds, my father made good the loss to his neighbor, and no more was ever spoken of the incident."

"How could you have been on the river? It was in the opposite direction from the wood," Kenneth objected.

Grandfather shrugged, and suddenly chilled, drew a thick, woolen blanket closer around his stooped shoulders.

"I have told you what happened. Believe it or not as you will."

"You have told a pagan story,' Uncle Jasper declared, sipping his warmed brandy. "You were a child, steeped in the nonsense of slaves. It is as I have often said - white children should not be exposed to such stories. Your father should have sold the old woman and sent you away for your education."

"And so he did," Grandfather McKinnon agreed. "But I am here to tell the tale, whereas perhaps I would not have been, had not our kitchen contained such magic herbs."

"Magic herbs," Uncle Jasper snorted. "A fine tale, indeed for such a cold night. But not fit for impressionable ears," he added, indicating the boy.

The child flushed with anger and stood, hands clutched at his sides.

"I am old enough," he announced, "to believe or not to believe as I see proper."

"You will not raise your voice to your elders," his father warned, sending him to bed without having the comfort of a second cup of cider.

****

Red stirred in his sleep, his lips still moving in silent protest. It was not the end of the story which finally woke him, but the prickling of a small, hand-sewed bag pressing against his breast. Scratching his irritated skin, he came to full awareness, sitting bolt upright, senses attuned to the sounds of the magic night.

When assured the wind and the sleet were no more than the howling of nature, and that the thunder and lightning had not released ghosts and goblins upon the earth, he placed his right hand over his heart, whispered an invocation found in no Book of Common Prayer and withdrew that which hung suspended around his neck.

Reverently kissing the mojo bag filled with rosemary and sage, he replaced it into the hidden recesses of his past and drifted off to sleep, to dream no more.

CHAPTER 10

The morning brought no relief from the cold and the rain.

Eric Anheiser was up early. In two days, he had swept the cellar, rearranged the crates and barrels, collected the empties and begun the arduous task of bringing down the remaining stock of beer and whisky which would last the new owner of the Lowdown until winter, or "maybe longer."

"Come on up and have some coffee," Cougar invited from the head of the stairs. She was rewarded by hearing the heavy thud of footsteps, then seeing the top of Eric's head as he emerged from the darkness.

"I could use some," he admitted, wiping his hands on a clean, white handkerchief taken from the recesses of a hidden pocket.

"How long have you been up?" Cougar inquired, sitting at the round, green felt-covered table near the bar.

"Since dawn. Maybe a little before."

"Why so early?" she complained, stifling a yawn.

"Did I disturb you with all my banging around?" he asked, concern in his voice. "I never once though. I'm sorry."

"Oh, no," she protested, only half convincingly. "I slept right through it. But the girls complained. It woke their customers up. A grumpy man doesn't remember to 'thank' his companion with a little extra."

Eric nodded wisely while he poured them both a cup of coffee from the still-steaming pot on the bar.

"How'd you get in, anyway?" Cougar continued, accepting the cup.

"Last night before he left, I asked Steve to meet me at the back door of the saloon as early as he could. He unlocked for me."

"After which I hope he had the good sense to go home to bed."

"I suppose he did," Eric chuckled. "I ordered the coffee myself, then forgot about it. Good thing you reminded me. And I'll make it up to the girls," he added, drawing up a chair beside her. "What would be fair? A dollar apiece?"

"That would be fair. And then some."

Eric reached into his pocket, withdrew a fancy, embroidered purse and took out several coins.

"How many girls?"

"I have four at the moment. Three dollars will do it. One wasn't working."

Eric pushed four dollars across the table toward her.

"Well, it would seem mighty ungenerous of me if I were to forget her." He started to add something else, then changed his mind. "I didn't expect you to be up this early, or I would have ordered breakfast."

"Don't you eat?"

"Sure. But I wanted to make a dent in unloading my wagon before I broke my fast. You want me to have something sent over from the Regent?"

"No. I'm not the breakfast type."

"Lunch?"

"I don' think I want to be seen eating with a man all covered with dust and straw," Cougar teased. "Better make it dinner. After you've washed up."

"Dinner it is." Eric leaned back in his chair, drank his cup dry, then waved a hand across the vista of the room. "You going to add onto your business? A fancy new roulette wheel would draw in the customers. I could teach Steve how to operate it." He laced his words with significance, so she took his meaning clearly.

"I can teach him that, myself."

"I forget. You're from -"

"New Orleans."

"That's right. Play the big houses?"

Cougar shrugged, running a fingernail of her left hand under one on her right.

"Passed through a few of them. Enough to learn the ropes."

"Ever work the steamboats?" She hedged, by holding out her cup for a refill. "The gaming tables, I mean," he clarified, too late to do himself any good.

"No."

"How'd you end up in Hellhole?"

"End of the line."

They both drank in silence for a moment.

"Turned out to be a lucky thing," he said.

"You can never tell about luck," she admitted.

"Wish I had been here to see you beat Bix Bradley at cards. I bet he took it pretty hard."

"You'd win that bet," she agreed with a fond smile of reminiscence.

"Give you any trouble?"

"He thought about it."

"Didn't know Hellhole had law. He here, then?"

"Claw Kiley? Yes. He was here. Standing right over there the whole evening, as I recall. Watching how things went."

"How good's his watching?"

"Depends on what you mean."

"Card playing."

"He sees what I want him to see."

Eric nodded, stroking his cleanly-shaven chin.

"He's young."

"He'll learn."

"About card playing and roulette wheels?" he joked. She smiled and shook her head.

"Someone's got to teach him."

"You?"

"I didn't say so."

"You know, Cougar, ever since I saw you, I thought you were the prettiest thing west of the Mason-Dixon Line."

"You did, did you?"

"You bet I did."

"I don't remember you telling me that."

"I don't remember having the opportunity. Bix kept you pretty close."

She shrugged and yawned again.

"I guess he did, at that."

"These last few months, since I was through - they've changed you, Cougar." She arched an eyebrow in his direction. "For the better. You were always a woman, but now you're - extraordinary."

"Thank you. A lady never turns down such flattery."

"I'm not saying it to be flattering. I mean it."

"Don't they have girls in St. Louie?"

"Plenty. I think my brother's just about talked himself into marrying one."

"Really? Who is she?" Cougar inquired, leaning across the table with interest.

"Her name is Belle McClendon. Pretty little thing. You'd like her. I do. She's nice."

"Belle?"

"Belle," he repeated, with shared emphasis. Not "Katherine," or "Phyllis," or "Patricia," but Belle. "Belle McClendon."

Cougar hesitated, then looked toward the closed doors of the saloon.

"Where'd he meet her?"

"At the High Tide Tavern. On the riverfront, about sixty miles down the Mississippi. Ever hear of it?"

She shook her head.

"No. Big place?"

"Sixty barrels of beer a month and thirty-five crates of whisky. Run by an old poler named Jacques Tournier. She was working there; that's where Chad met her."

"Lucky for Miss McClendon."

"They're talking about going to Europe for their honeymoon. The wedding ought to be a big affair."

"I imagine."

"Lots of people will be there. I'd like you to come, too. As my guest."

"To the wedding?" He grinned and nodded. "When is it?"

"I'm not exactly sure. Can I write you with the date?"

"Well, you can write me anything you want."

"We're going to have several huge canopies all spread out and music all day long. Ought to have the governor, and several state senators there, too. Plus a group from Washington, if they can make it. Chad says he wants more entrees than they serve on the River Queen. I'd put that at twenty or twenty-one. Beef, lamb, foul, deer, lobster brought down on rail from Maine."

"Sounds nice. What about oysters?"

"Ever hear of a wedding without oysters?"

"Try and find an oyster in Kansas."

"Oysters by the cart load. And flavored ices. Pineapples, oranges, lemons, coconuts. And fresh-brewed coffee all day long; with chicory. I bet you miss that, coming from N'Orleans."

"I do, indeed," she confessed. "You're making me hungry and it's too early to think about food."

"I'm designing a champagne float. Comes up out of a spigot and cascades down. Real pretty and party-like."

"Very lucky, this Miss Belle."

"She's pretty, but not as pretty as you."

"I'm liking her more and more."

"She'll make Chad a happy man."

"I can't see why she wouldn't. I always liked Chad. He's a good man. You be running things while he's away - on that honeymoon trip?"

"I expect. We're thinking of buying a brewery, you know. Set it off the river a bit."

"I heard something of that."

"Ever seen a brewery? A big one, I mean?"

"No. I haven't. Like to, though."

"Thought you would. By the time you come, we ought to have it just starting up."

"I didn't say I'd come. I said I'd think about it."

"I could show you our warehouse, too. Right now, I've got thirty-six roulette wheels, an entire floor of furniture - saloon chairs and tables - some nice ones, too. Just took an order from the owners of the Floating Palace to outfit her as a first cabin steamer. The gambling parlor they're setting up will make the River Queen look puny by comparison."

"Good for you."

"We're importing glass for the staterooms and Italian marble for the dance floor."

"It will float with all that aboard, won't it?"

"They say so. She ought to take up two docking spaces, she's so big. They're running a double engine in her.

"Speaking about furniture - I see you've got a room full of busted chairs and three-legged tables. I'll get to them once I've got the wagon unloaded. Where'd that deputy go, by the way? He was a good helper."

"The marshal sent him away. On business."

Eric nodded, then pushed away from the table.

"What about that marshal? He go away on business, too?"

"No."

"I surely do enjoy providing for the new owner of the Lowdown. Going to change the name, by the way?"

"I wasn't planning on it anytime soon."

"I'll get to work, then."

"Yes," Cougar agreed. "You do that."

As he scurried away, rubbing his hands in anticipation of the hard labor ahead, Miss Bradburn marveled at her life. It was not the one she might have chosen for herself, once upon a time, but it was more than she had ever dreamed.

***

Eric Anheiser had a melodic voice and he liked to sing as he worked. Running through his repertoire of ballads, seasonal carols and an occasional tune of a more bawdy nature, he occupied himself with unloading his wares from the heavily stocked wagon.

As he worked, he slowly became aware of eyes watching his movements.

Which made him sing louder.

After an hour of such personal entertainment as one generates when singing in a deep wood, he finally paused to wipe the sweat from his brow. Facing the loose-fitting canvas covering of the wagon, he tightened a stray draw rope, then spun on his heels, making a one hundred and eighty degree turn.

The eyes, lulled by his seeming inattention, magically developed a face and body.

"Hello, there," Eric said to the stranger he had not expected to discover. "What's your name?"

There were in his words, the tone of condescending an adult adopts with a child.

"Frankie."

"Frankie. My name's Eric. Nice to make your acquaintance."

The man so addressed made a low, cultured bow.

"The pleasure is all mine," he stated with perfect sobriety, though he was far from sober.

"I've seen you around Hellhole before, haven't I?"

"That is entirely possible," Frankie acknowledged.

"You wouldn't, perhaps, be a deputy, would you?"

"I? A deputy? No, sir. I am not, although I have been known to assist Marshal Kiley on occasion."

"You have, have you? I wonder if I would insult you by asking for your help in assisting me. My back is beginning to hurt and I have a long way to go before I finish my work here. I would, of course, *recompense* you for your time," he added, purposely using a ten dollar word unsuitable to the slow, carefully enunciated conversational style he had adopted.

"At what rate of pay?"

"One dollar a day."

"At that rate, I would be foolish to work with any urgency," Frankie observed. "In a week, I would be a wealthy man - according to Hellhole standards. He who jingles seven dollars in his pocket may eat at the Regent, sleep in the Hellhole House and buy drinks for the house in the Lowdown.

"If I were you - and in a hurry to finish my task - I would offer as an inducement two bottles of whisky if the job were finished today and one bottle if it were finished tomorrow."

"I beg your pardon, Mr. -"

"MacPhearson."

"MacPhearson."

"You need not apologize," Frankie continued, looking down at his well-work black frock coat. "My appearance would not induce a man to judge me kindly."

"Well," Eric began, then sighed. "Will you work for me at your own salary requirement?"

"I think not."

"Why not?" the wagon owner asked in considerable surprise.

"Your terms are not generous enough. But I do thank you for the offer."

So saying, Mr. Frankie MacPhearson tipped what might have been a long out-of-style Philadelphia judge's black hat, smiled benignly and strolled away.

"I'll be damned," Eric observed with reverence and went back to work, no longer feeling eyes upon his back.

***

Having never developed an appreciation for the finer cultural events in life, on the order of high theatre or operatic song, Claw Kiley avoided the territory owned by and surrounding the Lowdown. Such an absence did not, however, allow him to escape the same feeling of disquiet suffered by Eric Anheiser.

There were eyes watching him, as well. Not the same pair of orbs, for the lawman would not have been conscious of Frankie's curious retrospections. The unseen man or men watching him were of a far more dangerous character.

Pausing in front of the general store, Claw adjusted his hat while using the reflective, front pane glass, as a mirror. No one was behind him, not even his shadow, for the gloom of the day was thick enough to obscure both shadows and substance. Turning suddenly, he glanced, right to left, then upward, into the threatening sky.

Nothing.

It was as quiet, Jim Carey used to say, as coins not being dropped into the collection plate.

It was that quiet, Claw silently admitted to himself, and equally deliberate. In the purposeful withholding of that which was, by tradition, a preacher's rightful expectation, his listeners were making a statement as loud as thunder.

We do not like your sermon, they were saying. *Or the cut of your cloth.*

We do not like the stance you have assumed.

Or the side you are defending.

"Heaven," Jim Carey used to say, "means different things to different people."

With the emphasis on "mean."

As a boy, Claw Kiley had not understood his mentor's words. If heaven were a place where souls went after death, then the argument over how one spent one's time - playing a mouth organ while sitting on a cloud, or drinking from a five-dollar bottle of whisky while holding a hand full of aces - seemed unimportant. As a man, he had come to comprehend the difference.

One man's drink was another man's poison.

One man's peace was another man's hell.

He was not a preacher and did not pretend to know what the misty shroud covering the Gates of Paradise hid from mortal man. He was only a marshal, pretending to know the Letter of the Law. Pretending, because the rules one man held sacred were the rules another man broke with impunity.

"Christ and the anti-Christ," Dan Cord had joked.

Jack Duvall, on the other hand, had seen things differently.

"Claw," he had said, "There has to be a constant in life; a set of guidelines all men follow. That's the Law. Men may not like it; they may not trust it. The law is fallible and, being written by men, is prone to injustice. That's where the lawman comes in. He's a sort of preacher with a gun. He enforces the law because that's his job. All men are equal under the law, just like all men are equal under heaven. Men breathe; men eat and drink. You see to it they walk upright while they're going about the business of living."

"Live and let live," Jim Bennett had added after a significant pause. "If only it were that simple."

The other men, the men in the small gathering around the fire, had laughed. Claw had not laughed. He saw no humor in it.

One man named Red had come to Hellhole. No one invited him, no one asked him to stay. He had come to live. He had not broken any of man's laws. His face was not depicted on any wanted posters. No railroad detective sought him, no special agent carried papers demanding his arrest. If he had broken God's laws, it was not for man to punish him.

Neither Jim Carey nor Jack Duvall had ever said a marshal had to enforce God's laws.

Had either of those men stood beside Claw Kiley as he tarried in front of the artificial looking glass, he would not have asked their opinion on this particular interpretation of justice.

He was through asking questions. He was no longer a boy. The badge pinned to his shirt made him a man.

If only it were that simple.

Ada Duvall would have agreed. The difference being, she would not have said so.

Turning away from the window, Claw crossed the street and walked with long strides toward the livery stable. Without bothering to ask Bark Barker, the proprietor, to saddle his horse, as was his right, Claw threw saddle blanket and saddle over the animal's back, then led it outside. The horse's ears flattened against its head.

"Don't think that animal wants to be taken out on a day like this," Bark remarked, slipping out from behind a stall and staring into the threatening afternoon sky. "Looks like the storm ain't over."

"Looks like," Claw agreed, swinging his leg over the horn and slipping into the curved leather seat. Too damned bad, he added, but did not say so. He was not in the mood for conversation. He had already played it out.

North. South. East. West. It was a litany, a mindless repetition, asked by the not-so-repentant sinner. Which way? Where were they, those men on the prowl? The men who had tried a criminal en absentia and were now determined to act as executioner.

The black men Doctor Ward had identified, not by name, nor by face, but from the look of stark terror found in the eyes of their victim.

As Claw walked the horse, eyes turning first to the right, than the left, he wondered at his own audacity. He had joined the army to fight a war against slavery. Call it what you like: call it the War Between the States, the Late Unpleasantness, the War of Northern Aggression. It was still a conflict about human bondage.

Substitute any word you wanted for that expression and it would always equate to one basic concept.

Slavery.

Claw had gone to a Southerner to explain the significance of the dead rabbit's ear, not to receive advice on what to do with it. Yet he had gotten an earful, and the meaning of Fiz's words rang in his memory.

"You can't stop them"

Maybe you shouldn't stop them.

He understood what Fiz meant; he wasn't deaf. He had eyes; he could see. He understood guilt. The problem was, he had not expected it. Not from Fiz; not from the physician dedicated to saving human life, alleviating suffering, treating wounds of both body and mind.

Fiz did not know for certain Red had done anything wrong; he did not know whether Red had committed senseless murder, unjustly whipped bare backs, savagely branded cheeks, or cruelly severed off the ears of runaway slaves. Fiz did not even know his name. It did not seem right to single a man out for blame when you did not even know what to call him.

"Master" was not an acceptable substitute. Not even for a Northerner.

Claw understood that his original judgment - Fiz's fear for him - was legitimate. He also knew, upon sleepless retrospection, that Fiz had been using one excuse to hide another. No matter how he disguised it, Fiz was angry. He had set himself up as judge and jury.

Bitterness had a long reach.

Longer than the arm of the law.

It was a disquieting thought.

Exactly why Fiz was bitter, Claw did not know. Certainly, it did not tax his imagination to believe the healer had treated black men in his career, most of them slaves or former slaves. Hailing from Maryland, a border state, as Cougar so tersely reminded him, Doctor Ward would have had some professional cause to involve himself in the issues surrounding the "Peculiar Institution."

A short trip over the Potomac River would have brought him into the confines of the wealthy and the renowned. Washington, Jefferson, scores of other Founding Fathers had owned plantations on what was to become "Virginia's bloody soil." Slaves by the hundreds would have been worked in the fields, used as blacksmiths, drivers, household servants, mammies. Mistresses.

Black "pioneers," as his army regiment called them, had felled trees and smoothed roads. They graded the line for antebellum railroads, served as clerks, cooks, errand boys.

Fiz could not have failed to notice Negro children playing with white children in the yards of great houses, never equal, even in adolescent games.

He would have received his meals by a black butler, eaten off china washed by black hands, slept in a bed made neat by black labor. His horse and his buggy would have been cared for by a black stableman, while the very hounds used to track runaways would have served double-duty when baying after foxes.

Claw had never talked to Fiz about his views on slavery because the point had seemed academic. In reality, it had never occurred to him. Claw was a Northerner by birth and breeding; slavery was an evil he had risked his life to eradicate. Fiz was his friend, his ally, his father-figure. Claw's faith had been so great, he had never questioned the stand of one so like himself. It would have seemed blasphemous.

Now, those illusions were shattered. Not by the fact Fiz supported a former slave owner, but by the fact he did not.

Guilt by association.

Punish another to punish yourself.

String up Henry Wirz. Make a public spectacle of his mock trial and execution. Punish one to clear the consciousness of the many.

Claw Kiley did not want to know whether Phillip Ward ever owned a slave. Or what his views had been. What he did comprehend, was that he would not allow his friend to assuage his own guilt, no matter how indirect, by the blood of another.

Red, the stranger, the man with a past, would not be persecuted in his territory. If this man without a name had broken the law, punished those under his charge who were innocent; if he had shed blood without due cause; if he had maimed, mutilated or taken that which was not his right, then let him be held accountable for his own sins. Not those of a country.

Let him be sentenced for what he, himself, had perpetrated.

Not for the High Crimes and Misdemeanors committed by those of a generation past; not for those venerated for their "liberty and justice for all," which omitted, not by word, but by intent, all those not born a Caucasian male.

The law, Marshal Duvall had said, made strange bedfellows.

The spirit of the law, Marshal Kiley amended, made even stranger ones.

CHAPTER 11

With the pain in his arm growing worse by the moment, Red had a decision to make. He dared not remove the bandage placed there by the skilled hands of Fiz Ward, but it did not take a trained surgeon to smell infection. If the burn had festered, it would poison his blood. Once tainted, fever would set in, followed by chills and delirium.

Blood poisoning was the kiss of death.

It was a slow, lingering, agonizing, painful death. A man's body, wracked by this black sickness, jerked and twisted like the toys, suspended on strings, boys received at Christmas. It was possible to survive such an ordeal, but not likely. The patient would require a warm bed, tender nursing, frequent bleedings, ice chips placed between compressed lips and sips of broth poured, drop by drop, down a constricted throat.

To obtain that kind of care, Red knew he would have to return to Hellhole and seek the assistance of the doctor. He would have to be put to bed, covered with down-filled comforters, and possibly restrained, to prevent flailing arms from doing himself damage.

Such a protracted treatment would not come cheaply. Red was a proud man. It was unthinkable to demand such service without paying the piper. If he were ill a month or more, the bill could reach as high as fifty dollars.

Fifty dollars. The thought brought a grimace to the runaway's face. At one time in his life, he had left that much as a gratuity for a particularly fine meal.

Fifty dollars. The cost of a first cabin trip by steamboat from St. Louis to New Orleans. The cost of feeding a slave for one year, including the obligatory pair of brogans each was issued at New Year.

Fifty dollars. A man could buy a blue-blooded hound for that price, or put a down payment on a brood mare. He could purchase five bottles of French champagne, buy a fine pair of riding boots, or order a suit of clothes, imported from England and brought into Charleston Harbor on a clipper ship named Swift Lady or Cotton Bole.

For less than fifty dollars, a man could buy a scrub slave for use in the kitchen, or as a washer woman.

For five hundred dollars, a former slave owner could not buy his freedom.

For five times five hundred dollars, he could not buy his life.

What price Doctor Ward' services?

Red had not paid him for the treatment of his wounded arm. He owed him and he did not like to owe a man. He had always paid for what he took. Early training. If he were to return to Hellhole, he would have to offer the physician restitution. Ten dollars ought to cover it. That would even the score between them. Once that was settled, Red could ask for more.

But only if he could pay for it. He was not one to rely on blood.

"A man can't run his plantation on good deeds," his father used to say. "So don't expect the overseer, or the grocer, or the banker to run his business on credit. Pay what's due and you'll never owe anything to anyone. That's how an honest man holds his head up."

"You don't sin, an' the Lord don't have a score to settle with you when you die," the preacher had lectured.

How easy it had all been once.

To reach help, Red knew what he had to do. The first order of business was to mount his horse. Failing in that, he was doomed to walk.

"Goin' to the grabe by foot takes a man a mighty long time," an old servant had once advised him. The child Red was had taken that to mean a man on horseback rode more quickly to his death. He had therefore resolved to travel only by own energies. That was before his father, a practical man, had waved away his explanation and sent him back to work astride the fastest horse in his stable.

It had been a particularly fine steed, a tall, black horse, with wild eyes which shone white when it was riled. Ordinarily, such an animal was reserved for the master, or the master's favored guests, not the transportation of a boy. On this occasion, his father had saddled the beast himself, then left it reined to the hitching post. Red accepted the loan as a gift, vaulted into the saddle from the mounting block and rode like the wind.

When no ill came to him, he had forgotten the slave's warning. Two months later, as his family celebrated his birthday, he had been presented with a wild, spirited horse of his own. This animal, the color of which Red likened to the tips of whitecaps forming on an angry sea, had been his constant companion for many years. He spent so much time in the saddle, his mother used to chide him by saying, within his hearing, "There goes the white horse," meaning, "There goes Kenneth astride his white horse."

The horse, christened "Lightning" at birth and "Whitecap" by his new owner, was then and forever after, referred to by the family, as "Kenneth."

The animal grazing on a short tether was not Whitecap. It was a common brown horse, without a name. He had bought it from a scratch farmer who needed money more than he needed a horse. Red had paid more than it was worth, hoping the man would remember his kindness and steer any who came after him in the wrong direction.

Whether the dirt-poor man had done so or not was a question only the angels could answer.

Angels, Red seemed to remember, were the heavenly remains of spirits, rewarded for their good earthly deeds by being given the ability to visit the living. He could never quite understand why that power was desirable, inasmuch as he had never seen one substantiated act of mercy any angel had ever committed.

Men spoke of angels in much the same way they revered saints, but he had never known a saint to intervene in the affairs of men, either.

Which, for the rest of Mankind, neither stopped the supplications nor tarnished their image.

Red supposed that had something to do with the oft-quoted expression, "best of both worlds."

He was not a praying man, himself. If men were on the side of the angels, and angels stood on the right hand of God, it seemed an unworkable equation to his analytical mind.

He was, as a preacher in his cavalry regiment described him once, a heretic.

He was soon to be unbeliever who traveled on foot.

The horse without a name drew back its lips and stomped its right forefoot as he approached. Holding up his hands, Red tried soothing words he did not feel. The horse, seeing through his deception, back-stepped, arching its heavily muscled neck in defiance.

"Whoa, boy," Red pleaded. "Steady."

He did not have the strength to saddle the animal. Fever had stripped him naked. He would, therefore, have to ride bareback, maintaining his position by balance and thigh muscles. Failing in that, he would be a short time getting to the grave.

In his mounting delirium, Red was no longer certain whether that was a good thing or a bad thing.

"Easy," he begged.

The horse switched its tail and flattened its ears.

Grabbing the mane with his good right arm, Red attempted to pull himself up onto the horse's broad back. His legs had turned to lead, however, and did not rise more than an inch off the ground. Frightened by the unexpected failure of its master to demonstrate proper technique, the horse reared, then nipped him in the arm.

Crying aloud, then sobbing shamefully, Red grabbed his wounded arm and stove off the pain by the application of killing pressure. As the jangled nerves died from lack of blood, he gritted his teeth and tried again.

This time, he miraculously succeeded, straddling the horse, then holding onto its neck for balance.

"Easy, boy," he soothed. For all the disembodied eyes watching from afar, he might have been addressing himself, and not the horse. "Easy, boy."

His self-congratulation was short lived.

He had forgotten to take off the hobbles from the animal's front legs.

There was no way he could perform that type of mechanical act while sitting astride the horse. With a low moan of resignation, Red drew his leg back and vaulted down, forgetting, for the moment, his legs would not hold him. He fell, face striking the wet earth, pinning his crippled arm beneath him. The horse danced away, out of reach.

"Hells's bells," he cursed, before remembering himself. But in remembrance, there was no comfort. "God damn it!" the heretic shouted.

The horse moved further out of reach.

Pulling himself out of the mud and onto his knees, Red made a gallant effort to steady his ragged breathing, then wiped his runny nose on the sleeve of his shirt. It was an abhorrent gesture which spoke of poor upbringing. He had learned it in the War, much as he had learned to kill with impunity, though no one of his acquaintance considered killing a poor reflection on a man's breeding.

"All right," he acquiesced, more for his own benefit than the horse, in that horses did not understand the spoken word. "No more. Not again."

The whites of the animal's eyes diminished into large, mud-brown pools of iris.

Red had been given a chance and he had squandered it. With a resignation born of despair, he unsheathed his knife, then crawled the remaining distance to the steed. Quickly severing the leather tong, he waved the beast away.

"Go on!" he ordered. "You're free." Appreciating its release, the horse wandered several steps away, then turned its head to stare at the man on the ground. It was an unusual sight, bearing some contemplation. "Go on!" Red shouted with animation. Then, considering the fact the horse was as lost as he, he nodded in the direction of Hellhole. "That way. There's a warm stall and a bag of oats waiting for you in Hellhole."

Still, the horse did not go. In anger, Red turned his hunting knife inward and threw it, striking the hilt harmlessly against the brown hide. This, the animal seemed to understand, for it trotted away, to look back no more.

Freedom was a wonderful thing.

Kenneth "Red" McKinnon would have been the last to deny it.

"What yuh gonna do now, masta?" a deep voice inquired. There was a softness, almost a tenderness to the interrogative.

Spinning around, Red gave a gasp of utter terror, then bolted into the underbrush, blind to anything but his need to escape. An echo of raucous laughter pursued him.

"Yuh gonna run all da way to Hellhole, Masta Kenneth?"

"Yuh think yuh got friends dere, Masta? Ah wouldn't be a goin' there mahself, Masta. Yuh ain't got no friends there. None a-tall."

"We done got to dem, Masta," another voice bragged, its tones far different than the others. There was no false jocularity, no familiarity, no mercy. It was the voice of the Grim Reaper; the Angel of Death. "Dey's none what will open da doors to yuh, yuh debil. None what will remember da old days an' let you in. Da old days be gone, Masta Kenneth. Yuh a smart man, yuh oughta know dat. Come on out, now, boy, an' take yuhr punishment."

The man who had assumed the name "Red," perhaps from the color of his hair and perhaps from the color of his spilled blood, made no reply. It was too late for replies; too late for speech of any kind.

In the beginning, at the start of his new life as wanderer, fugitive, hunted animal, he had tried to reason with them. Failing in that, he had met their taunts, thrown back jeer for jeer. But while they seemed not to tire of the game, he had wearied of it. There was no common ground between them, no possible basis for understanding. They meant to have his life and he desired to prolong it.

"No one asks the fox if it wants to die," his father had said once, upon seeing tears of sadness run down the cheeks of his sensitive son. "That's the way it is, Kenneth. There are masters and there are men; there are hunters and their job is to kill. And there is the hunted. Their job is to provide sport for the superior.

"That is God's Law, Kenneth; that is the way He set up the rules of His earth. You would not question God's wisdom, would you, Kenneth?"

The snuffling boy had decided he would, and was therefore banished from all future fox hunts, to the extreme annoyance of his father.

The boy had not gotten his cowardice from the McKinnon side, Master McKinnon had decided savagely. Therefore, he must have inherited it from his mother's side - the Hawkins side of the family. Such awareness was a great shame to him, for Kenneth was his only son. Why God had punished him with three daughters and only one heir - and he a disappointment - was inexplicable.

Because he could not lay the blame at God's feet, the senior McKinnon chose the collected "feet" of the Hawkins family. It was regrettable, but there seemed no other explanation. And to think, their blood went back to the kings of England.

Red plunged headlong through the low brush and thorn-festooned bushes, cutting his hands and face until they streamed crimson. Gasping for breath, his lungs nearly bursting from the demands his sudden exertion placed on them, he staggered on. To stop was to die. They had made that promise the last time they caught him.

"Da nex' time will be da las' time, Boss Man. We catch yuh ag'in, we gonna skin yuh alibe."

They had made similar threats before. Red never failed to believe them. Their voices haunted his sleep, their faces, blurred by erratic firelight, invaded his dreams.

"Da nex' time will be da las' time."

For a doubting man, they had succeeded in instilled belief into his being. Something his father had failed to do.

Perverted justice.

They trailed him, six in all. They were in no hurry. Their prey was on foot and wounded.

All things came to those who waited.

That was what the preachers said.

"Where yuh be, Masta? Cum on out an' git it ober wid. Yuh cain't run no mo'. Yuh's done runnin' Masta Kenneth. We done run yuh to bay. Like da hounds. Rememba da dogs, Masta? Yuh want us to set da dogs afta yuh?"

He remembered the hounds. Not the high-spirited, blue-blooded dogs his father and his father's neighbors ran, but a pack of mean, snarly curs, whose barks and bays, long into the night, had sent shivers down his spine.

The dogs - the black men's dogs - had found him once, come up upon him while he lay, half stuporous from fear and exhaustion. Unafraid of his human scent, held back only temporarily by the dying embers of his campfire, they have come, first one, then another, until the half dozen of them had attacked en masse, ripping at his arms, tearing the flesh of his thighs.

That had been six months ago. The brutes would have killed him, then and there, by finally tearing at his throat, but he had succeeded in knifing one of them, more from luck than skill. With the hot blood of the dead animal staining his arms, Red had stood, like Atlas, with the dog, held in both hands, suspended over his head. As its living companions charged again, he had thrown the carcass into their midst, temporarily scattering the dog attack, which had *moved in echelon,* like trained soldiers.

Frightened, then cautious and finally intrigued, they sidled up to the dead cur, ruffs bristling, tongues lolling. When it became apparent the prone figure offered no resistance, the pack had amused itself tearing it apart. He had escaped while they consumed one of their own.

No. Red did not want the dogs set after him. He was not even certain his pursuers still kept dogs. He had not heard them in weeks. He had cocked his attentive ears and listened at the time of the full moon, but all was silent. Another man might have prayed that, like the dogs, the former slaves were nowhere near. Red knew better. They were out there, warming their hands over a blazing wood fire, or cooking their victuals in a round, black pot.

Because he could not feel them did not mean they had given up their quest. The dogs may have been sold, or eaten, or run off, but the men persisted.

That was the truth of God's gracious world.

The fact he had not heard the dogs did not lesson his fear of them. Without conscious volition, the images of the barred white teeth, the matted fur, the stale scent of their breath came back to him with all the horror of his first encounter, so that his agony was as great as if they had actually been attacking him.

The dogs had drawn first blood. Their masters would draw last.

What was it his schoolmates had said?

He who laughs last, laughs best.

Red McKinnon had never been one for easy laughter.

Born with credulity but without a sense of humor. That is what his maternal uncle Jasper had said.

Perhaps he had been right.

A shot rang out, striking the rotting stump of a tree trunk not fifteen feet from where Red crouched. They could not know where he was, but the bullet had come close. Not close enough to kill, but deliberately fired into the tree as a warning.

We will not let yuh die as easy as dat, they were saying. We want to watch while da breath goes out ob yuh an' yuhr lungs rattle in death. We wanna grab da spirit escaping yuhr body an' send it anudder way.

No rest fer yuh in life, Masta Kenneth. No rest fer yuh in death.

Another shot rang out, this one spitting up a pile of soggy wet leaves. It went further to his left. In a moment, a third shot would go to his right.

It was wonderful to know one's enemy.

It made the anticipation of capture that much greater.

We'll fill yuhr mouth wid salt, Masta, they had promised. An' sew yuhr lips shut. We'll cut off'n yuhr hands an burry yuh face down, in the deep, dark earth. We'll strip yuhr body naked, so's yuh'll know what it's like to face da Debil on His own terms.

We'll burn white birch bark over yuhr grabe, Masta, so's yuh'll neber git out. We'll say da old prayers an' chant da church hymns to Sweet Jesus, while we're markin' yuhr grabe wid da wild onion.

Yuh'll neber git out, Masta, but yuh'll know what's happenin'.

Yuh'll see da flesh rot off'n yuhr bones, an' on da black ob da moon, yuh'll roll ober an' ober in dat grabe, while da wolves an' da ebil spirits dance ober yuhr head.

He waited, like a fox. Not a crafty, wise old fox, but like a young, panicked pup, chased until it was trapped in front of a sheer wall or at the edge of a cliff. He waited for the third shot to come, and when it did, he bolted, using the loud retort to disguise his noise.

It was a technique Red had mastered, not from the trapped fox hunted for sport, but from the War, when, like so many Rebel soldiers, he had learned what it was like to taste leaves and mud while slithering on his belly, snake-like, away from an enemy one-hundred-thousand strong.

There was no comfort in familiarity. Familiarity bred contempt.

That, too, was from the Bible. Man's bible. In a chapter Gutenberg failed to print.

Then came a fourth and a fifth and a six shot, frightening him by its unexpectedness. They were firing blind, now, firing so close the earth shook under his hands. It was only when the rain came again that Red realized it was not shots from human guns, but cannon from heaven: the thunder of the gods.

Then there was lightning, striking so close he could smell the sulphur singe the ground, see the flames of the burning wet grass and sodden trees no earthly power could have set ablaze.

September, he thought madly. It is too early for such a storm. Do not look for storms until October.

With the water rising to his mouth from sudden flash flood, Red rose up, like Lazarus, and crawled away on hands and knees. The sun, obscured by low-hanging clouds, blinked out the light, causing night to fall preternaturally. With the world thus turned upside down, the fugitive made good his escape.

Unlike Lazarus, there were none to welcome his return from the dead.

Like Lazarus, he was made mad from the miracle.

CHAPTER 12

With visibility no more than hand-before-his-face, Claw Kiley reined in his horse and dismounted, soaked to the skin by the unexpected drenching. Within a quarter hour, the land beneath his feet was covered with water, forcing him to move to higher ground.

As he was tying the reins around a low-hanging branch, a clap of thunder, then a jagged bolt of red-hot lightning struck within fifty yards of where he stood, spooking his horse with its ferocity. The animal whinnied in terror, pulled the slippery leather from his grasp and plunged headlong into the rising water.

Claw made a futile dash after him, then stopped and let him go. With a man on its back, the horse would not have gone a step further into the ever-seeping muck, but on its own, would be in Hellhole by sundown of the next day.

Such was the logic of a horse. Claw decided he could not damn him for it.

Which did not prevent him from cursing.

Shivering from the penetrating cold, Claw looked around himself for shelter. With the trees making a leaky roof, and no overhanging rocks to hide beneath, he was compelled to stay where he was. Briefly removing his hat to throw off the accumulation of water which dropped from the brim like a waterfall, he succeeded only in soaking his hair.

He should have turned back when signs of the storm became unmistakable. He could not hope to trail men in the rain. He could not hear their whispered conversations, smell smoke from their campfire, nor could he hope to scare them away with the rays of a bright sun sparkling off his badge.

Of that much he was certain. It did not ease his conscience knowing they were caught in the rain, too. Men obsessed with the idea of murder did not feel the elements. Hunger was nothing to them. They fed on hate.

Red was out there, too, trapped somewhere in the wood, or wallowing through the torrents of a rain-swollen baranka. The thought occurred to Claw that if the fugitive drowned, the situation would resolve itself. The hunters would leave Ford County, the wild dogs or the coyotes would feast on Red's bloated body and he could catch up with his horse, or else walk the distance back to Hellhole.

All would be as it was, without his intervention.

But that would be too easy.

It would also be a lie.

All would never be as it was.

Claw Kiley did not like lies; his life was predicated on truth. He would find the man called Red and see he received justice. When the marshal returned to Hellhole, he would have to have a heart-to-heart talk with Fiz. There was much which needed explaining. On both sides.

Once the air was cleared, he would look up Eric Anheiser and find some reason for ordering him out of town. Littering. Loitering. Annoying the Law.

Truth in all things.

That was the way he ran his office. Cougar Bradburn would understand. She was a truthful woman, herself. Vengeful, too. He supposed her sense of humor and fair play would save him.

It would be a pity to be spared from the ravages of weather, the danger of hunting men, the bitter sanctity of the doctor and the confrontation with a former slave owner, only to be felled by a blow from his gall.

With that thought failing to warm him, Claw hunkered down against the side of a tree trunk and closed his eyes. Time would be long in passing.

***

The whipping wind blew inward, sending spray into the Lowdown Saloon. Tiptoeing carefully over the slippery, sodden sawdust, Steve grabbed the double doors and drew them shut. They did little to keep the storm at bay.

"Close the full doors," Cougar ordered, coming out from her small work room in the rear of her establishment.

He complied immediately, then blew on his hands.

"Cold, today," he needlessly observed. Then, "I didn't see the Marshal ride in."

Cougar shook her head.

"Neither did I. I suppose he got caught out there. Knowing Claw, he's burrowed into some cave, snoring away the afternoon. I expect we'll see him in a day or two, and he'll wonder why we were concerned."

She moved fluidly behind the bar, reached for a bottle sitting under the counter and cracked the top. She poured herself a shot of brandy, sipped it, then replaced the high-priced gift into its hidey hole.

"Why don't you go home, Steve?"

"It's early, Miss Cougar."

"Maybe. But no one'll be out on a day like this. If someone does stagger in, I think I can handle him myself. Go on. Call it a day."

"Thanks. Mary'll be making dinner at four. Why don't you come over? Bring Eric with you, if you want to. She likes company."

"I might. Thanks."

Steve retrieved his coat from the rack in the rear of the saloon, waved a friendly departure, then hurried away, glad for the time off. It was unusual to have the day to himself and he determined to take a long nap, rise to eat a full meal, then spend several hours on his hobby. It was not a pursuit he talked about, and one his friends would have been hard pressed to explain.

Sharpshooter Steve, circus attraction turned barkeep, collected stamps. They were his true passion in life. Where other men sought treasure in gold, or in the collection of rare paintings, he saved stamps. Not the kind steamed off letters and pasted between the pages of books, but those still affixed to their original messages.

There was history in stamps. Some were on letters of affection, while others were from businesses. Some stamps were set crooked, while a few were put to paper upside down, the result of a careless clerk, or a heart-sick lover. Stamps were living history, binding together people with a uniqueness all their own.

They were a marvelous invention, part and parcel of communication, as great as the printing press or the weekly newspaper. For two pennies, a man could send a stamped letter to his wife, away visiting family. He could announce the birth of a child to distant relatives, send an invoice to a reluctant customer, spread the news about home life to a lonely soldier, or inform a brother on the loss of his wife.

For a ha'penny, a man could buy two dozen used stamps from Hector, at the post office, who dug them out of the dead letter bin.

Coming to Hellhole had been a bonanza for Steve, the stamp collector. Nearly one hundred letters arrived yearly which went uncollected. "Hellhole" or more formally but less correctly, "Hellhole City, care of General Delivery," was the address, while the names ranged from "Mr. Tobias Kamer," to "Miss May Williams." Perhaps Mr. Kamer had decided not to come to Hellhole, after all, diverting his investment business to some other prairie town. Perhaps he had been killed in a stage coach robbery, died from bracken water poisoning, or changed his name and did not want to claim any remembrance from his past.

Possibly Miss May Williams was a saloon girl who did not know a letter from a secret admirer awaited her. Or, she might have been a woman, traveling alone, who did not care to find the written orders, summoning her home. She could have been a woman tearfully awaiting notification from the War Department on the safety of her husband, never to learn his fate, because the letter from Colonel Johnson or Captain Billingsley went uncollected.

Steve never opened the missives from the dead letter office. He merely examined the stamps, categorized them by state, or cancellation, or face value, and put them under glass. It was not for him to pry into the affairs of others. It was enough to wonder, for therein lay the value.

To know too much was often to regret. He had enough in his own life to put aside, without adding the burdens of strangers.

***

"I suppose," Eric said, joining Cougar at the bar of the Lowdown, "our dinner engagement is off."

"If I'm closing up, I can't imagine why the Regent would stay open. The weather's just too bad for people to venture outside."

"Got any food? A cook stove? I flatter myself I have some talent with a skillet. Besides," he added, seeing her hesitate, "you have to eat. Just because a storm's come up doesn't mean you won't get hungry."

"Are you trying to tell me you're hungry?" Cougar inquired in the quintessential way she had of phrasing a rhetorical question.

"Starved," he confessed. "There's no point my unloading any more supplies today, anyway. It's too windy and wet out there. And those steps of yours will be as slippery as ice. So, I really have nothing better to do. Unless...."

He trailed off his words while gently raising his right eyebrow. Cougar hesitated, remembering Steve's kind dinner invitation. But Steve was family and Eric - at the moment - was still an interloper. It would not do to "bring him home" just yet. She pointed to the back.

"The stove's in there. You'll probably have to clean it out, though. I doubt anyone's used it since last winter. I have no idea if there's anything edible. I know there's a box of rock salt. We use it to melt the ice out front. If a man falls on his face, we prefer he do it inside - after he's spent his poke," she added with a smile.

"I'll look real hard to find something a little more appetizing than that," Eric promised. "See you in a bit."

"See you," she agreed, lowering her voice so he had to stop and turn around. Rather than repeat herself, Cougar waved him off. He smiled and trotted away.

If Eric managed to prepare some palatable food, Cougar decided she would invite the girls to join them. In this case, six was company while two was a crowd.

It would be a cowardly deed, and one Eric certainly would not appreciate. She knew he wanted to be alone with her, and the opportune threat of continued rain and wind suited his purposes perfectly. As she settled into her chair, Cougar mused on the situation.

Eric Anheiser was a good looking man. He was well bred, polite, friendly and understood the value of a dollar. He was no one's fool, had a head for business and a driving force compelling him forward at all times. She liked his brother and she understood clearly the message Eric was trying to get across when he told her the story about Chad and Belle.

All the elaborations about honeymoons to Europe, the preparation of twenty-one entrees, flavored ices and champagne floats were window dressing. What he was actually telling her, was that he and Chad were not blue-blooded Boston snobs. If a former saloon girl was good enough for one brother, another would be equally suitable.

It was not as though she had never noticed him, never spent a futile night wondering what it would be like to catch his fancy. He was fun, had a sense of humor and he paid well. More experienced than Claw, he knew how to be gentle or forceful as the occasion dictated.

In business, there was much they could teach one another. That made a partnership all the more appealing.

A year ago, six months ago, Cougar Bradburn would have been walking on air to realize she had done more than catch Eric Anheiser's eye. Her head would have been filled with dreams of fancy dress balls, long sea voyages and the prospect of getting a new brewery up and running.

At the moment, however, she could not quite fathom why her mind kept going back to San Francisco.

***

Red woke every ten minutes, stiffening his muscles as he strained to differentiate storm noises from those indicating a stealthy encroach of his enemy, then shifted positions and dozed again. He kept telling himself he had shaken them; that the rain had been a blessing in disguise. Without the storm to cover his escape, he would probably already be dead.

And then, as the cold numbed his body, he became aware of a disquieting realization. For the first time in his life, he had not shivered at the thought of his own demise. The idea of death seemed logical, even desirable.

More frightened now than he had ever been in life, Red hugged himself and tried to cry. He had an awareness that if he could work up some emotion, however unmanly, he would begin to feel again. The blood would rise in his veins, the prospect of escape would once more assume its rightful predominance in his brain, and his ever-active mind would begin working on plans for escape.

For the life of him, no tears came into his eyes. To help them along, he awkwardly - and without aforethought - pushed his hat back on his head, letting the rivulets of rain wash down his cheeks.

His nose ran but his eyes remained dry. They were, he decided, the only things dry in the entire world.

With his heart pounding , Red stretched his cramped legs, flexed the muscles in his right arm, then snuffled again. His mind was as sluggish as his desires, however, and a drop of clear, salty fluid formed at the tip of his nose.

"Wipe it away," he ordered himself, but suddenly, his arm would not obey. "Get up and move around." His legs had apparently gone to sleep. He tried to whistle but no sound came from his poorly puckered lips. He tried to sing but could think of no songs, remember no tunes.

He tried to cough but the mucus clinging to the sacks in his lungs refused to give up their prize. He tried to blink, but the eye lids refused to close.

"It's the fever," he told himself. "Fever has taken hold of me."

It was hard to think. He struggled a long moment before bringing to mind the words "blood poison."

"I am thirsty," he thought, although the idea sounded more like, "Th... thur... I - I am tirsty."

"I must drink, to bring down the fever," came out "I - I - I.... I dink... to feber."

He was regressing into childhood.

Which was better than thinking he had lost the will to survive.

The next thing Red realized clearly was that he was on his feet and walking. He was drenched to the bone, his feet splashed through ankle deep water.

Frightened to discover himself out in the storm, he paused to take his bearings. How and why he found himself traveling east was a puzzle he lacked the strength to solve.

"Walk. Keep walking," was all he could think. "Move one foot in front of the next. No trail to leave in this tiny river."

The thought struck him as funny and he laughed. The more he laughed, the funnier it became, until he was nearly convulsed.

There was no such thing as a "tiny river."

He would fool them, yet, those black men who had grown as close to him as his own shadow.

"Walk. Keep walking."

East was not the direction he had intended to take. If he were to escape their clutches, then he must go north, into the high country, where a man's name and his past bore no relevance. Or south, to Mexico. Hundreds of former Confederates had fled to that country. He could explain his plight to them and they would band together to protect him.

That was the way with vanishing species.

North. South. His two choices. He laughed, again, at the new joke. In his delirium he had discovered his sense of humor.

He had been reborn.

Tears poured from his eyes, reminding him he had left his hat behind, in the rising water of his former sanctuary.

Why, then, was he walking east? Turning around, Red suddenly became confused. He could not be certain that he was actually moving east. Without the sun or the stars to navigate by, he might just as easily have been traveling in a circle. Yet he was utterly convinced he was heading east.

Why?

The answer was as clear as ice.

Hellhole.

"No," he cried, stopping his forward movement by grabbing hold of an outcropping branch. "No!"

His break was not much help, as he discovered, too late, for it was a dead limb, broken off, but fallen at such an angle as to deceive him into thinking it alive. Still clutching the wood with his right hand, Red was nudged along, forever forward, by the angrily rising tide of the newly born waterway.

If the rains continued, the rising water would be a full-blown river within six hours, perhaps less. Rushing with the indomitable strength of a newborn, it would wash away everything in its path.

Everything except sin, for this was not holy water, but rather the muddied, soil-laden, debris-filled spawn of bemused gods.

By morning, a man who had lived in this God-forsaken territory would not recognize one single landmark. Mighty trees, which had served extinct Indian tribes as sources of firewood and shade, would be uprooted and dragged away in a matter of minutes; ancient rock formations, blunted by the sands of time, would be whittled down to pebbles, the size a poor child could substitute for marbles.

Lean-tos, shanties, shacks and mud-brick homes would be torn apart by the undirected rage of the river. A nail, manufactured in Philadelphia, sold to a dealer out of Wichita, transported by rail to St. Louis, then crated to Hellhole by a four-up, sold by a dry goods store to a homesteader, then hammered home into the side of a barn, was likely to come to its final resting place at the bottom of a sink hole twenty miles away, there to rust away to nothing.

On a hot, dry summer day, when yearling scrub cattle, which had never witnessed water falling from the sky in their lifetime, came to sniff out a drink or perish, they would eagerly lap up this brackish puddle. Within a day, they would perish from unintentional poisoning.

It was the cycle of life and death on the prairie. The following season, more scrub cattle would be born, and they, too, would wander aimlessly, in search of water. The herd would come upon the sink hole, pass by the bleached carcasses of their kind without recognizing them as such, and drink from the shrinking pond, polluted, not only by rusty nails, but by the rotten bodies of those which failed to crawl out before the breath of life deserted them.

This second generation of cattle would die, depositing their bodies on top of those which had come before.

Unless an unusually wet spring kept the grasses green and the water holes filled, all the scrub cattle in Kansas would perish.

Propelled forward by the water at his knees, Red was shoved into a still-standing tree, bloodying his nose from the impact. He did not seem to notice, for he was laughing.

It took human beings four long years of bloody conflict to end the existence of scrubs, while it would only take Mother Nature two generations to dwindle the population of scrub cattle to a point where their existence would be rendered meaningless.

It seemed the funniest joke Red had ever heard.

Ascribe it to blood poisoning.

***

He might not have awoken at all, had not the horse shoved its cold, wet nose into his face. Pulling back, Claw fought off the dream which had encased him, slew the dragons of his past, then came to full awareness, hand on the butt of his gun.

His sudden movement frightened the horse, which retreated a step. Eying the man before it, the animal whinnied piteously, then tried once again to endear itself to him by extending its nose.

"Easy, boy," Claw said, accepting the offer of friendship by tenderly rubbing the outstretched nose. With his heart beating at quick-step, he slipped his fingers around the bridle, thus attaching the horse to his arm.

"So, you decided to come back, did you?" he asked, drawing himself up to his full height. "I'm mighty glad to see you."

The excitement in his voice caused the horse to swish its sodden tail, like a dog. Since the days when primitive human beings first domesticated its diminutive ancestors, there had been an implicit promise of care. This beast standing before the lawman was a product of thousands of generations of horses which had been bred to expect hay and oats after a hard days labor, a lump of sugar from a cupped hand and a rubdown to remove the scratchy burrs from its short-haired coat.

Anything less was a denial of responsibility, a promise broken.

Brushing his own cheek against that of the horse, Claw threw his arms around the animal's neck and hugged it.

"Don't know that I could have walked all the way back to Hellhole," he admitted. There was a quiver in his voice, a shaking in the admission he would not have felt free to express in front of any but those dumb brutes who did not share secrets with Claw's kind.

Claw felt a chest cold coming on and he was near frozen from exposure. Five miles of dry, rolling terrain had become one hundred in this flooded, angry land. A two hour return trip by foot had been magically transformed into one of two days, or two weeks.

He coughed, spit out the greenish phlegm, then shook himself like a wet dog.

"Sure am glad to see you," he repeated. "I sure thought you were back in Hellhole by now, brushed and dry and eating -"

He did not finish the sentence as awareness washed over him like clear-flowing water. This animal was not his horse; it was not the horse he had bought from Bark Barker on his arrival in Hellhole. Not the one he promised to replace when spring grasses grew high and ranchers looked to sell, at a reasonable price, the herd they had so carefully primed for market.

This was another man's four-legged beast.

The horse was unsaddled, but the well saddle-soaped leather reins attested to the fact the animal had, until recently, been tended.

By the light of the suspicious, cloud-pocked sky, the marshal inspected the horse for a brand. Finding none, he went back to the reins. Nothing there to tell a story.

"Where'd you come from, boy?" Claw asked, after the manner of horsemen, who never failed to speak to their mounts as though expecting an answer.

Turning into the wet gloom, Claw raised a hand to his eyes to shield them from the rain and called out.

"Hello? Anyone there?" He paused no more than half a beat before abandoning the effort. "Well, boy," he continued, turning back to the horse. "I don't know about you, but I think I want to get out of here." No words were necessary to announce its agreement, though it whinnied, just to be certain. The remembrance of abandonment was too fresh in its mind to take chances.

Claw walked the horse through the rising water, noting with relief, it was not limping. It had not, therefore, been released due to injury. As the horse walked, however, Claw noted the broken leather hobbles still wrapped around its forelegs. Removing his pocketknife, he quickly severed the remnants, thus freeing the legs from the water swollen, tightly constricted restraints.

Holding the two leather pieces close to his eyes, Claw furtively inspected them.

"Break free, did you?" he inquired, but the evidence in his hands spoke otherwise. The horse had not escaped, it had been set loose, for the hobbles had been cut clean, with one stroke from a sharp hunting knife.

"We'll take it slow, boy," Claw promised. "Don't want to find ourselves plunged headlong into a swollen baranka."

The animal nodded its head wisely, then rippled its hide in anticipation of the tall man mounting its back. Claw did so with a seamless effort, paused to cough and spit again, then, reins in his left hand, military-style, kicked the brute with the tips of his boot heels.

"Let's go," he urged. "There's a stable waiting for you in Hellhole. And a nosebag of oats."

The later was an implicit promise, the animal's due. Flicking its ears in annoyance at the delay, it plunged forward, into the rainy afternoon.

It never occurred to Claw to do more than shout for the horse's owner. Survival was his first instinct. He was catching cold, he was near frozen and he had a horse to take care of. His duty now was to return to Hellhole.

It was a situation, Dan Cord might have said, of not looking a gift horse in the mouth.

CHAPTER 13

The dinner, as Eric prepared it, consisted of thick sliced bacon, fried to the point where the fat retained its whiteness but the streaks of meat were crisp; hard tack fried in grease with melted cheese poured over it, with canned peaches for desert.

"Not bad," he admitted, spreading the last of the cheese over a cracker. "Considering what I had to work with."

Cougar gave him an odd look, then agreed.

"Well, you'll never make a cook at the Regent, but if you're ever out of work, I'm sure they'll employ you at the Hellhole House."

"That, Miss Bradburn, is a left-handed compliment."

"Let's just say you're a better beer hawker than a chef. But," she added quickly, and with sincerity, "I enjoyed it."

"We all did, Eric," Rosemond agreed, wiping her lips with a napkin as she had seen her betters do. "How nice of you to invite us."

"No," he demurred politely, "it was your Boss who invited you."

The girls looked clearly startled.

"Thank you, then, Miss Cougar," Rosemond repeated, this time to the proper person. "I've worked a lot of places an' never once been said a kind word to by the boss, let alone received an in-vite to sup with him."

"I wager you've received an 'in-vite' or two," Cougar replied, "but I'm not surprised none of them were for an innocent dinner."

Cougar looked at the pretty, young, shop-worn woman sitting to her left. Rosemond could not have been more than twenty-five years old, but looked ten years older than that. Her hair was dyed to the color of off-season raspberries, while the rouge she skillfully applied to her cheeks had faded to what Doctor Ward might describe as "three days post fever."

Like so many of the girls employed at the Lowdown, Rosemond Jones was fresh off the stage. When applying for the job, she had explained to former owner Bix Bradley she was from Hays, which could have meant she passed through that city on her way to Hellhole, or that one of her customers had described it well enough for her to claim kinship.

Sitting in on the interview, Cougar had not minded the deception, for, in fact, neither she nor Bix had seen it as such. Asking where a girl hailed from was no more than mere formality. She had lied herself more than a few times, in her younger days, when places such as Natchez or Vicksburg had sounded more glamorous than Dry Hole or Muddy Waters.

Cougar liked Rosemond and she pitied her. Rosemond was a girl going nowhere in one hell of a hurry. Long past the age where she could hope to snag a young farmer or catch the eye of a back-east salesman, she was fodder for the blackjack dealers, the stinking hiders and the gold seekers, for whom Kansas was as close to Sutter's Mill as they were ever going to get.

Rosemond was one of many who had long ago stopped requesting the bartender to water their drinks, or who refused an offer to go upstairs because a man had an evil reputation. She was nearly at the end of her track, never realizing the miserly clerk back at Home Town had failed to sell her a through ticket to Happiness.

Bix Bradley had employed three type of girls and Cougar Bradburn would be no different: those fresh and young enough to make a man feel both fatherly and lecherous; those experienced in the ways of selling drinks, dealing cards and handling four men a night, and girls like Rosemond, who knew better than to take the last dollar from a customer's purse as he snored away his time beneath her covers.

"Never take more than a man'll miss," a friend had told Cougar Bradburn once, long ago.

"Never take more than a man expects you to pinch," a wiser acquaintance had informed her, in her own younger days. "No man but the rawest, youngest steamboater expects to go to sleep and wake up as wealthy as when he closed his eyes. Help yourself to what's owing you, and then take a bit more. If that don't leave enough for him to buy a bottle in the morning, then just take your cut. Never leave man nor beast high an' dry; that's what turns 'em ugly for the next gal down the line."

At eighteen, Cougar had seen little point in worrying about anyone else but herself. She had followed the advice, however, for it had been spoken with a wisdom she respected, if not appreciated. She had not gotten wealthy by erring on the side of prudence, but she had managed a ticket to the "end of the line."

Her mentor had not told her the trip would end in Hellhole.

Foresight was occasionally a blessing but more often a curse.

Eric Anheiser was the half-filled bottle of whisky in Cougar Bradburn's life. He was the clerk at the ticket office, smiling as he handed her that for which she had abundantly paid.

Ride the stage a bit longer, he was saying to her. Hellhole City doesn't have to be your final resting place. There's a whole world beyond this water-trough town. You've tarried long enough to make a mark: that's more than most, who do no more than settle into unmarked graves, their dreams cold before their body's dead.

I have more to offer. More than a lawman who knows there's a bullet out there with his name on it.

Those were not Eric's exact words, of course. Better educated than she, he would have phrased his sentences with champagne words, while punctuating them with breweries and distilleries.

They were not his exact words, but they contained the amber truth of his meaning.

You're better than the rest of these girls, Cougar. You have brains as well as looks. You're a woman worthy of possession.

Yes, Cougar agreed, in her silent, one-sided conversation. I am. Or, at least, I always thought I was. My winning this saloon, my settin' myself up in business, my status as an owner, rather than as an owned, makes any man give me a second look. Like you, Mister Anheiser.

A second look.

And therein lay the problem. Eric had been through Hellhole half a dozen times during her tenure as saloon girl. They had shared drinks together, had a few laughs and gone upstairs twice, last spring, when Bix Bradley was in bed with a sick stomach. Eric had teased her, demanding that whatever it was she put in Bix's drink, she refrain from adding to his. Cougar remembered retorting that if she put something in Bix's drink, he would not be "expected to recover."

They had snickered over her statement, snuggled under the covers and made a night of it. In the morning, Eric made a point of washing his state mouth out with the contents from the bottle on the nightstand they had failed to finished, then paid her without once checking his purse. Cougar took his meaning, and thought him the most desirable man in the world.

That had been last spring. They had seen each other several times since, but as Eric reminded her, Bix had "kept her close." True enough. Bradley had been a mean, son-of-a-bitch-bastard, who hated to think anyone had more than he did. While it would never have crossed Bix's mind either of the Anheiser boys would drop more than a twenty dollar gold piece at the foot of a Cyprian, that twenty dollars was more than he figured she deserved.

"Girls are like beer," he used to say. "Give them a head and they go flat faster."

Old Bix. He had a way with words.

"Cat got your tongue?" Eric asked, rousing her from her reverie.

"Cat? No," she answered, brushing away the fur balls of her past.

Looking around herself, Cougar was shocked to see that the table had been cleared of both dishes and companions. While she had sashayed down memory lane, Eric had tidied up, while the girls had slipped away to an early, empty bed.

"How about I stoke up the fire and we warm ourselves by it?" he suggested. She appeared not to understand. "There's no stove in that upstairs room at the end of the hall, and it's getting mighty cold down here."

"What?"

"I thought you looked as though you were shivering. We could go into the back office and warm ourselves by the stove in there. There isn't one out here, and there isn't one upstairs in your room."

Cougar smiled, melting his heart.

"Now, how would you know there isn't any stove upstairs in my bedroom? The last time you were through Hellhole, that room was occupied by Bix Bradley. Don't tell me you tarried in there, paying your compliments to Bix. I didn't think - he - was the type."

Eric flushed red, looked shocked, then finally grinned.

"Oh. I see what you mean. No, nothing like that. There's no stove pipe leading outside. Unless he liked smoke in his room, he'd have a vent. I've been around this building more times than I can count, and I've looked it over pretty well. The only vent for a stove is the one in the back room - the office."

"I guess Bix expected your whisky to warm the customers," she observed, matching his smile. "You're right, though. I hadn't thought about that. In winter, the only room kept warm was his office. He said his ink froze if he didn't keep it proper. As for upstairs, I imagine he used hot bricks under the bed clothes to warm his sheets."

"You'll need something more substantial than hot bricks."

"I'll put in a stove."

"You want, before I go, for me to knock a hole in the wall so you can put up a chimney?"

"I don't know. I don't want you working for nothing, Eric. I already owe you so much for your offer to fix all that broken furniture."

"You don't owe me for that. I volunteered. Chad and I call it 'customer relations.' Besides, I like to work with my hands."

Cougar blew on her fingers, which, she noticed, had grown cold.

"You must have a schedule to keep. Chad'll be expecting you back."

"He'll keep. How 'bout I have a look? Won't take more than a few minutes."

"Tonight?"

"I can't cut through the wall tonight, but I can see where the best place would be."

Cougar already knew where the "best place" would be. But then, she was no carpenter.

"All right. I'll go with you."

"Let me grab a lamp."

"I already know the way."

He laughed on cue.

**

Claw coughed, spit, then rested his free hand on the neck of the horse. The animal responded by flicking its ears, then stumbled as its right foreleg hit a snag obscured by the rising water. Pulling in the reins, Claw hesitated, then looked around himself in despair.

The landscape had changed, altered literally within hours. The low-hanging sky cast a pall over the rolling hills, making apparitions appear solid, while deceiving the eye as it calculated distances. Near became far, while far seemed impossibly distant. It was, he thought, easier to reach the clouds, than Hellhole.

At least he knew in what direction the sky lay.

There was only one prudent course of action and that was to lay low, wait for the water to recede, the clouds to part and the sun to shine. He was, after all, Claw told himself, in no hurry to return. Those in Hellhole worrying about him would have to wait for news. Better see him ride in, wet and weary, a day or a week late, than have a posse find what remained of his water-bloated body.

He remembered, in extreme annoyance, he had sent Joshua away. That meant there was no law in Hellhole.

"Well, that would suit Eric - and all the rest of those damned people who keep saying they didn't know there was law in Hellhole," he groused aloud. "For the next two or three days, there won't be any. Put that in your pipe and smoke it."

That was an expression of an old trapper Claw had wintered with back in '60. It meant, he said, "take your time before deciding on a course of action."

Claw had heard other men use it with decidedly different connotations.

At the moment, he could not have put anything in his pipe and smoked it. Even if he had a match to light the tobacco, the constant drizzle would extinguish it before he had managed one single puff.

That, he grimaced, would please Fiz Ward. While Claw did not doubt the physician had used that expression a time or two himself, he was equally certain he never followed his own advice.

Patience was not a virtue west of the Mason-Dixon Line.

Nor anywhere else, he guessed, though he had been no further east than the Carolinas, and anyone suggesting those states were "east" was likely to get a bullet in his gut.

Claw was not even certain what time of day it was. He thought it might be late afternoon, but as the night was hardly darker than the day, he supposed it did not matter. What was of concern was the rising water. If he camped in the wrong location, the changing tide of a flash flood would sweep him away before he had time to grab his hat.

"A man without his gun still has his wits about him, Claudius, but a man without a hat is at every man's mercy, because they think him a fool."

He had forgotten who said that.

Someone with a hat, no doubt.

"We could sure use a fire, old boy. Got any suggestions?" he inquired of the steed. The horse sneezed, causing Claw to do the same. He figured if the horse began yawning, they'd both be floating, face down, in the Kansas Ocean, by morning.

And both hatless.

A fate to be avoided at all costs.

"That's it!" he shouted, startling the horse into a quick-step. It moved one hundred yards through the water, then slipped, throwing its rider. Claw plunged into the rising tide, went under before he could take in a breath of air, and came up sputtering, ten feet away from the animal.

The horse, too, had fallen, and was slow getting to its feet. Claw swam to him through the thigh-deep water, grabbed the reins and began wading. A horse, he knew, would either refuse to take one step forward into flowing water, or it would plunge ahead without questioning the consequences. A man on foot was wiser, although not necessarily luckier.

This time, and for the foreseeable future, the rider would lead and the riderless horse would follow.

Claw decided they would keep moving until finding some ground above water. Then, they would set camp, no matter how grim their situation appeared. Walking without direction was the worst thing anyone could do. It wasted energy, wore on the nerves and made a man prone to walking in circles, like a cur chasing its tail.

Claw did not favor reading on his tombstone, "Died like a dog."

***

Red was no longer cold. Nor did he mind the blood dripping from his nose. Nothing mattered, anymore.

He had heard them.

He had not seen them, for they were a quarter mile off, moving, he decided, on a parallel course to his own. One had fallen into the water, then come up splashing, in anger. Red had heard the sound of a horse whiny, then more splashing. It was an interesting observation. Negroes were hardly susceptible to the malaria occasioned by the miasma of the low country so favorable to the cultivation of rice and cotton, while their white brothers - and sisters - suffered terribly from that dread disease of fever and ague. Yet both races were equally prone to drowning.

It would be high irony, indeed, if his pursuers perished from the rising waters while he died of the fever.

He took comfort in the thought. That was when he knew he was truly ill.

"Drown, you bastards. Drown. Out here on a Kansas prairie, so far from home."

It was the first time Red vitriolically wished them dead. He had engaged in hand-to-hand combat with his pursuers, struggled to kill them with a knife, one-on-one; taken took pot shots at the group from long range with a Yankee rifle he had bought from a carpetbagger, yet those instances had been no more than self-preservation.

The black hunters were now predators to him, equated to starving mad dogs, or circling wolves. They were grizzly bears, never in a hurry, never frightened, never put off. In the beginning, it had been different; it had been a game, little more than hide and seek. At stake was his life, though he had appreciated the hunt. Let them come. He would outfox them.

It was time that wore him down; the ever slow passage of days, then weeks, turning into months and now years. He had hoped they would weary of the chase and go home; expected them to make an end of it, then merge back into the swelling tide of their restless, homeless kinfolk.

His harriers, these former slaves from his beautiful, beloved plantation, had done neither. They had kept coming, ever cautious, ever ruthless, but always as men; always as vengeful, recognizable agents of God's justice. It was only now, when Kenneth McKinnon had dissolved into a nameless, countenance-altered farce of a man that he finally saw the blacks for what they were: his negative, his opposite side. And in so being, they became one with him.

Had James McKinnon fully understood his son's capacity for reason, he would have disowned him and left Flowering Tree to his eldest daughter's husband.

It was unfortunate, Red decided, that his father was long dead. What was that song lyric: a smoulderin' in the grave.

John Brown's body lies a smoulderin' in the grave.

Something else to laugh it.

His father would not have seen the humor.

Knowing they were out there in the storm, only a quarter mile from where he stood, was suddenly a perverse comfort to the man called Red. Had he lost them, really shed them from his trail, his life - what was left of it - would have been useless. They - his former slaves - had unwittingly given him purpose. And what was a man without purpose? He was a dead man.

He laughed again, pleased at the sharpness of his wit. He had been mistaken; the fever had not dulled him, it had brought out the quickness of his intelligence. It had opened his eyes to his world, previously hidden by magnolia and crinoline, fine brandy and scientific journals discoursing on the merits of crop rotation.

Red McKinnon was born again, baptized by the muddy waters of a Kansas flood.

Divided Kansas; bleeding Kansas. In 1856, John Brown had killed five pro-slavery men at Pottawotamie Creek, Kansas.

In 1856, no one could have told James McKinnon the Younger he would have anything in common with that fiery abolitionist, yet three years later, they were both dead, both destroyed from what might be styled "natural causes." John Brown had been hanged from the neck until dead for inciting a race riot and taking over a Federal arsenal in Harper's Ferry, Virginia. James McKinnon, Junior, had died from injuries sustained during a fox hunt on his own plantation.

Neither had lived to witness the Great Bloodletting they had so inextricably begun.

It was just as well, Red decided, his head drooping to his chin. The world was a changing place. There was no room in it for those who could not grow with the times.

It was an oddity. Cotton grew. Rice grew. Children grow into adults, but men did not grow. They merely died, hoping their ideas would grow for them, only to discover - if there was a life after death, which Red reverently doubted - that ideas, like men, were stolid, un-transmutable things.

Ideas could not die, for they had never lived.

Giving them something in common with men, after all. Most men had never lived, either. They just plodded through a dreary, predestined course, then dropped by the roadside, to be heard of no more.

Red did not feel like a man or an idea, but in his suffering, he knew he had lived.

Making him one up on his father.

CHAPTER 14

Red knew why those men wanted to kill him. He understood it with the simple acceptance of one who had lived life. He comprehended it on the level of nature, the same way he accepted the fact he must breath, eat and sleep to survive.

He had never once questioned their motives, stayed awake worrying about their actions, tried to reason out the best way to explain himself. Hatred needed nothing to sustain its evil; it maintained a symbiotic relationship with its host: fester, erupt in violence, sate the anger, begin again. The cycle of death functioning within the cycle of life.

Hatred was a fungus. Scrape it away and it would appear again, in a new shape, a different color, just as virile.

Hatred functioned like the locusts of the field. When a man saw one insect, soon he would see ten million. A field of green growing rice, or corn, or wheat, would be reduced to stubble within a day and an hour.

The difference was, fungus and locusts did not possess intelligence. They merely existed.

Hatred reduced men to the state of the lowest forms of life.

Weak men hated and weak men sought excuses. Weak men accepted God's Will as Divine, without ever looking to see if they had the Message right.

Red had heard so much discussion on the Biblical texts, he might had stood for a preacher. As a Southerner, he could recite, by rote, if not by heart, the well beloved Titus 2.9: "Bid slaves to be submissive to their masters and to give satisfaction in every respect."

He could recite equally well, though with less practice, Colossians 4:1: "Masters, treat your slaves justly and fairly, knowing that you also have a Master in heaven."

The irony - and the tragedy - was that both quotes came from what was commonly known as the "New Testament."

Jesus, who had come to free Mankind, had become the leader of a religion He would never have recognized.

The man known as Red McKinnon was not a religious man. He had always believed that actions spoke louder than words.

Which was why he did not blame the former slaves for their actions. Nor even for their hate. They, too, had heard the Bible preached.

"...an eye for an eye and a tooth for a tooth..."

That, too, was from the New Testament. Matthew 5:38.

No one in Red's memory had ever followed up that admonition with the remainder of the text: "For he makes his sun rise on the evil and on the good, and sends rain on the just and the unjust."

With the rain pouring in buckets over those men both evil and good, and the sulphuric stink of lightning stinging the eyes of both the vengeful and the fugitive, how could he deny it?

It was enough to make a believer out of the doubtful.

Enough, almost, to convert a sinner.

In the story of his life, Red had been cast as the evil and the unjust. He did not question why such a thing had transpired, nor did he wonder why he had been singled out for special punishment. This was a new world, where scientific logic superseded tradition. A fact was a fact.

Or, as his grandfather would say, a spade was a spade.

Red McKinnon had a decision to make. His quandary was not a new one; it was as old as time. Kill or be killed. That was not from the Bible, but it could have been.

Such was the phenomenon and the danger of the literal translations of words written by fallible men.

Holy Ghosts not withstanding.

The black men were less than a quarter mile away. He had heard them. They had lost his trail and were worrying now only about their own survival.

The man who runs lives to fight another day.

He had learned that in the War. It was jocularly referred to as the Living Bible.

With a bit of luck, skill and the Powers That Be on his side, Red could sneak up on them, shoot them at point black range and be free. He had six bullets left, a full chamber. There were six former slaves seeking to take his life.

Six: a Holy Number doubled. Twice the Trinity. He had come a very long way to enact a very old drama.

Was it not written, "In the beginning God created the heavens and the earth"? And also, "Let the waters bring forth swarms of living creatures,"? And again, "So God created the great sea monsters and every living creature that moves, with which the waters swarm, according to their kinds..."?

That was Genesis.

Was this flood, then, a re-creation of the beginning, when God said, "Let the earth bring forth living creatures according to their kind"? Red was a living creature coming out of the waters like a great sea monster, a representative of his kind. The black men were also creatures of their kind. It was preordained, then, they meet like this, under the heavens and upon the earth.

Six bullets. Six men. One Fate. He was living his dream and called it Revelations.

***

Fiz awoke with a start, sweating so profusely his first thought was that a window had broken, admitting torrents of water into his bedroom. His candle had melted down and extinguished itself some time during the night, leaving his room shrouded in blackness, so that he could not, at first, confirm his suspicion.

Only after ascertaining the bedclothes were dry did he realize his condition was the result or an inner, rather than an outer, tempest.

Throwing off the covers, he swung his legs over the side of the bed and set them on the floor. This time, he could not shake the feeling he was adrift in a boat, the slippery wooden deck covered with slime, the vessel upon which he temporarily resided pitching and heaving, at the mercy of the storm.

Phillip Ward did not like the ocean. He did not favor traveling by water. Given the opportunity, he would go by stage, or train, and failing that, by buggy or on foot. Prone to sea sickness, and born in a landlocked state, he had never trusted sea-going vessels.

If man were meant to travel the watery highways, he would have been given fins.

Fiz could not tell what time it was, but supposed it close to two o'clock in the morning. Bone weary when he retired, he was no longer sleepy. Going back to bed now would only mean tossing and turning for hours before finally arising, more exhausted then when he had first lay down.

Drawing his two strong arms through the sleeves of his robe, he cinched the belt with a deft knot, then padded silently into his outer office. The room smelled vaguely of aseptic, alcohol, blood and coffee. To him, they were the reassuring scents of his profession. Lingering a moment to take in the shadows, he oriented himself to the room, nodded familiarly to himself, after his manner of comforting a patient, then crossed to the stove.

The fire had gone out, the embers barely warm, struggling for life amid the choking mass of grey ash.

Carefully, ever so carefully, Fiz swept away the dead and blew life's breath upon that which was alive. When he saw the tiny sparks glow red, he added a shiver of paper, blew again until it flamed yellow-orange, then added a bit of kindling. As the wood splinters caught, he added more, then finally dared place a quartered log on top. Smoke stung his nostrils as the small flame engulfed the remnant of a long dead sapling .

Not content to leave the fire until he was certain it would catch, Fiz waited with the patience of Job. In point of fact, he used that expression often, although its generally accepted meaning was a misnomer. Of all the characters out of classic literature, Job was certainly one of the least patient. Given a boil on his backside, he howled through 42 chapters before his inexplicable redemption.

As the life-giving warmth spread throughout the room, Fiz peered skeptically into his coffee pot. There was still half a pot of coffee left, simmered down from the full one he had made the morning before. This fact annoyed him and he gritted his teeth in distaste.

No matter how many times he warned himself to wash the pot and leave it filled with fresh water for the morning, he never once obeyed his admonition. He was either too tired, or too busy or he forgot. Poor excuses, all. In any event, Fiz despised excuses. Excuses were for others, not for himself. Pity the weak, the infirm, the homeless, the fools, yet spare not the rod for himself. That was the philosophy he had lived by for forty odd years, and the rule of thumb he would die by. Phillip Ward looked at the world through the eyes of one who understood imperfection in every man but himself.

Now fully awake, Fiz did not have to go to the door to ascertain the rains still fell. He could hear the water beating away on his roof, hear the rivulets cascading down, there to merge into ever-growing flooding on the street below.

To reach the pump and refill his coffee pot, Fiz would have to dress in his rain slicker, navigate the ice-slick stairs and wade through puddles ankle deep. By the time he primed the rusty pump and drew water, he would be soaked to the skin. By the time he re-climbed the steps, he would have spilled half the water out of the pot, for the lid was a lid in name only. The round top had lost its shape long ago, after an irate patient had flung it across the room.

Fiz had never seen fit to have the lid set to rights by the blacksmith, who would have charged him twice what it would have cost to buy an entirely new pot and lid.

Coffee pots were like old friends. The aged gracelessly, they ceased to function long before they were pockmarked by holes, and their stained innards tainted whatever good came out of them.

Fiz loved his coffee pot with a passion bordering on idolatry. He had purchased it from a tinware man in St. Louis, long before he had decided where, or if, he would ever set out his shingle again. The pot was used when he bought it. There were chips in the enamel and the spout had begun to rust. A dent in the side might have been caused by normal wear and tear, but Fiz always imagined someone had kicked it.

His coffee pot was a cast off like himself, and he would have rather parted with his surgical instruments than it. German steel scalpels, sponge sticks, retractors and curved needles could all be replaced by others of the same ilk, selected from a back-east catalogue and ordered by mail. Within three months, he could re-outfit himself with entirely new, shiny instruments which had never seen the sight of blood.

He could not replace his coffee pot in three months or three years. Man could live without blood-letters and forceps, but he could not survive without the companions of his heart. That was a lesson learned more bitter than any coffee Fiz had ever brewed.

He was not in any mood to get soaked to the skin for an error of forgetfulness. With a grunt of caustic irritation, Fiz opened the door, tossed the old coffee out into the flooded world of Hellhole, then stuck the empty pot under a stream of water pouring from the roof. It filled in seconds, rewarding him for his broken promise by providing him with an easy way out.

Well satisfied for his cleverness, Fiz dumped an incalculable number of full and half-full scoops of ground beans into the pot, fitted the lid precariously on top and set it on the hot burner. In a moment, the scent of fresh coffee superseded the other odors of his occupation and his habits.

Waiting impatiently for the coffee to boil, Fiz poured himself a cup before it was quite brewed, blew on the liquid to cool that which he had so laboriously heated, then settled into his chair. The cup he used was a black tin enameled mug he had purchased in Hellhole shortly after his arrival. He used it exclusively, though he had a fine set of matching, white porcelain mugs laid out beside the stove. Those he reserved for patients, their relatives and the odd friend who occasionally dropped in.

The porcelain mugs had been a gift from a wealthy developer, waylaid on a journey to San Francisco. He had inadvertently been run over by team of horses and broken his leg. The resulting wound had been a compound fracture, which healed poorly. Fiz had managed to save the leg, though it provided little service to its owner. He had given the traveler a cane left from a patient whose outcome had been less successful, and received for his trouble twenty dollars, the gift of six mugs and a promise that if he should ever care to visit the city built on a foundation of sunken wrecks, he would be a welcome guest.

That promise and a dollar would buy him five pounds of coffee in the dry goods store.

The rain falling outside had lasted two days and was likely to last as many more. Claw was out in it somewhere, holed up, he hoped, at a scratch farmer's house or a horse rancher's homestead. Joshua, too, had failed to return, but Fiz was not looking for him. Joshua was a mountain man, capable of taking care of himself. He did not wonder that the deputy was regaling the residents of some isolated farm with stories of how he stopped bank robbers in their tracks, rode two thousand miles to return a penny's change to a hider he had inadvertently overcharged while working at the livery, or discoursing on the benefits of a good paint pony.

There were others, caught out in the storm. Fiz's concern for them, he told himself, was merely clinical. The former slaves, the black men on a holy quest, were undoubtedly squatting by a roaring fire, placidly waiting for the rain to stop. They were in no hurry and were unlikely to have been caught unawares by the coming rains.

These were men who had lived outdoors all their lives. They were hardened field hands, probably, who looked upon the elements as extensions of their own bodies. Summer heat, winter cold, spring and fall rains were natural events, accepted with the calm resignation of a people used to adversity.

They had trailed Red for three years and would track him through eternity, if needs be. They would draw near and watch him panic, then fall behind and listen as their quarry breathed a sigh of relief. They would catch him in a trap, have their fun with him and let him go.

Fiz supposed Red would understand. He had become the red fox, and the black men, the hounds.

"Sport" was not a word to a Southerner: it was the living, breathing embodiment of Natural Selection.

The survival of the fittest. The excuse for one race to hold another in bondage.

For Red, Fiz told himself, he cared not one wit. His life was forfeit, in any case. No use crying over spilled milk.

However white.

Fiz had not been out for two days and he did not expect to go out any time soon. It was unlikely anyone would summon him and it was not his nature to go looking for trouble. The Regent was closed "due to inclement weather," which read, to Hellhole residents, as closed "due to weather," and the Lowdown, while still open, did little, if any business, he supposed.

It was a peculiarity of the times he lived in, Fiz mused. Restaurants, banks and businesses were closed, the stage line had ground to a halt, the telegraph office shuttered, and if there had been a church, it, too would have shown a closed door to the world. Only the watering holes, the marshal's office and the doctor's office were still in operation.

And of those three separate and distinct places, only the Lowdown actively solicited business.

He heard the noise and told himself it was nothing. Just a changing pattern of rain or the new creation of a waterfall off his roof. He heard the noise again and told himself he was growing old. He heard the noise a third time and wished he had thought to lock his door and draw the shades.

Had he not just congratulated himself on the fact he was not looking for business?

Rising with a weariness born of gifted insight, Fiz shuffled to the door and opened it. A man, or the shadow of a man, hung over the foot of his railing like a corpse, too long suspended from the rope. Closing his eyes a moment, Fiz prayed for strength. Not the kind required to lift the wounded body and drag it upward, but the kind which fortified the will.

Fiz Ward was a praying man, a devout man, a man of the cloth. Not the kind of black cloth a preacher wore, but the kind who used cloth to bind the hurts of the just and the unjust alike.

The kind who would never turn away any who came to his door, man or beast.

Not even when the man was a beast.

"Who are you?" he asked, not as a demand, but rather as a reassurance he had correctly guessed the man's identity.

"Red McKinnon," came the reply, giving Fiz one additional piece to the puzzle he had not hitherto known.

McKinnon.

By itself, it was a name which meant nothing to him. It was the "Red" which held the significance.

Fiz made a move to pass through the portal of the doorframe when Red spoke again.

"I killed one of them. In the dark. Don't know which one it was. Don't suppose it matters." The effort to speak cost him. Fiz waited in frozen animation for him to finish what was so clearly of importance to the man on the stairs. "Thought they were all together. I was wrong. I came upon this man after he had fallen from his horse. Couldn't make out his face... too dark.... What does it matter?"

"I suppose," Fiz growled from deep in his throat, "it matters a great deal to the five who escaped."

Red made a low guttural noise then spoke no more. Fiz hesitated, thought to go back inside for his rain slicker, then abandoned the idea and went out, clad only in his underthings, a robe and slippers.

Gingerly walking down one step at a time, he came upon the man, cocked his head one way, then the other, then grabbed him by the arm. Red flinched in pain but said nothing.

"Can you move? Do you have the strength to go up, if I help you?"

"I don't know. Don't know how I made it this far."

Looking down into the murky dimness of the street, Fiz saw no other living thing.

"What did you do with -"

"I left it out there."

"The horse."

"I... left it with the dead man."

"You didn't take it?" Fiz exclaimed with obvious incredulity. "You left it out there to starve? Or drown? What kind of a man are you?"

"I left it out there for..." Red trailed off his words and did not finish his thought. Fiz, however, was not so understanding.

"You left it out there for what? For the dead man's ghost? For your information, dead men's spirits don't need horses. They travel on the air."

"I know that," came the annoyed response.

"Then I ask you again - why did you leave the horse out there?"

"I... had to."

"You had to?" Fiz demanded, his ire overcoming his awareness that he was rapidly becoming soaked with cold, wet rainwater. "Why did you have to? Did the others come up? Is that why you left the horse?"

"No. None of the others came up. After I killed the man, I didn't hear any of the others. I didn't hear anything at all."

"Then what in thunder did you leave the horse out there for?"

"I had already given it its freedom once. I didn't want to break a promise and go back on my word."

"You're talking in riddles. What does that mean? 'You didn't want to go back on a promise'? What promise could you have made to a black man's horse?"

"It wasn't a black man's horse, Fiz. It was my horse."

Before Red could elaborate further, he fainted dead away.

CHAPTER 15

When he returned to consciousness, Red became aware of coffee being poured between his clenched teeth. Coughing up that which had already entered his throat, he sputtered, choked, swallowed, then gagged, spewing the physician with coffee and bile.

Fiz did not give an inch. When he saw his patient swallow the rest of his stomach contents, he placed the black speckled drinking mug to his lips.

"Try again," he ordered.

This time, Red obeyed and the resultant effort admitted the coffee down his throat.

"Thanks."

"Think nothing of it. I'm just doing my job."

"How long was I out?"

"Just long enough for me to half drag, half pull you into my office and set you on a chair."

"I'm sorry. I thought I could make it."

"Did you?"

"At one time. Maybe not any more," he admitted, hanging his head and closing his eyes. "I'm tired."

"Fugitives usually are. That's the nature of the beast."

Red snorted through his stuffy nose, then accepted the handkerchief Fiz offered him. After blowing his nose, he had the good manners to keep it, stuffing it into his trouser pocket.

When Fiz ascertained his patient had recovered sufficiently to speak further, he tapped Red's boots with the toes of his own shoe.

"You've ruined your boots," he observed.

"You know," Red grimaced, staring down at his feet, "I was thinking that as I was walking. Where I come from, a man is judged by his possessions. His plantation, his cash crops, his worth in - coin. The manner in which he dresses. If I were back home right now, I'd be a poor man, indeed."

"What happened to your plantation?"

It was not the time to demand answers to meaningless questions, which was exactly why Fiz inquired.

"It was burned to the ground."

"Sherman?"

Red shook his head slowly.

"Can't say that it was. The slaves burned it after they were liberated. The soldiers watched it burn. Didn't lift a finger to stop them. So I'm told," he added, without a trace of bitterness.

"Times have changed," Fiz observed, removing the leaden jacket from the man sitting in his beloved desk chair. "Three years have gone by. I understand many former owners have applied for redress from the Federal government. And gotten it."

"So I've heard."

"Why didn't you?"

"By the time it might have been worth my while, it was already too late. Flowering Tree had been sold for back taxes to some damned carpetbaggers. Broken up into lots. Farmed by freedmen... so I understand."

"Is that a fact?"

"So I'm told," the slumped man repeated, slurring his words from extreme exhaustion.

"You could still try. Some reimbursement would be better than none. If you've taken the Oath of Allegiance."

"I took it. Same as you took it."

"You have your Pardon, then."

"Had it. Lost my papers. Lost everything."

"Lost your horse, too, you said. Or 'gave it its freedom.' How did you get back to Hellhole?"

"I walked."

Incredulity.

"You walked?"

"Yes, sir."

"You walked all the way back to Hellhole when you could have ridden a dead man's horse?"

"Yes, sir. That's just what I did."

"Your own horse, in fact."

"That's what I said," Red replied, growing weary of the game.

"Well, it beats me," Fiz concluded, rubbing his forefinger across his mustache in a nervous gesture of long standing.

"I... I didn't mean to come back here. To you. My presence here means danger. It'll stop raining by and by. They'll find the man I killed and come looking for me. When they don't find my body on the trail, they'll end up back in Hellhole. They'll kill anyone who stands between them and me."

"Are you telling me to give you up?"

Red shuddered, coughed, then nodded his head wearily.

"I would, if I were you."

"So would I."

"What does that mean?" the former Kenneth McKinnon demanded angrily.

"You've been running for three years. You've suffered hardship, torture, despair. You've got a festering wound in your arm and possibly blood poisoning. A bullet's maybe more merciful than an amputation and a long convalescence."

"I - I've thought about all that," Red agreed slowly and with a stammer of shame.

"You've thought about that, all right," Fiz agreed. "That's why you walked all the way back to Hellhole in a tremendous thunder storm. That's why you killed a man out there on the trail. Just so you could have me turn you over to them."

"What do you want of me?" Red demanded, the fire slowly rekindling in his eyes.

"The truth."

"Go to hell."

"You want to tell me about it?"

"I shouldn't have come here."

The wounded man struggled to rise from the chair and failed. Had Fiz not caught him, he would have fallen flat on his face.

"No. You shouldn't have," the healer agreed. "But you did. You battled unconquerable odds to barge your way back into my life, and I'll have the whole story, before -"

"Before I die?"

"You owe me that much," Fiz stated calmly.

"Owe...." Red muttered, his brain filling with waves of disorientation. "I owe you that much. I was taught... to pay what I owe."

This time, when he lost consciousness, Fiz did not bother summoning him back to the land of the living.

***

"No, ma'am," Bark Barker confessed, shaking his wrinkled face, while shoving his gnarled hands into his pockets. "The Marshal ain't come back. Thought when the storm let up a bit he'd be in, but I ain't seen hide nor hair of him. Joshua come in, though."

Cougar jutted her chin forward before speaking.

"Did he say he had seen Claw? Heard anything from him?"

"No, ma'am. He sure didn't. Said he was bone tired and close to starvin'. I reckon he went over to the Marshal's office to clean up, then went in search of a bite to eat."

"Thank you," Cougar replied, her tone flat and emotionless. "I'll look for him."

"I see the Marshal, you want I should send him over to the Lowdown?"

"You do that."

Her journey to the Marshal's Office was long and arduous. Main Street was knee deep in mud, compelling her to step carefully lest she twist an ankle in an unseen hole, or slip on a clod of floating manure and plunge, head first, onto her face.

Caution was the better side of valor. It also delayed the inevitable.

The door to the office was unlocked, testimony more to Joshua's unconcern for intrusion than the fact Claw had never replaced the lock he had bent and twisted six months ago when breaking into his own office. Cougar paused, hand held in a fist at the door, then knocked and went in.

She did not immediately see the deputy, but his gentle snores alerted her to the fact he was asleep in the back. Following his muddy tracks to the jail cells, she saw him in the middle cell, curled into a ball, his mountain man's hat doing poor service in keeping the sun from his eyes.

"Joshua?" And again, "Joshua?"

He roused slowly, the soft, familiar voice failing to bring him to the alert as would that of a stranger's. When he finally did open his eyes, he swung up so suddenly, his hat fell to the floor. He retrieved it as he spoke.

"Miss Cougar! I thought -"

"No. I'm not Claw."

"I reckon you ain't. He over at yer place, sleepin' it off?"

She understood that he was referring to Claw's trek and shook her head slowly.

"He hasn't come back."

"Bark tolt me he had gone out to look fer them yahoos a'most directly after I left. I figure he got caught in the storm, like I did."

"I supposed maybe you stayed put with a farmer; maybe that Timmons fella."

"No," Joshua scoffed, running his hands through his close-cropped hair. "I se'd him early on, then went a callin', jest as the marshal tolt me to. Paid my respects to a family called Earnhart, then went on to a rancher by the name o' McGowan. Se'd it was gonna storm pretty good an' declined an invite to stay put. Should have, though," he admitted, yawning and blinking his eyes to drive sleep from his brain. "If that weren't the worse floodin' I have ever saw, I'll I don't know what was."

She smiled thinly.

"You should have," she agreed.

"That's probably what the marshal done," he tried, reading her expression.

"Yeah. That's probably what Claw did."

"He'll be back directly, Miss Cougar."

"I guess he will."

Joshua rose from the bunk, stretched out the kinks in his sore muscles, then rubbed his stomach.

"I suppose it wouldn't do no harm fer me to go lookin' fer him. Might be his horse threw a shoe."

"You ought to get something to eat."

"Shoot, Miss Cougar, the sun never rose on a – Jackson - what knew the meanin' o' hunger."

"You'd know that better than I," she admitted. "But just to be on the safe side, why don't you come over to the Lowdown with me and have a bite to eat. I ordered breakfast early and it's still sitting over there."

"The Regent open now, is it?"

"They opened this morning. I can't vouch for the freshness of the meat, but charred the way they cook it, it's hard to tell."

"I could jest about eat the side o' a barn," he confessed. "An' drink a keg o' coffee. Nice an' hot, if you got it.

"Left a pot on the stove."

"I'll join you then, an' thank you kindly fer your offer."

When he made a jerking motion toward the rear door, then backed away, she waved him off.

"See you there directly," he finished and slipped away.

Ten minutes later Joshua arrived at the Lowdown, his face and hands washed, the mud brushed from his clothes. The sound of a hammer hitting a nail rang true to his ears as he joined Cougar at her table.

"Sit down," she invited, knowing he would not impose unless asked to do so.

"That Eric?" he inquired, leaning his head toward the sound of the hammering.

"He's fixing up some of the broken furniture. He promised he would before he left Hellhole. I'll pay him a bit for it," she added for no apparent reason.

"I wouldn't pay that feller nothin' I didn't have to," Joshua observed, helping himself to the steak, fried potatoes and corn bread set out on the table.

"Why is that? I don't like to be beholding to anybody."

"Cain't say I blame you. But in his case, I'd make a 'ception."

"Why is that?" she repeated.

Joshua stroked his weeks-worth of beard.

"Fella like that has all the money in the world. He calls time his own. He owes you, mebbe," he added, then made a show of cutting his meat.

"Mebbe," Cougar agreed, shrugging her shoulders. "Mebbe he does."

When Joshua finished two portions - his and the order which would have been Claw's - he wiped his face on a faded red cloth, then pushed back from the table.

"'bliged, Miss Cougar. I'll be goin', then."

"But... where are you going to look? And what will I tell Claw if he comes back right after you leave?"

Joshua grinned easily.

"Tell him I done went out to haul his mangy hide back to Hellhole fer skinnin'. I'm told ol' Jacob at the general store's payin' top dollar fer marshal's skins this season."

She smiled despite herself.

"And what else shall I tell him? Of a more useful nature?"

"Tell him I went out a lookin' fer him, an' not pickin' up his tracks, went on and done some socializin'. It was his orders, after all, that I call on them homesteaders an' advise them the law's done cume to Hellhole."

"All right," she agreed, knowing she would do no such thing. "I'll tell him. And Joshua -" The deputy turned and paused at the batwing doors. "Thank you."

"What's one more saddle sore added to the heap I a'ready got?"

When she had no answer for him, he departed quickly, leaving Cougar alone with her grim thoughts.

***

Phillip Ward had an option. It was not one he normally accorded himself.

In the annals of medical practice, he had one choice and one, only. His patient, the man named Red, and christened Kenneth McKinnon, had blood poisoning, caused by an infected wound in his left arm.

The first time Fiz cleaned away the burned tissue, he considered the possibility of infection. The burn had been a deep one, going clear to the bone. Any time a man sustained such an injury, there was always the chance of the physician leaving contaminated tissue behind. Having no more than his eyes to judge, how much to cut and scrap away was left to his experience.

This was no more or less complicated a decision than removing a bullet from a man's spine, or severing the tightly stretched skin of a woman's body while performing a cesarean section.

In neither example was the life of the patient assured. The extraction of a lead object from between masses of nerve endings and intricately knit bones required a steady hand, an intricate knowledge of how the vertebrae should fit, and the skill to fit together that which a foreign object had so wickedly torn asunder. The extraction of a fetus, coming into the world upside down, was an equally risky procedure. Once the doctor complicated the birth with a scalpel, he immediately ran into the difficulty of contamination, un-staunchable bloodletting, and the unintentional tearing of internal organs.

The odds were long, and no physician willingly entered a surgery or a birthing chamber with a light heart. Never was the weight of his obligation to "do no harm" far from his thoughts.

Removing a bullet from the spine held the tacit threat of paralysis, protracted suffering and eventual death. Taking out a fetus, which, in medical circles was also considered a foreign object, risked the life of the mother and the baby. In many cases, only one life could be saved.

If there were a difference between the two emergencies, it boiled down to one word: choice. A man under anesthesia could not be aroused and asked his preference: paralysis or death. A woman, however, could be questioned: your life, or that of the your baby?

Medical philosophy was clear and well documented in scientific journals. Save the life of the man, and help him adjust to near or total loss of movement. Save the life of the woman, for she was an adult, aware of what she stood to lose. The woman had a husband and probably other young children to tend. The unborn, which had never drawn independent breath, had no comprehension of passing from one existence to another. Accepted practice placed her death as the greater of the two tragedies.

In the field, however, the value of life and death was not so easily defined. A surgeon who knowingly preserved the existence of a man while destroying his identity, did his patient no good. For him, the offer of a bleak existence confined to a couch was worse than death.

A doctor who saved a sickly mother, whose uterus he had cut apart, and whose body he had bled to a near fluidless condition, ran the risk of losing both. It also denied the woman, a free thinking human being, the right to make her own sacrifice.

Doctor Ward did not want to think he was to blame for Red McKinnon's deteriorating medical condition. He had, he told himself, as he paced the small confines of his examination room, done all he could. The patient had presented himself at his door with a burn of too long standing. He had operated, excised that which his training had taught him was poisoned, and sewn up what he supposed to be healthy tissue.

He had, he told himself, done no more or no less than he would have done for any other patient. He had based his decision on sound medical and surgical knowledge. He had detached himself from who and what the man under his scalpel was - from whom he had been.

Fiz relived the operation, arguing with himself that he had performed a skilled job. He remembered thinking, at its conclusion, he had done his best.

What he faced now, however, was the tormenting idea that he had not.

Red McKinnon was suffering from an advanced case of blood poisoning from which he would not recover. This was not, the physician angrily reminded himself, a case of the doctor playing God. He had seen too many patients like Red in the past. He knew, without a doubt, the man would die.

Infection had gone too far; the fever sustained at too a high degree. The brain was already affected. In a day, two days, Red would be reduced to a raving maniac. In a week, he would lie, insensate, on the bed. Inside two weeks, the last earthly transaction involving the former master would be the passage of coins to the undertaker for a cheap coffin and a bumpy ride to Boot Hill.

Red McKinnon was going to die. A layman could make that prediction with absolute certainty. A child who had never seen death could look at the prostrate form on his surgeon's couch and describe his imminent passing over from one existence to another.

Red's enemies, the men who had taunted and pursued him for legitimate and perhaps not so legitimate purposes, would acknowledge their victim's rapid decline into hell.

Phillip Ward could describe with infinite, clinical detail, exactly what was happening inside the still-warm clay. He could elaborate upon the lung sacks filling with fluid, restricting oxygen to the body. He could analyze the tainted blood by smell, determining the contaminant which had reached from head to toes. He could watch with professional detachment, as a spot of black grew up his patient's arm, destroying circulation to all affected parts.

Professional detachment was a wonderful thing. He had attended lectures on just that subject as a student. He could recall with vivid clarity his professor standing in the lecture hall, discoursing upon the dangers of attachment.

"It is your duty, as future physicians, to maintain a healthy distance from the emotional turmoils of your patient. To become involved is to lose your objectivity. To abandon scientific principal for one of emotional suggestively is the worst crime you can commit. It clouds the judgment, weighs options more heavily on one side of the medical scale than the other. It prevents you from diagnosing accurately what which a clear-headed doctor would have no trouble seeing.

"Maintaining decorum, professional and personal, is an absolute necessity. Let your hands be guided by your heart, and you will fall victim to superstition and unrealistic hopes. If you take away nothing more from your studies than a firm belief in the triumph of cool logic over the undisciplined actions of one who is guided by hot-headed illogic, than I will have set you on the course of success. I will have transformed you from uneducated men into healing physicians."

As a medical student, Fiz had believed his professor; had held those words dear to his heart. As a young, practicing doctor, he had maintained his composure, looking upon the body not as belonging to a living, thinking, feeling individual, but merely as a casing for injury and disease.

Scientific principal had been his guiding light. Through research, knowledge and a strict adherence to the balances of nature, Phillip Ward had forged his name into the annals of the competent and the skilled.

Aesculapius, the god of medicine, had blessed his work with magnificent triumphs. His waiting rooms were filled with those seeking him out as their best - their only hope.

Compassion, empathy, an identification with those in pain, had been as far removed from his technique as if those concepts were the exclusive realm of ministers and nursing sisters.

It had always been said that Doctor Ward was a good listener; that he was gentle, kind, sensitive. He had believed that himself, while secretly congratulating himself on his ability to shield his true emotions from others.

Ironically, Dr. Ward had discovered, by a cruel twist of Fate, that scientific study alone was not enough to make a competent healer. It had taken a fatal blow to his heart, a failure of unforgivable proportion, to shake him from the foundations of scholarly detachment.

The man who paced the small outer office located in an out-of-the-way hider town called Hellhole was not the same man who had graduated medical college. He was not that student, whose head had been so full of knowledge; not the young practitioner who had earned fame by treating disease as an entity separate from the soul. Not the famed surgeon who operated on tumors no others would attempt. Not the same man who quoted the *Lancet* as though it were Scripture.

For nearly ten years, this month, Dr. Ward had been a changed man. His former colleagues would not have recognized him as the promising young surgeon from Baltimore, nor would his wealthy, renowned patients from Boston have identified him as the physician who climbed the socially prominent register with ease.

Not even the men who served with him for four arduous years in the Confederate Medical Corps and knew him well, would have thought to find him so changed. Gone was the surgeon who could work twenty-four shifts amputating arms and legs as though the task was no more complicated than sawing the limbs off trees.

Forever altered was the doctor who scribbled death certificates without number; the dry-eyed physician who had written letters home for boys who would never see their wives; the healer who had admonished the weary and the sick to hold up their chins and get on with their lives.

Vanished into thin air was the man who had gone to War to die, because he saw no reason to live.

Suffering had paid its toll on Phillip Ward. His own pain had miraculously transformed him into a true healer; a man of Apollo, the physician, and Hygeia, the goddess of health; a disciple of Maimonides. A follower of Jesus of Nazareth.

Suffering had mutated him but he had not resurrected from his cocoon of isolation into a perfect human being. He was as flawed as any sinner, capable of committing high crimes and misdemeanors, whether knowingly, or by turning a blind eye on the truth.

Red McKinnon had come to him, seeking help, in the time-honored tradition of patient to physician. Red had asked for no more or no less than the sum of Fiz's knowledge, the skill of his hands and the faith of his heart.

Fiz had given him his professional expertise, yet he had failed to offer him the full measure of his faith. He had treated Red's wound, operated to remove the damaged tissue and bound the new incisions with clean gauze.

Yet now, as Dr. Ward paced, he was uncertain whether he had chosen the correct - the precise treatment required. It was unclear to him if he had fallen back into his old ways, by treating the disease and not the man.

He had done what was required, no more. And in failing that, he had not done enough.

The wound he had cleaned was now poisoned. There were numerous reasons why Fiz could conclude the arm had become re-infected after his surgery; Red had left his care without the prescribed follow-up. He had done some hard riding, exposing his arm to the air and mud kicked up by a horse's hooves. He had camped outdoors, lying on the ground, where an open cut could have been exposed to insects, flying sparks from a campfire and dirt. He had gotten soaked from rain, further soiling the bandage. He had sweat from fever, and become chilled from the elements.

Fiz could have enumerated the potential causes for a recurrence of the poison until he was blue in the face, and still not convinced himself. There was nothing, no way to prove, one way of the other, why the arm had turned black.

He had either cleaned the burn sufficiently and Red had inadvertently contaminated it again, or he had not scraped away all the infection and the deadly disease process left behind had come roaring back, more virulent than before.

Guilt was a terrible burden to bear.

No one would have agreed more than Fiz's patient.

CHAPTER 16

"How bad is it, Fiz?" Red asked.

He had been awake for some time, lying on the bed with his eyes closed. It seemed to take more energy than he possessed to lift his eyelids. When he did not receive an immediate answer, he tried again, this time with a rueful smile.

"I'm as weak as a kitten."

"That's because you haven't had anything to eat. I'm going to fix you some good, strong broth in a moment and I want you to try and drink a little of it."

"I'm not hungry."

"You are, but you don't know it." Fiz approached his patient, fussed with the pillow, then managed to leave it in exactly the same position as before his ministrations.

"That's a lot like life, isn't it, Fiz?"

"I'm not in any mood for philosophy," came the tart rejoinder. "Especially not yours," he added.

Cruelty was often used as the spokesword for remorse.

"Are you gonna tell me?"

Fiz noticed Red's dialect became more apparent when he did not have the strength to fight it. Also that his grammar suffered.

"Tell you what? It's ten o'clock in the morning. You've been asleep for hours. The date is October first."

"That explains it, then."

"Explains what?" Fiz demanded, his irritation mounting.

"Why it's so cold. By October, the weather always turns nasty."

"Is that what you were waiting for? For October to arrive?"

"To explain my nastiness, you mean?" Red smiled up at the physician.

"Don't play games with me, mister. Stay put. I'm going to heat the broth."

"Yes, sir."

Fiz spun on him as though he had been stung.

"And don't call me 'sir.'"

"No, sir."

Fiz stomped his foot, his patience hovering between emaciated and starved to death. He presumed Red was mocking him, meant to chide him again, but his patient had already lapsed back into a semi-coma.

McKinnon had changed much over night. Normally thin and wiry, his face now more closely resembled a skull. The skin was pinched and drawn, and of such a pallor as to make his light-colored stubble appear dark, almost blood red. Whatever excess flesh he had carried in life had been eaten away by fever, hollowing out the deep crevices beneath his eyes, while making his nostrils appear large and cavernous.

His breath was stale, and a thin discoloration had formed over his teeth. A lock of particularly straight hair fell over his brow, while another at the back, curly and unruly, stood at attention like a convict awaiting execution, giving him both the innocence of youth and the playfulness of an imp.

The most disturbing aspect of the picture, however, was the whitish film over his eyes, resembling the cataracts of death. They mocked Fiz, taunted him, as though his patient had prematurely painted them over his dying portrait, knowing they did not, yet, belong.

"Keep your eyes open," Fiz ordered, hoping to confound Red's disobedience by demanding the opposite of what he desired.

Red obediently forced his eyelids open. The effort cost him, and his eyeballs rolled into the back of his ever-enlarging skull. It was not until he gasped, sucked in a deep breath through partially opened lips, then coughed a deep, near-death rattle, that Fiz understood he was still alive.

"The light hurts," Red whispered, although, for the life of him, Fiz could not fathom how light could penetrate those sunken orbs.

"Never mind. Close them. That's all right. I thought it would help you stay awake until you had taken some nourishment.

Fiz was a poor liar. If his patient noticed, he did not express the observation.

He did not speak again until Fiz had left the room to reheat the broth he had ordered for his own breakfast.

"Is it still raining?"

Annoyed that he could not make out the words, Fiz retraced his steps to the bedroom.

"What?"

The patient did not answer. Fiz hesitated, started to turn, then paused, listening, as was his professional habit, for the sounds of breathing. He did not move until he ascertained the weak exchange of gasses.

The fire in his stove had gone out. Fiz continued to stir the broth without realizing it was not warming.

Playing his patient's last question over in his mind, his lips moved in remembrance. It was like the poetry his late wife had so lovingly collected. While she seemed to understand it completely, it took him several re-readings to divine the most basic observations from the carefully structured lines.

When he had complained to her that most of the writing was garbled nonsense, she had sat him down and read it aloud. It was only then, as he listened to her rich, sweet tones enunciate the ancient language of "thees" and "thous" that their significance tumbled over him in cascades of beauty.

Fiz had never forgotten her unintentional lesson. Now, standing before his cold stove, a lifetime removed from their warm Boston sitting room, he used her technique again to decipher the unknowable.

"Yes," he whispered across the universes separating the living from the dead. And again, "Temporarily."

When the soup was sufficiently warm to his cold fingers, Fiz poured it into a bowl, placed it ever so carefully onto a tray, then set a spoon beside it. He changed the position of the eating utensil six times before satisfying himself it was just right. Discarding the red and white-checkered cloth which had come with the tray from the restaurant, he covered the last supper with a linen napkin from his own supply.

Where emotions failed, resorting to technique was the final resort for the weary.

"Yes," Fiz said, setting gingerly into the sick room, carrying on the conversation as though there had been no lag in their exchange of words. "It's stopped raining. The sun came out for a few minutes this morning, but there's more rain to come. I heard from a rancher earlier that there had been some pretty bad flooding outside of town. Trees uprooted, huge boulders washed away. He said he didn't recognize the landscape and he'd lived out there for twenty years."

Fiz did not expect his patient to answer. When he did, the physician nearly dropped the tray held so precariously in his two good hands.

"That's the way it goes. It's nature's way of starting anew. The old dies to make way for the young."

"You are not going to die."

"Do you know Shelley?" Red sighed, summoning up from the recesses of his mind, his days of youth and introspection.

> "The beaten road
> Which those poor slaves with weary footsteps tread,
> Who travel to their homes among the dead
> By the broad highway of the world, and so
> With one chained friend, perhaps a jealous foe,
> The dreariest and the longest journey go."

"You're a poor one to quote Shelley."

"I'm sorry."

Fiz bit away tears, made a horribly contorted face, then set the tray down.

"I suppose I'll have to feed you. Open your mouth."

Red did as he was requested, after the manner of hungry infants. Fiz dipped the spoon into the broth, blew on it cold liquid, then placed the lip of the spoon to his patient's lips. When Red gave no indication of being aware of his obligation in the unfolding play, Fiz carefully dripped the liquid into his mouth.

"Swallow."

Red swallowed. The procedure was repeated two more times until Red no longer seemed to remember how to work his throat. Fiz replaced the spoon on the tray and covered it with the white raiment.

"Thank you," Red whispered, causing Fiz to jump from the unexpectedness of his words.

"You're welcome."

A gloom settled over the room. From the front, Fiz could hear his wall clock ticking away the seconds. Sixty times a minute. The rate of a heart at rest.

"I'm going to have to operate," the physician announced suddenly. "I'm going to have to amputate your arm." No reply. "Do you hear me?"

Thirty more ticks of the heart over the course of one full minute. The rate of a dying heart.

"I'm waiting."

"For what?" Fiz remanded, shaken by the renewed strength of the voice.

"For you to finish."

"Finish what?"

"You were going to say something else."

Fiz blushed, not from emotion, but rather from an awareness that dying men were often gifted with flashes of insight, inaccessible to those whose time had not yet come.

"I can operate and save your life for a day or a week. No more. Or you can spare yourself the agony and use what remaining time you have left, to tell me the truth."

"The Truth," Red smiled. It was a ghastly gesture. "He knows not what he asks."

"Clear your conscience. Make confession."

Fiz's ventricles pounded at one hundred and fifty times a minute, out of synchronization with the rest of his heart. The rate of a frightened man.

"Forgive me, Father, for I have sinned."

"I am not a minister. I cannot forgive you," Fiz snapped.

"Nor am I god," Red replied. "Though I can forgive you."

The muscles in Fiz's jaws tightened, drawing his mouth shut like a farmer's purse.

"It is not I on death's door," he continued through clenched teeth. "I'm merely offering you the chance to -"

"Assuage your guilt," Red completed for him. "I do understand, sir."

"You understand nothing!"

"If I tell you the story - it will take... time. Do I have the time to finish it? I should not like to begin and leave you hanging. I have done that to you once, already. And is it not true, a man cannot die twice?"

Red smiled at his joke.

"No. It is not true. A man may die one thousand deaths and yet live."

"He may die one thousand deaths in his mind and yet live. I agree. We are the same, you know, sir."

"We are not the same." Said with less conviction than intended.

"I meant no offense."

To reply, "None intended," would have been a lie. Fiz was tired of lying. He was also afraid any response would put the man off, and he did not wish to do that. He wanted only what he wanted, and that was the reason - the explanation - whether for good or evil - of Red McKinnon's flight from life.

Fiz wanted the story to validate his own judgment; to make clear to him the cause of his own strange detachment. He needed the details - the agony, the torture, the inhuman cruelty - which drove former slaves to hunt a man after the fashion of a beast.

He had to have a justification for his own peculiar attraction.

Fiz needed to understand Red McKinnon's dying words so he could live with Phillip Ward.

"Please," he begged, but Red was beyond hearing, past the call of his own kind. He had returned to a swirling, never-changing world which survived on the level of clouds, no longer of earth, yet far below heaven.

"My father died in 1860. The same year the Democratic Party met in Baltimore and nominated Douglas for President. The same year the Southern Democrats convened in Baltimore to nominate Breckinridge to run for President on a platform which protected the right to own slaves.

"Baltimore was an interesting place in those days, wasn't it? A Southern State caught in the middle."

"I wasn't in Baltimore in 1860. I was in Boston," Fiz snarled, but Red was not speaking to him. He was addressing his own ghosts. And only he could hear them answer.

"The year 1860 was tumultuous. John Brown made a fool of Federal authorities by taking the Harper's Ferry arsenal, then hanged for his crime, appeasing no one. Do you know who was there, in Harper's Ferry for that execution? Some very famous names - or rather, names which would become famous in the coming year.

"Robert E. Lee was there, commanding the Union soldiers. I understood he hid behind a tree while the arsenal was attacked by a head-on, frontal attack. Superiority of numbers. Ulysses Grant wasn't there, but he won the War by using those same tactics. Lee never had superiority of numbers, and he lost by failing to understand that very concept."

"I don't need a lesson in military strategy."

"Thomas Jackson was there, too. He was a major at the Virginia Military Institute. He taught natural and experimental philosophy. It was a dry, nearly incomprehensible subject. He was held in low esteem by the students and the other teachers. He also taught artillery. I don't suppose they paid him any more for it."

"I know this."

"Thomas Jonathan Jackson. T.J. Jackson. He was there with the Corps of Cadets because he was the only professor at VMI with any real military experience. The rest were paper soldiers. He witnessed the execution."

"Good for him."

"JEB Stuart was there, too, I believe. James Ewell Brown Stuart. He had been serving out west... in the Dragoons, if I'm not mistaken. I might be. Memory fades."

"I don't need a history lesson. I remember it." And then, to explain why he remembered it, "It was in the newspapers."

"The United States of America hanged John Brown like a curtain. No one was appeased. If my father had been well, he would have attended the concluding ceremonies. One of our neighbors did. His name was... I forget what his name was. He wrote an editorial about what he saw. It was published in the Richmond Inquirer. He was quite famous because of that.

"None of us read it, of course. We lived outside Charleston. There was a great deal of coverage in the Daily Courier. My father read the Mercury. The same man from Boston - who worked for the Daily Journal during the conflict - went to Charleston after the War was all over. His name was Charles Carleton Coffin and he wrote under the nom de plume 'Carleton.'

"HEATHEN TEMPLES AND OTHER RELICS OF BARBARISM was the headline, all in capital letters. I read it."

Fiz found himself listening to the ticking of the clock. Time was running out. He leaned forward impatiently.

"Yes, yes, you read it. After you returned from the War. I understand. It upset you. But it doesn't explain -"

He might have been talking to his coffee pot.

"I didn't have to go to War. I was a 'one hundred Nigger Man.' By law, I was exempt. That was because my father died," he added needlessly. Fiz remembered. He felt as if he had known the elder McKinnon, supped with him at his own table, ridden with him over the beautiful rolling hills of Flowering Tree, thought he had never heard of man nor plantation before listening to Red's story.

Red continued, the film over his eyes growing whiter as he talked.

"I inherited the plantation and all its assets. All its debits," he added, suddenly chilling the physician's heart. "My father, the late James McKinnon, Junior, had been a great man in life; an oversized man. There were hundreds of men at his funeral. The former Confederate governors of South and North Carolina; the lieutenant-governor of Virginia. Three officials from the state of Georgia.

"There were a handful of legislators from the Congress, in Washington. I heard it said the ghost of John C. Calhoun was in attendance."

Fiz's mind, already in a swirl, wondered idiotically, whether Eric Anheiser's illustrious relative had been there, as well, and realized, with a start, he did not even know whether the Anheiser clan was Southern or Northern. While Missouri had "gone for the Union," its leanings were less than lily white.

His own question disquieted him.

"John C. Calhoun. Yes," he agreed, calling to mind the intense, powerful senator with the burning eyes. He had met the man once, at a dinner party in Washington, in 1849. That had been shortly before his death, which had occurred the following year. Several of his acquaintances had journeyed to Charleston to attend the funeral. Fiz remembered they had complained about their accommodations, making him glad he had not gone with them.

"The funeral, as I said, was very well attended." Red had continued talking and Fiz's mind scrambled to catch up with the narrative. "It also cost a great deal of money. I had to arrange ten carriages with perfectly matched black horses for the procession. There were..." His voice trailed off, forcing Fiz to shake him gently. When he finally continued, his thoughts had gone on ahead of his lips.

"... name was Albert Jakeo. I think he had been involved with my father in several business dealings, as well as being his banker and investment advisor. I made an appointment to see him a week after the funeral. He was a hard man to find."

Red groaned, grimaced as a spasm of pain shot through his emaciated frame, then settled down into his pillow. Sweat rolled from his forehead in torrents, causing him to blink repeatedly as it pooled his eyes with salty fluid.

Instinctively, Fiz looked at his patient's arm. The bandage had slipped down, revealing a small portion of the blackened tissue. His stomach turned and he found himself holding his breath for fear the odor would cause him to wretch.

"When I finally sat down and went over the will and my father's finances, I was horrified. Aside for small legacies to my sisters and a stipend for my mother, he had left everything to me. Everything amounting to a hill of debts as high as Mount Sinai."

Red shook his head slowly. He coughed, tried to spit, then swallowed the greenish mucus. Fiz had not thought to offer him a handkerchief.

"I was shocked. Stunned. I had no idea my father had been living on credit. I don't know what happened... exactly. Bad business investments. Poor crop yields. He never was much for science. None of those great plantation owners were. 'Just so much Yankee intervention into our ways of doing things,' he used to say. 'What was good enough for our forefathers is good enough for us.'

"But it wasn't, of course. I never saw my father read a book. He wasn't a book-reading man. He read the newspaper. I remember an article he read aloud once. It was about -"

"Never mind!" Fiz snapped, his nerves strung to the breaking point. "You inherited a bankrupt plantation. Go on."

He was close to tears himself. Fortunately, Red was beyond noticing anything of this world.

"I owed the Factors the entire cotton crop. Everything was pledged. If I had gotten a full crop, I might have been able to get the Factors to refinance me another year, but the weevils were bad. And cotton prices were off in Liverpool. I had a good rice yield, but that wasn't a cash crop. Not like the cotton.

"You would have thought - with a war coming on - England would have been hot to buy any cotton they could get their hands on, but that wasn't the case. No one believed there would be a war, you see. No one. Not the cotton growers, not the politicians, not the English markets. Men had talked of armed conflict so long, it was like crying wolf.

"No one believed it would come to war. It was 1860, Abraham Lincoln was the Republican nominee for President, and men's tempers were as a hot as an Independence Day firecracker, yet no one really foresaw what was coming."

Phillip Ward remembered. He re-read the newspaper editorials, revisited the parlors of old friends, listened to the conversations of learned, aristocratic, blue-blooded Boston men. Had he been a speculator, he, too, would have bought the A-1 rated cotton shares.

"I had to do something to save Flowering Tree. It was my home," Red continued, his voice fading into a whisper.

Seeing Red's lips were dry and cracked, Fiz wetted his finger with cold broth, the only liquid he had within arm's reach, and ran them over Red's mouth. His patient seemed not to notice the taste, salty, like the dregs of weeping.

"The home of my mother. I could not fail her. She had her dignity to maintain. I only had two options, as I saw them. Sell the plantation and move her permanently into our town house in Charleston, or sell off some of the property and use that money to convince the cotton factors to stake me to another year's seed.

"Selling the plantation was not to be considered. It would have killed my mother, ruined our name. 'If a man don't have a name, then he's nuthin' but a dirty sharecropper or a nigger lovin' Yankee,'" Red quoted. He did not say whose words he repeated and Fiz did not ask.

"I sold some bottom land to Mr. Ellis and I leased other land to Mr. Jakeo, the banker. It wasn't enough. I had some jewelry of my father's I sold in New York, enough to give me some breathing room. I put some of it on the debt I owed the Factors, but they didn't know me, you see. They had only dealt with my father. Him, they would have trusted. Me - I had to prove myself.

"I had never handled money before; nothing more than my allowance. Before I went off to college, I had worked in the fields, beside the overseer. Not *as* an overseer, mind you, but with him. He was a well hated man. With good reason, as I had cause to discover. But he knew how to make men work. His name was..."

"Never mind what his name was!" Fiz snarled, drawing back from the man on the bed, whose radiated body heat as great as any Yankee cannon.

"Bilkins. Theodore Bilkins!" Red recalled suddenly. The remembrance seemed to calm him. "He made eight hundred dollars a year and earned every penny of it. I believe he made more than the governor."

"Good for him."

"I worked in the fields and I spend time in the quarters," Red continued, a faint smile lingering on his sunken face. "I knew those people. They knew me. I used to listen to them tell their stories about the Old Country. There were some who remembered... the old ones. Not personally, you understand. The remembered what their mammas and pappas had told them. The ones who had come over on the great slave ships, right into Charleston Harbor.

"After the War, I took a walk down on those very wharves. The Federals had destroyed most of them. There was so little left. I had seen many a slave auction at -"

Fiz shook Red's shoulders. As he left off, the patient's head rolled to the left and remained in that unnatural position, tongue lolling out from between half-closed teeth.

"For God's sake, there isn't much time left," Fiz warned.

He had heard a noise outside and it frozen his blood. His own hands trembled and he drew his arms around his body for warmth.

"I had to sell the niggers." Red spoke so suddenly and with so much verve, Fiz nearly fell from his carefully perched sitting position. "I didn't want to, but I had no choice. They were the most valuable assets I had; the ones most easily converted into cash. I tried to do it fairly, sell them in family units, but it wasn't easy. You know what I mean," Red pursued, opening his eyes suddenly and staring fixedly into Fiz's.

"The men - the young, healthy men - were easy enough to liquidate," Red continued, speaking now in a conspiratorial tone. "The women of child-bearing age fetched a good price, too. But the older ones - there never was any money to be made off them. Nor the children, especially the infants. A man might as well give them away as try and sell them."

"All right," Fiz agreed, craning his head toward the outside window. He hardly dared breathe, for fear of missing that which he did not want to hear.

"There was a lot of conversation, naturally," Red added. "By my father's friends. They were shocked I was selling the off the stock. But, of course, they were eager for a bargain. I sold all those I could to the neighbors - to keep them close. I did the best I could. It wasn't much. The market was flat. No one believed a war was coming," he added.

"The market was flat," Fiz repeated, feeling nauseous and light-headed.

"I sold fifty, maybe sixty. Some I made over eight hundred dollars a head on. Those were the good field hands."

"The ones with two ears," Fiz whispered, biting off his words to keep down his acidic stomach contents.

Red smiled in agreement.

"Those with two ears," he repeated. Fiz vowed silence.

"It wasn't enough. Once my father's creditors got wind of the fact I wasn't sitting on a treasure chest, they came knocking on the door. Politely, mind you. Southern men are always polite. They were also impatient. I needed to raise more cash.

"That's when the fire broke out."

Fiz heard a footstep on his outside stairs. He tried to tell himself it was no more than a charred log settling in the stove.

He had forgotten the fire had gone out long ago.

Giving him something else in common with Red: a mountain of ashes from to look back upon from a long past lifetime.

CHAPTER 17

The fire bell rang at exactly nine-fifteen. Kenneth McKinnon remembered the time because he looked at his watch. These was no particular reason for him to have done so. He performed the action more from habit than curiosity.

9:15 P.M. on the first day of October, in the year of Our Lord, 1860.

"Where's the fire?" someone shouted.

Kenneth did not have to ask. Although it was too dark to make out human shapes, he had seen the flames from his upstairs bedroom.

"The slave quarters!" he informed the questioner tersely. "Organize a bucket brigade and for God's sake, send a courier to Twin Towers. Tell them to send all the men they have. And hurry!"

Kenneth McKinnon was the owner of Flowering Tree Plantation. As such, his word was law, transcending even that of the mayor of Sumter County, should such an elected worthy have stepped onto his property and attempted to give an order.

The red-haired, freckle-faced man was twenty-eight years old when his father passed and he became master of his own destiny - and that of six hundred-odd souls - including his mother and three sisters. During the first two months of his mastership at Flowering Tree, he had replaced his overseer, earned the grudged respect of his neighbors and established himself as a fair and reasonable taskmaster with his slaves.

The second two months of his tenure - when his financial condition became common knowledge around Charleston, South Carolina - he had drawn skepticism from the same neighbors who had, until recently, admired his work. As the situation worsened, Kenneth raised eyebrows and doubts among his father's creditors, while earning the enmity of his black laborers, a fact that bothered him more than all the other criticisms combined.

An incredible turnaround for one destined, by birth, to follow in James McKinnon, Junior's footsteps.

Huge debts, poor crop returns, a pending lawsuit by the Southern Cotton Factor, and an overdue mortgage payment on the family town house in

Charleston had done nothing to improve young McKinnon's temper. Considered a hot-head from birth in consequence of his fiery red hair, Kenneth had developed into an unruly child, then an imaginative youth, and finally a liberal young man in an age where conservatism was spelled with a capital "C," and revered, alongside God and John C. Calhoun, by all Southern Democrats.

It was commonly held that Flowering Tree would have been in better hands had the late James McKinnon gifted the plantation to Rufus Murphy, one of his sons-in-law. To have disinherited his only heir, however, would have meant flying in the face of tradition, and James McKinnon was known as a man who respected the "tried and the true."

It was also familiarly speculated that he did not want his son cursing him throughout his journey in the After Life. Kenneth had always displayed a credulous belief in the folk tales of his father's plantation slaves, and had, on rare occasions, been invited to share a meal and linger afterwards, when spells were cast and destinies written.

While his youthful eccentricities had not endeared him to his relatives, the neighbors, or the family minister, it had been hoped Kenneth would grow out of his fascination with the occult and turn into an upstanding Episcopalian, a God-fearing Democrat and a pillar of the community.

A good marriage to a strong, steady, son-bearing woman from a respectable Southern family was considered the cure for Kenneth's ills.

More than a few of the local belles were paraded in and out of Flowering Tree, attending summer dances in their finest dresses, or brought around on bell-bedecked carriages to celebrate a spot of Christmas cheer with the McKinnons. While several were whispered to have the inside track to the younger McKinnon's heart, he never expressed such thoughts himself.

"Let him come of age," the wise old men predicted. "When Kenneth reaches his majority, then the fillies had better stand ready at the gate. It'll be a race to the wire."

If men did not speak in terms of crops, by predicting that any girl catching Kenneth's fancy would be in "high cotton," they used horse racing statements, for what was a plantation owner if not a farmer and a horse breeder? Next to a nursery full of sons and ten thousand acres covered with white-tuffed cotton balls, the greatest love of a Southern man's life was his horses.

Kenneth did not marry at twenty-one, nor did he display much attention to the eligible young women paraded past his starting gate, prompting some white-haired old sages to speculated he found better amusement in his father's slave quarters, where so many good men before him had gone to sow their wild oats, but if they were correct, no issue was ever attributed to the future master.

Others guessed that when Kenneth went abroad on Tour, he would marry an English heiress, or a hot-tempered Irish lass, most suited to his taste than the well-bred, placid girls of Charleston. They waited impatiently for two long years, but when the prodigal returned, he came home empty handed, taking up residence, once again, in his boyhood room overlooking the water pond at Flowering Tree.

All three of Kenneth's sisters were married to local men, but the festivities surrounding such high times did not seem to inspire the bachelor. He gave no more indication of marrying than before his European trip, appearing quite content to assume his role as the elder McKinnon's representative in the fields.

As the heir-apparent to Flowering Tree, he oversaw the day-to-day workings of the plantation, seeing the machinery was in proper working order, the crops properly harvested and the bundled cotton safely transported to market. He fell naturally into the role of intermediary between his father and the laborers, settling disputes, creating work assignments, dispensing clothing, sustenance and distribution of the small plots the slaves were allowed to farm for their own private use.

As time progressed, Kenneth became the sole buyer and seller of his father's valuable two-legged assets, eventually doing away with the small freelance buyers occasionally employed to maintain the stock, while dismissing the services of the larger trading houses in the city. He was a man known to both buyers and sellers as one who "knew the business," a designation only begrudgingly given to the very best slavers in the state.

All of that changed when the prince ascended the throne and discovered, to his shock, the true state of his late father's affairs.

Kenneth had performed the physical labor necessary in running a plantation one hundred times the size of Manhattan, but he had not been privy to the financial side. That, James McKinnon kept for himself. His business practices were no more or less complicated than those of his neighbors, no more or less speculative. Like those of his peer group, he lived high, spent lavishly and prayed to God for a high yield to pay that which he had already squandered.

Had James McKinnon lived to a ripe old age, it was likely none of his financial woes would have come to light. As a man respected by those with whom he did business, his local creditors, the factors and the bankers from Boston and New York would have continued their arrangements from year to year, depending on the passage time, the slow accumulation of interest, and his good name to make right what nature did not provide.

His son, however, was a stranger, an unknown, a man untried. No one at the First Bank of Charleston knew what to expect from him; the lenders at the Southern Cotton Factor could not be certain the son had the savvy of the father. None of the stiff-collared investment men from Back East cared to extend credit to a man who carried the name but not the reputation of the patriarch.

Therefore, they called their loans, which was perfectly within their legal rights. Teams of couriers arrived at Flowering Tree, setting out signed contracts dating back to the time when the import of Negroes from Africa was permissible under law. Telegrams of condolence were followed by letters, written on blue embossed paper and sealed with red wax, informing the new owner of debts, now due, of credit rate increases and promises of future good will "when all was put to rights at your earliest convenience."

Selling and leasing parcels from his vast holdings at Flowering Tree shocked the neighbors. They might have borne that indignity, had not the horses and hounds followed. A plantation owner had certain obligations, specific dignities to maintain. Fly by coach to New York and pawn, in private the family jewels; arrange for new contracts at higher interest rates; hold private auctions to rid yourself of the old and the young slaves; consign one hundred of the best field workers to the MART in Charleston for quick sale to the sugar mills in New Orleans, but never, ever part with that which made a man a king in this brave new world.

Kenneth McKinnon did not give a damn about what those in the Low Country thought. It was his perverse nature, his status as an outsider, though he had been one of them from birth. It was his red hair, his freckled face, his temper, his disdain for tradition which caused those who had earlier supported him to withdraw their approval.

These neighbors, the men whose ancestors had fought in the Great War for Independence, pitied the widowed matriarch, clucked their tongues at the three sisters who were deposed from their status as princesses by their brother's actions, hated Kenneth for his independence.

All this Kenneth might have accepted with indifference had he not lost, simultaneously, the love of his slaves.

"I will sell them in family units or not at all," he vowed. That was when he determined there was no other way to pay the mounting debts and save the plantation. "I will not sell the old, for I have an obligation to them. I will not sell the young, for they have a human right to be raised by their parents."

It was a noble sentiment, oft expressed in Southern editorials, spoken of from the pulpit and on the court house steps, and then ignored. It was, as one statesman noted in private, an idea doomed to failure.

"Give me one hundred of your best field hands, and I'll auction them off for six, eight hundred dollars apiece, to local buyers," Mr. Brody, half-owner of the largest House in Charleston promised. "I understand how things are with you; I'll only take five percent commission. Assuming," he added, "they all have paper," meaning proper ownership title. "Or, I'll sell them by lot to a House in New Orleans. Prime hands in the sugar cane business command top money. Maybe over $1,000 each."

"I want them sold in family units - and none outside South Carolina."

Mr. Brody, a man who had sat in James McKinnon's study many a night and played poker until dawn, scratching his whiskered chin and shook his head.

"Can't be done, son. Once I sell stock, it goes where the new owner takes him. And no one - no one in his right mind - sells in family units. Whatever put that idea into your head? You've been to enough slave auctions in your life to understand the business."

Kenneth McKinnon understood the Business and had never questioned its principles. He had walked the crowded aisles of the MART thousands of times, inspecting those for sale, judging them by the condition of their teeth, the strength of their muscle, the sharpness of their eyes. He had passed on those bearing marks of whipping, for as every master knew, placing a permanent scar on the back of a slave reduced his value by half by signaling him as a trouble maker.

He had discussed the merits of taking a chance on an older slave, purchased children on the basis of their long-range potential, and bought the women of child bearing age to replace those of Flowering Tree who had perished in childbirth.

He had sold young black boys when his father's plantation had a surplus, just as he dispensed baled cotton to the shipyards, or arranged for the rice crop to be auctioned at one of the great Northern ports. He had found places for the occasional slaves who did not fit into the family unit at Flowering Tree and had, when the situation called for it, disciplined those who would not put in an honest day's work, or who escaped on the ill-advised dream that freedom from bondage was purchased by the will to escape.

Never had he been faced with the prospect of a "fire sale": of the wholesale breaking up of family units for the sake of raising huge sums of money.

"I will not do it," he vowed.

That was in his second month of proprietorship of Flowering Tree. In the third month, when the letters of demand became more frequent and more insistent, he had capitulated, offering for sale fifty of the prime men and fifty of the prime women, regardless of where or to whom they were sold.

It was in the fourth month that he bowed to pressure, putting on the block three hundred men, woman, children, and the elderly, hoping like a fool, they would be auctioned to those owners living in the county. Hoping, like a blind man, to see them stay in the area, so they might bargain for the opportunity to visit relatives left behind.

Praying, like an atheist, for forgiveness.

The slaves of Flowering Tree did not understand McKinnon's predicament. They were not privy to the stresses, the burdens placed on his shoulders. Nor would they have understood had they been told. Understanding was the providence of the white man. Suffering and betrayal was the lot of the black.

The understood what they saw and felt and touched. They comprehended only that their lives were being destroyed, their loves ripped from their bosoms, their security sold "down the river," to a plantation in a foreign nation called Georgia, or a sugar mill across the world in Louisiana.

On that first day of October in 1860 when Kenneth McKinnon heard the mad ringing of the bell, he was the only man alive who did not understand why no one came to fight the fire. White men with gangs of black slaves did not come from Twin Towers, or Sweet Wind, or King Harry's plantations. The fire engines from Charleston were not hitched to their horses and rushed to put out the conflagration. The remaining field hands from Flowering Tree did not hurry with buckets full of spring water to quell the flames destroying what was once their home.

Kenneth McKinnon was a man alone. He had lived that way; thought he could survive on the outside of a very tight-knit group. He had wanted everything, and in the end, he had nothing.

"For God's sake, hurry!" he urged, grabbing a black man by the shirt and shaking him until his teeth rattled. "What's the matter with you?"

The man had no answer. He felt none was owed.

Turning from him, McKinnon ran to a group of slaves standing by the pump, hands on their hips.

"Prime the pump, you goddamned fools," he cried. "And fill those buckets!" Turning to a cluster of children, he implored them to "run to the house for more buckets, pots, pans, anything that will hold water!"

None of them moved.

"What's the matter with you?" he cried again, screaming into the hot breath spewed forth from the massive fire. "Get a move on!"

"Dat an order, Masta Kenneth?" a tall, stately black man demanded, emerging from the darkness, more shadow than man. "Yuh gibbin' us orders? Yuh askin' us to put out dat fire?"

"It's your own quarters," Kenneth cried in desperation. Then, seeing the man unmoved, he grew angry. "Come with me! We have to try and get in the quarters. There may be people trapped inside."

"Wad yuh mean, people?" the slave demanded, cool and untouched by the flying embers which had singed Kenneth's hair into a grotesque combination of red and blacked strands.

Unable to comprehend the simple question, he tugged at the slave's arm in desperation.

"Come with me! They will burn up if we don't get them out!"

"Mebbe it's better to be dead than alibe," the man responded.

Kenneth thought him mad.

Turning around and around like a dog chasing his tail, he implored one after the other to help him. No one accepted his plea.

"They're you're own people. Let us try and save them. Let us try and save what buildings remain."

The fire spread rapidly, going from one hut to another, the thatched roofs catching fire as easily as a black Cuban cigar. Perhaps it had begun when a spark from a cooking fire ignited the straw used for bedding. Possibly a coal, used to rekindle the ashes of the morning fire, had been carelessly passed from one hut to another, and dropped onto the dry grasses growing at the perimeters.

Less likely but not without probability, the fire had been arson.

"That was what the insurance investigators said," Red McKinnon explained to Fiz Ward, his voice weary and depressed. "Arson. I told him he was insane. Why would I set fire to my own property?

"The answer was obvious. It was commonly known I was in need of money. He brought forth half a dozen witnesses; men with whom I had dealings. They all said the same thing. The price of slaves on the open market was falling; there was fear of war. No one wanted to buy what I had for sale. It was all lies, nothing but lies. But what could I say? How to explain I would never destroy that which was mine? That which I... loved?"

A tear rolled down his cheek and he bowed his head, overcome by guilt.

Fiz hesitated, then placed a hand on Red's unaffected right arm. He had no cause to perform that act; his professional interest lay in the blackened left arm.

"How many died?"

"Twelve perished; two men, three women, seven children. The slave quarters were ruined. Nothing left. Burned to the ground. The stench was unbelievable. No one helped me," he continued, looking across his right shoulder. "No one came. I went in alone... to one of the huts. It was filled with smoke; I couldn't see anything. I tripped, fell over something, landed on my face, burning my cheeks. I called out, cried out... searched until my hands were too numb to feel. I crawled out with a child in my arms.

"It was dead. A baby. Just an innocent babe.

"Why, Fiz, why? Why is it better to be dead than to be alive?" Red sobbed.

"I think you can answer that better than anyone," Fiz answered slowly.

He waited a moment, then removed his hand. His fingers were cold, numb, as though he had been gripping so hard he had cut off the circulation, though he had barely touched the man's burning flesh.

"Go on," he ordered. "Finish it."

"I'm finished."

"Tell me the rest."

"I've told it all."

"Not all."

There was that sound again. A creaking of weight on wood. Outside, on the stairs. Closer, this time.

"Hurry," Fiz demanded.

"There's nothing more to tell. I was ruined. The insurance report stated the cause of the fire as suspicious. They wouldn't pay on my claim. My mother moved into the town house in Charleston. I buried the dead. No preacher would come out for the services, so I read it myself. What could I do, Fiz? I'm no minister, but no man of God would set foot on Flowering Tree.

"It wasn't the first time I'd read that service," Red added. "But it was the last. The next time I hear it, it will be read over my body. Unless, of course," he laughed bitterly, "no one bothers. It doesn't make any difference to me. I don't care. I don't believe."

"If you didn't believe, why did you read it over the graves of the dead slaves?"

"Someone had to."

"Why?"

"It seemed the proper thing to do. The dead - they believed. Christianity is a wonderful tool of the white man. Do you know that, Dr. Ward? We teach Jesus to our slaves, not to save their souls, but to lull them into subservience.

"'My Kingdom is not of this earth.'

"That's what Christ taught. 'My Kingdom is not of this earth.' Powerful words. To a white man preaching to a black man, what he's really saying is, accept your lot in life. Your reward is not here; it is in heaven. Work in the fields, in the Big House, in the smithy's shop, behind the counter of your owner's store; obey your master. Your freedom is on the other side of the grave. When men believe that, they grow docile. They work for their earthly masters, to be worthy of a new - a better master - in heaven."

"You're only just finding this out?"

"What would you have had me do, Doctor? Give it all up without a struggle? It was my heritage," he added softly, weeping into his hand.

There was so little left.

Doctor Phillip Ward did not reply. Instead, he stood up slowly, walking away from his patient noiselessly, on the balls of his feet. He left with room without making a sound.

Fiz stood in the narrow hallway and shivered. It was cold. There was going to be an early winter.

Without hesitation, he padded into his own small room at the rear of the hall. Opening the unlocked door, he admitted himself. It was dark. He crossed the floor with unerring certainty and brought forth a shotgun. He did not have to crack it to assure himself it was loaded.

Fiz was not a hunting man. This was not a sporting piece.

Weapon in hand, he left the room and walked down the hall, silently, on cat's feet. He paused at the sick room and listened. He heard nothing.

No sound.

Fiz went into his outer office, then moved quickly to the door. Jerking it open, he leveled the shotgun and pulled the trigger. A nose of horrific proportion shattered the silence. Without waiting, he discharged the second barrel, then paused and listened.

He heard two soft thuds. The sound of two bodies falling from the height of a staircase onto the earth below.

He paused again and listened.

No sound.

For all he knew, every man, woman and child in Hellhole was dead.

"'The Lord gave, and the Lord hath taken away; blessed be the name of the Lord,'" he quoted from The Order For the Burial of the Dead, memorized from the pages of his Episcopal prayer book. And then, out of order, "And yet this body be destroyed, yet I shall see God: whom I shall see for myself, and mine eyes shall behold, and not as a stranger."

Both the strange and the strangers had come to Hellhole to die.

CHAPTER 18

It had stopped raining, but the sky was a threatening steel grey. The wind, from the north, held a sting to it, which found a way to worm up arm sleeves and through button holes, snake around protective collars, and crawl in at the waist, biting any and all exposed flesh.

"If a man has to die, it ought to be on a day like this," Vernon Trask, the undertaker observed, rubbing his hands together and stamping his feet, not from cold, but from impatience.

Fiz shot him a venomous look, which, to a more sentient soul, would have sutured his tongue to the roof of his mouth. This man, whose main - though not sole - occupation was preparing the dead for burial - had long ago learned that nothing he said, outside of suggesting brass, rather than copper handles for the coffin, meant anything to anyone. He was, therefore, immune from criticism.

The dead had never been known to complain, and they were his principal customers.

The fancy coffin, the one he had finished so recently, sat atop two wooden sawhorses, adjacent to the yawning, open hole. Vernon was secretly glad the ground had not frozen after the last rain, or he would have had to hire an extra digger to break through the hard earth.

He did not think Fiz Ward would have paid for that labor, forcing him to absorb the cost out of his profit margin. Had anyone but the physician refused, Mr. Trask would have taken his case to the law, but Fiz was a good client, and the marshal had not yet returned from wherever he had gone. It was not Vernon's business to pry, and therefore, he had not. Especially as time pressed.

It was not proper etiquette to leave a dead body sitting in the back room of his shop.

Silence was another trait he had developed in his avocation. Not enough to suit Fiz, however, who was still seething about the undertaker's remark concerning the weather. He determined to go over the coffinmaker's bill with one of his fine-toothed combs - the kind he used to remove head-lice eggs from the hair of children each and every spring. Like clock-work.

Another cycle, from which neither Men nor insects could escape.

The thought did not improve his temper.

"Who's going to read the service?" Cougar asked, to no one in particular. She was wearing black, which matched the circles under her eyes. She had heard some exchange between Fiz and Vernon but had not caught the words. The howling of the north wind obscured what she was not meant to hear.

There was no minister in Hellhole; none had ever seen fit to settle in their God-forsaken hider town. Occasionally, an itinerant preacher passed through, on his way to Caldwell, or Hellsbane or Wichita. He was usually imposed upon to say a few words for those who had passed on since the last time one of his kind performed the last duty for the dead. In the absence of the ordained, that meant either Fiz or Vernon would have to repeat the prayers.

She wished they would hurry. Not because it was cold, for she felt nothing. Rather, it was her lack of emotion which scared her. Cougar hoped the too familiar words from the Book of Common Prayer would stir some feeling in her breast, though, like the certainty of resurrection, she doubted it.

"I will," Fiz said.

Cougar was not surprised, for Fiz had arranged for the funeral, ordered the coffin and driven her up to this desolate place in his buggy. When the deceased was a friend, an acquaintance or a patient, Fiz always read the service. Unless there were any surviving next-of-kin who cared to do the honors.

"Then read it, for God's sake," she ordered. Her words were terse, chipped, commanding. It was her right to assume such a stance; she was the only woman present and therefore by tradition, if not by law, she oversaw the proceedings.

That was a Southern woman's lot in life: to give birth and to consign the dead to the ground. What occurred in between was not her domain. Cougar did not consider herself a "Southern women," but at the moment, assumed that mantle to hurry things along.

Glancing over at Fiz she noticed he was not holding the prayer book. The realization gave her heart a thump. While she knew he had memorized the requisite words, it seemed sacrilegious, somehow, not to hold the good book for comfort.

He had always done so before. If the assemblage had to send back to Hellhole for the book, they would be at the graveside another hour.

She had never felt so alone in her life. Without Claw at her side, comfort, warmth, love, faith were no more than man's false words.

Fiz began so suddenly, Cougar nearly jumped out of her skin.

"'Hear my prayer, O Lord, and with thine ears consider my calling; hold not thy peace at my tears; For I am a stranger with thee, and a sojourner, as all my fathers were. O spare me a little, that I may recover my strength, before I go hence, and be no more seen.'"

"That's not how it starts," Vernon complained.

"Dixi, custodiam, Psalm xxxix," Fiz remarked sourly, and then added, "I have completed the service."

"How can you be finished when you didn't even say 'Amen'?" Vernon gasped. As a minister to the dead, he was shocked to the marrow of his bones by the impropriety of the moment.

"We have two more to bury. Let us get on with it," Fiz continued, not hearing or not caring to respond to the undertaker's question.

The small gathering moved one hundred feet away from the first open grave, to stand beside the other, newly-dug holes in the earth.

Two more coffins, both a match for the first, lay snuggled into the shallow excavations which were to become their final resting places. The mourners resumed exactly the positions they had taken at the first grave.

"I am the resurrection and the life, saith the Lord; he that believeth in me, though he were dead, yet shall he live; and whosoever liveth and believeth in me, shall never die.... We brought nothing into this world, and it is certain we carry nothing out. The Lord gave, and the Lord hath taken away; blessed be the name of the Lord. Amen."

Fiz gave the signal and two men from town crept forward steadily, shovels at the ready. When they had begun their task of filling in the cavities, Fiz made a curt signal with his good right hand. The services, such as they were, had been terminated.

Vernon Trask replaced his tall, Abe Lincoln top-hat on his head, muttered some words of consolation as behooved his status, and departed, enriched by the experience. Cougar moved a step toward Fiz's buggy, then waited for him to join her.

"Go ahead," he requested. "I'll be alone in a moment."

She had the disquieting impression his idea of "a moment," and her idea were lifetimes apart.

When Fiz was assured she would not follow him, he retraced his footsteps to the first grave, knelt beside it, then reached into his worn, shabby overcoat. While Cougar could not precisely see what he was doing, it appeared to her that he removed something from around his neck. She had never known Fiz to wear a cross or any other article of jewelry. His action puzzled her.

But not enough to dwell upon it. She had her own cross to bear. Claw Kiley had not returned from his ill-fated search for the man named Red and the former slaves who had vowed to take his life. Now, three of that group had perished and still Claw had not come back. Her concern was only for the living.

Opening the mojo bag with stiff, trembling fingers, Fiz sprinkled the rosemary and sage onto the shiny black coffin, then drew the mouth of the hand-stitched purse closed and knotted it. He then jiggled the magic bag to assess the weight of it, in an effort to assure himself the golden coin he had added had not inadvertently fallen out. With a silent "Amen," he tossed the lucky talisman on top of the herbs, bowed his head and wept.

Not for the dead clay, but for he who had gone on to another life, in another body, at some other time, far from the reality of existence that Phillip Ward was privileged to know.

Cougar's scream returned Fiz to his senses.

"Claw!"

Looking over his left shoulder, Fiz saw a scarecrow of a man on horseback riding toward them. Rising to his feet, he took a step forward, then held back as Cougar raced ahead of him.

"Claw! You're alive!"

For a moment Fiz doubted his senses. The hunched figure riding Red McKinnon's horse could have been anyone. It could have been Red himself, returned from the grave, not exactly as Fiz had prayed for, but flesh and bone, resurrected for a second chance at life.

He doubted his own eyesight but not Cougar's heart. If she were certain the ghostly apparition on the borrowed horse was Claw Kiley, then that was exactly who it was.

The prodigal had returned.

As Cougar reached him, Claw swung his leg over the saddle horn and slipped to earth. She caught him in her arms. For a moment they both swayed, unsteady in the cold winter wind, before their combined weight righted them.

"Claw, I thought you were dead!" she cried, tears running down her cheeks.

"I thought so, too," he admitted, wiping his own eyes with the back of his hand. Then, using that same hand, he pointed toward the newly filled graves. "Who are you burying?" he asked.

"No one," she replied. "It doesn't matter now."

***

They sat around a table at the Lowdown, the three of them: Claw Kiley, Cougar Bradburn and Phillip Ward. The saloon was closed, it's double-wide doors locked and shuttered to keep away the whistling outside wind, and smother the howling of the feral night creatures.

It was cold in the room, heated only by the pot-bellied stove roaring away in the antechamber used as a counting room at the rear of the building.

"Darndest thing I've ever heard," Fiz exclaimed, rubbing his mustache with the pointer finger of his right hand. His words held no conviction, but were spoken from habit, more obligation than meaning.

Claw nodded agreeably.

"I didn't know whether it was ghost or man," he continued. "It came out of the rain and the fog, so swiftly I didn't have a chance to defend myself. Didn't even know there was anybody out there, except me."

"Who was it?" Cougar asked.

"I don't know. It came upon me, screaming and yelling and waving its arms like a mad thing. Mistook me for someone else," Claw guessed.

Fiz presumed he was correct.

"We tussled a bit, then he discharged his pistol. I don't know how he missed me at that close range. I fell back, more from the shock of the blast than anything else. Scared the wits out of me."

He had forgotten, in his excitement, the first rule of being a lawman: never admit fear to the woman he loved.

"I guess he figured he killed me. I lay as still as I could; played possum."

"Good thinking," Fiz agreed, sipping the dregs of his cold coffee.

"Thought he'd go through my pockets... something. Take the horse. As far as I could tell, he was on foot. Didn't have a horse. If he had taken my horse, I'd be a dead man today."

"But that wasn't your horse," Cougar pointed out. "Your horse came back to Hellhole by itself. Scared the living daylights out of me."

"I hope Bark gave it some oats."

"I suppose he did," Cougar dismissed offhandedly.

"Found the horse wandering, all by itself," Claw continued. "Someone had severed its hobbles with a hunting knife."

"Must have run off," Fiz decided for them. They nodded agreement, proving Fiz was a better liar than he gave himself credit for.

"Then what happened?" Cougar asked. "After that man - that thing - that ghost - thought he killed you?"

"Nothing." Claw paused to stare up at the ceiling. "He just went off. Never said a word. I guess he thought he finished me. Why would a man do that, Fiz?"

"Why are you asking me? You're a lawman. You've seen men do peculiar things before."

"I guess I have. Doesn't make sense, though. You think it was that Red fella done it?"

"I don't think anything," Fiz sighed. He took out his watch and glanced at the time. Midnight. They had talked away the night. A new day had been born without their having any awareness of it. "It's getting late. I'm going to bed. Have to be up early."

"Why is that?"

Fiz pushed away from the table, tucked his pocket watch back into his vest pocket, then shook his head. He had not heard the question.

"Good night," Cougar called after him. She waited until he had let himself out before turning her shiny blue eyes back on the marshal.

"What do you say we turn in, too? I know a room at the top of the stairs which gets pretty cold at night. There's no stove in there," she added.

"Sounds good to me."

They went off together, up the long, lonely staircase, hand in hand.

It was a time to reaffirm life.

***

Ada Duvall finished her letter. It was late. After midnight. She had worked past her time. She was an old woman. Old women had no right staying up past the witching hour. They belonged in bed. Beside their husbands.

Her husband slept in a different kind of bed than the one Ada had prepared for herself. His was a cold, lonely grave.

They had waited too long, Ada and Jack Duvall. Waited for the perfect job, so they could buy a house and settle down. Waited for the children they would never have. Waited for the retirement they would never spend together.

Ada Duvall was a lawman's widow.

Dipping her pen into the cold, black ink, she scrawled her full name at the bottom of the letter.

Ada Carter Duvall.

She would mail it in the morning, with the realization that it would arrive too late.

It was always later than one thought.

The End

GSFE

ALSO BY: S.L.KOTAR AND J.E.GESSLER

A character based historical 1950's courtroom based murder mystery
entitled "**The Hugh Kerr Mystery Series**"..

- Book I   **The Conundrum of the Decapitated Detective**
- Book II   **The Conundrum of the Absconded Attorney**
- **Book III**   **The Conundrum of the Sins of the Fathers**
- **Book IV**   **The Conundrum of The Two-Sided Lawyer**
- **Book V**   **The Conundrum of the Clueless Counselor**
- **Book VI**   **The Conundrum of the Loveless Marriage**
- **Book VII**   **The Conundrum of the Executed Defendant**
- **Book VIII**   **The Conundrum of the Jettisoned Jury**
- **Book IX**   **The Conundrum of the Perjured Pigeon**
- **Book X**   **The Conundrum of the Haunting Halloween**
  - **Party**
- **Book XI**   **The Conundrum of the Tuneless Tunesmith**
- **Book XII**   **The Conundrum of the Meddling Motorcar**
- **Book XIII**   **The Conundrum of the Blundering Bear**
- **Book XIV**   **The Conundrum of Shooting Fish in a Barrel**
  -
  - **To Be Continued!**

Next a series is "New Beginnings" a 1950's medical drama.

- Book I   **The Believer**
- Book II   **The Heretic**
- Book III   **Arrow Song**
- Book IV   **Peas In A Pod**
-
  - **To Be Continued!**

"the ReproBate saga" is a character-based series in the 1860 American Civil War

- **Book I**   **Beneath the Rose**
- Book II   **skull and cRossBones**
- Book III   **Redefining Bastions**
- Book IV   **thicker than Blood**
- Book V   **prioR Battles**
- Book VI   **Requited Blasphemy**
- Book VII   **The waR Between**
- Book VIII   **To Richmond or Bust**
- Book IX   **carrying Battlescars**
  - **To be Continued**

"the Hellhole saga" is a character-based series from the American West

- Book I   **First Draw**
- Book II   **Audition for a Legend**
- Book III   **Strange Bedfellows**

"The Kansas Pirate Series" is another character-based series from the American West

- Book I   **Pirate Treasure**
- Book II   **Strawberry Fields**
- Book III   **The Drinking Gourd**

Stand-alone novels include:

- **Catman** *He was every man; he was no man*
-
- **ONE** Science Fiction space travel

- **Shepherd of the Kingdom** a modern-day horror classic

Non-Fiction

"The Kepi Magazine," A publication specialized in the Civil War and 19th century life.:

- **The Kepi Volume I and II**
- **The Kepi Volumes III and IV**